Woulds

by

J L Wilson

Woulds

Contact Information: info@thewildrosepress.com

Cover Art by *Kim Mendoza*

The Wild Rose Press, Inc.
PO Box 708
Adams Basin, NY 14410-0708
Visit us at www.thewildrosepress.com

Publishing History
First Crimson Rose Edition, 2018
Print ISBN 978-1-5092-2185-1
Digital ISBN 978-1-5092-2186-8

Published in the United States of America

I woke once and realized groggily I was snoozing on the couch. My face hurt and I shifted position, tucking a pillow under my ear so my bruised cheek wasn't pressed against the fabric. I drifted back into sleep, lulled by the sound of the air conditioner as it kicked on.

The brisk ringing of my phone woke me. I propped myself up on my elbow and fumbled for the receiver which sat on the end table near my head. "What?" I growled when I managed to find it.

"Tuck, I need help."

I sat up straighter and rubbed my left eye. Luckily I remembered in time and didn't touch my right one. "Rob? Is that you?" I asked around a yawn.

"I need help. Can you come here? Can you come to the cabin?"

"The cabin? Why are you there?" Rob had a cabin which his family owned for generations. It was situated north of town near the river in the middle of a tract of forest and near the flood plain. "I thought you went home."

"I had John bring me here. I need help, Tuck. Can you come out?"

I peered at the clock on the wall over the dining room table. One-ten. Damn. One o'clock in the morning and Rob was calling me. "Why?" I snapped, waking up more fully.

"It's Guy."

"Guy? Guy Gibson? What about him?"

"I think I killed him."

Dedication

For Dora "the Explorer" Pillado, who taught me that fans come in all shapes, sizes, ethnicities, geographical regions, and ages.

Chapter 1

"I'm going to kill that bastard." Rob Huntington's voice was breathy and low above me. "Move aside, Tuck."

"You're not killing anybody, Rob." I stood between him and Guy Gibson, one hand on each male chest, the men held arms-length apart—my arm's length.

It wasn't my strength keeping them separated. I'm barely five-feet tall and weigh about one-ten sopping wet and each of them were more than six-feet tall and probably topped two hundred pounds per man. "I told you guys to break it up. I won't have my pub get a reputation as a place where drunks go to fight."

"Get away, Tucker." Guy didn't sound upset, worried, or flustered. Like always, he was cool as snow and icily calm. "We're outside. Your pub won't suffer from our actions."

"Shut up, Guy. You started it." I sensed my tenuous authority slipping. I've been a bartender for more than thirty years and despite my size and sex, I've always been able to control a crowd through a mix of intimidation and humor. Tonight was an exception.

"All I did was tell the truth. Rob can't give his wife the things she deserves." Guy stared over my head at Rob, who looked like he was dunked in water. Sweat curled his thinning blond hair and splotched his blue cotton shirt.

In contrast, Guy appeared like an ad for *Town and Country* with his navy Polo shirt and crisp, creased khakis, his dark hair parted with military precision on one side. *How does he do it?* I wondered when sweat trickled down the side of my face in the June heat. *It's midnight and it's still hotter than hell. He's not even wrinkled.*

"I said break it up. This is stupid." I glanced at the parking lot behind the pub. It was half-full of cars but no people. Where was a nosey crowd when you needed one? "You guys are old enough to know better. People our age don't have fist fights."

"I won't let him talk like that about my wife." Rob's voice was slurred and he leaned against my hand. I was pretty sure if I removed it, he'd fall flat on his face.

"Need help?"

I twisted, glimpsing the bulky man emerging from the back door of the pub. My movement caused my hands to slip just enough to allow the two fighters to shift position. Guy swung a punch over me, aiming for Rob's chin. Rob ducked in time, but I didn't. Guy's elbow connected with my face and I spun back, landing on my butt near the narrow flowerbed framing the back of the building.

Guy didn't care that I was tangled up with his leg. He moved in, landing punches on Rob's ribs. "Damn you, Guy!" I shouted, grabbing his ankle. "Stop it!"

He shook me off, his foot connecting with the side of my face. My head hit the stone edging separating the petunias from the path, and I saw stars as blinding pain exploded in my brain. When I regained my senses, Guy lay a few feet away, stretched out on the mulch-covered path between the pub and the parking lot. He blinked at me, looking surprised and mussed. Rob leaned against the back wall of the pub, his feet planted in a flowerbed with his hands on his thighs while his head dangled.

I peered upward groggily, my vision blurred. "What the fuck . . .?"

"Come on, Tucker." A man leaned over me, his face coming into the light from the lanterns lining the path. It was John Smalley, a local farmer who supplied me with organic produce and meat for the pub's restaurant. He was a giant of a man, easily six-six, with shoulders broad as a doorframe. His hirsute appearance—dark hair with streaks of gray, black beard, dark eyebrows—added to his rough appearance, but John was a soft-spoken man with a kind word for everyone.

I took the proffered hand and he hauled me to my feet. I winced, my back and butt announcing the fact I was bruised. That's when the pain in my face kicked in, too, and I put one hand over my right cheek. "Damn." I glanced at my palm and the blood there.

John leaned over me. "I saw you leave and thought you might need some help."

"Rob and Guy started arguing in the pub and I told them to take it outside." I touched the skin beneath my right eye, wincing when I contacted swollen flesh. "I didn't think they'd do it."

John squeezed my shoulder sympathetically. "Testosterone knows no age limit."

"Lordy, we're almost senior citizens. What are those guys—fifty? Fifty-five?"

"They're both fifty-five," John said. "I went to school with them." He moved to Rob, who shifted from the wall, revealing the plaque and the inscription there.

The Oak's Acorn Pub and Parlor
Barnsdale, Iowa
Established 1990
Miller Muchson, Brewmaster
Tucker Frye, Proprietress
Alan Dale, Head Chef

As though summoned by the words on the sign, the back door to our restaurant, the Parlor, opened on Rob's left. Alan Dale peered through the clematis-covered arbor. "What's going on?" His gaze landed on me. "Tucker, are you okay?"

"I'm not sure." I tugged my dark gold Oak's shirt from the waistband of my jeans and dabbed my nose.

Alan walked around the arbor and joined me. "You look like crap. If you were fighting, I think you lost." He smoothed my thick curly black hair from my forehead and tilted my head so the light shone on my face.

"I wasn't a willing participant, believe me," I said in a nasal voice. I pressed my shirttail against my nose, stemming the flow of blood. "Give me an ice pack and I'll be fine."

Alan's gaze shifted to Rob. "Is he drunk again?"

"Probably. I only served him one beer but he must have been tanked before he got here." My vision began to blur when my right eye swelled shut. "What happened to Guy?"

"I hit him." John put a hand on Rob's arm, helping him step away from the trampled petunias and the building. "Not hard. Just enough to slow him down."

"I'm sorry, Tuck," Rob muttered. "I couldn't stand to listen to him anymore."

I went to him, still blotting my nose. "You have to get hold of your temper, Rob. You know how Guy is. You can't let him bug you."

Rob nodded, sweat rolling off his face when he leaned toward me. John moved to the side, giving us a bit of privacy. "Marianne told me tonight she wants a divorce."

"Oh, Rob." My fingers closed around his tanned forearm sympathetically. "I'm sorry." I knew his wife was unhappy. In fact, I knew far more about his marriage than I really wanted to know because he often confided in me. Being a bartender was akin to being a priest. People tended to give me their secrets, expecting me to hold them. Of course, there were really few secrets to be held in a small town like Barnsdale, population seven thousand.

Rob straightened. He was slender but muscular with thin, baby-fine hair tumbling on his head in curls. His long, oval face was tanned and barely lined and his blue-gray eyes, big and heavily lashed, tilted downward at the corners, giving him a sad, downtrodden look. Drinking and inactivity were taking its toll, but sometimes he still appeared to be the athlete he used to be.

I had heard all about his high school glory days. He and the others grew up together in Barnsdale and graduated from high school together. Rob was captain of the football team and Guy was captain of the tennis team, indicating their athletic and their social status since Guy's father was a banker and Rob's father ran the local hardware store.

"Sorry, Tucker. I didn't mean to hit you." Guy pushed himself up from the mulch, standing cautiously until he got his balance. "I was aiming for Rob." He brushed wood chips off his shirt and pants, frowning at the smudges.

I shot him a hate-filled glare. "If I wanted to hear from an asshole, I'd fart." As usual when I was under stress, my Southern accent kicked in.

Alan made a snorting laugh noise. "Good one, Tuck."

Guy smoothed his Polo shirt into his waistband, the taut knit fabric highlighting his muscular chest. "This isn't over, Huntington. You've been lying to Marianne and I'll make sure she knows it. She deserves better than you. You're her second choice and you know it. You'll see." He stalked away.

A dark shadow darted in front of him. The mother cat I was attempting to befriend chose that unfortunate moment to make a break for it. She skittered from us warring humans, trying to divert us from the nesting box I made for her in an alcove between the restaurant's arbor and our flowerbeds.

Guy drew back his foot to kick her. I started toward him, but John was faster, dragging Guy back with one massive hand on the other man's shoulder. "You don't pick on weaker creatures," John said when the cat disappeared into the shadows. "Didn't your father teach you anything?" The bitterness in his voice was at odds with the mocking smile he leveled at Guy.

Guy tried to wrest his arm free but John held him tight. "I owe you for this," he snarled, touching the bruise on his face.

John grinned, releasing his grip and pushing slightly so Guy stumbled. "Well, that's a change of pace, isn't it? The banker's boy finally owes somebody."

"Damn it, Guy. I just got the cat to trust me. Now you come along and prove to her again that humans are jerks." I checked the alcove, but the cat was hunkered in the darkness behind the wooden boxes I put there to give her privacy. Guy stalked off, pausing once to shoot Rob a murderous glare. "Has he always been such an arrogant son of a bitch?" I asked the world at large.

John laughed softly. "Guy's father owned the bank in town. He loved lording over all of us and he never changed." For one brief moment, his smile faltered but it quickly returned. I was a relative newcomer to town, having been in Barnsdale for only twenty years, but Rob, Guy, and John shared history going back more than fifty years. Who knew what memories lurked there?

"Well, thanks for stopping him from kicking her." I gave up on finding the cat. "It's taken me two weeks for her to let me get close enough."

"I meant it." John stared at the parking lot when headlights came on and an engine roared to life. "You don't pick on weaker creatures, no matter if it's human or animal." His voice was soft and his dark eyes held a faraway gleam, like he was revisiting a memory. Then he turned toward the shadows, extending a hand. "She'll forgive us."

"She won't let you get—" I stopped when a thin silhouette crept tentatively from the shadows and sniffed at John's fingers. "What are you, the cat whisperer?"

John rubbed the furry black head before straightening. The cat darted back to her haven. "I like animals and they know it." He turned to Rob, who watched the sleek gray Porsche speed from the lot. "Ready to go home, Rob? I'll drive. You can pick up your truck tomorrow."

"I think you should go to the hospital, Tuck." Alan went to the restaurant's back door.

"I'm fine, Alan. Give me a steak to put on my eye and I'll be good as new."

He waggled a finger at me. "I won't waste a perfectly good steak on your eye. I'll make sure someone can cover the bar for you. The crowd has thinned so there shouldn't be much to do." A triangle of light briefly highlighted Rob when Alan disappeared inside.

"I didn't pay my tab." John reached for his back pocket.

"It's on the house." I pulled my shirttail from my face then found a clean spot on the fabric and dabbed again. There was no blood this time, so the worst was probably over. "Come back tomorrow and I'll buy you another one."

John put a hand under Rob's right arm and started walking slowly to the parking lot. "I'll take you up on that. Good night."

"Tucker, I'm sorry." Rob leaned precariously near me. "I didn't mean for things to get out of hand. Guy is such a dick and when he started talking—"

"It's okay." I took up position on Rob's left, helping to steady him. "Somebody needs to slap Guy into next week and not give him bus fare to get home. If he's not careful, it'll be me."

Rob grinned lopsidedly. "That's a good one. You're too little to do it, but I'd like to see you try."

"I may be small but I'm mighty." I gently released him to John's care, watching them amble to the rows of cars, John nodding at something Rob said. Next to John, Rob seemed small, dwarfed by the other man's bulk. *Thank God John never gets upset. If he did, there would be hell to pay.*

"Ready, Tuck?" Alan leaned through the restaurant doorway, extending a plastic bag.

I eyed the label. "Peas?"

"Frozen peas are better than an ice pack." He gestured me ahead of him into the back hallway. "Trust me."

I hesitated near the shadows at the door. "I should refill her water. It's so hot."

Alan sighed loudly. "You get cleaned up. I'll deal with Missy Mom." He nudged me ahead of him. "The Pub is still crowded but the restaurant is closed so you might want to use the Parlor kitchen instead of the bathroom. Use the prep sink."

I eyed my bloody shirt and silently agreed with Alan's advice. We had to make a lot of compromises when we turned the old glove factory into a brewpub, but it was worth it to save the beautiful limestone building with the oak floors, massive wooden beams, and the trestle tables, now the bar counter in the Pub.

The shared restrooms between the Parlor restaurant and the Pub bar were one of those compromises. We wedged in the tiny bathrooms at the back of the shared space between the two businesses, accessed via a short hallway.

I followed Alan past the wall separating the dining room and the patrons from the bustle of the cooking area. He disappeared into the walk-in cooler at the back of the kitchen and I headed left, toward the prep sink. I pulled a wad of paper towels from a roll hanging over the sink as Alan emerged with a bag of shaved ice. "I'll fill her dish with ice and it'll stay cool all night." He grabbed the flashlight from a hook on the wall and left.

I leaned on the stainless steel sink, sighing when air conditioning surrounded me. It was only mid-June, but our weather continued to be crazy. Alan called it our Sweaty and Sweatered Spring, with warm temps in March, cool, wet days in April, and cold then hot days in May. Now here it was June and summer seemed to be settling in to stay. It caused headaches for farmers during planting season and now we were smack in the middle of growing season and people were anxious for rain to offset the heat.

I ran water in the basin and dabbed gingerly at my face with a damp paper towel while I regarded myself in the small mirror over the sink. My right eye was swollen and red, giving me a Christmas contrast with the green of my other eye. My face, normally somewhat oval with high cheekbones and a small pointed chin, was now puffy, the way it was four years and a hundred pounds ago, when I weighed two hundred and twenty. My thick black curls sprang in a halo around my face, tumbling to cover my ears and rest on my collar. I tried a multitude of hairstyles over the years, from waist-long to severely short, but this ear-length style suited both my new, thinner physique and my lack of time to care for something more sophisticated.

I washed up then tugged a stool from under the gleaming metal center island. I pressed the bag of peas against my face and slumped tiredly. I've tended bar for years, from fancy hotels to ocean-side dives, from one end of the country to another. When Alan approached me decades earlier after my divorce, I jumped at the chance to invest my divorce settlement into my lifelong ambition to have a place of my own, a place where *I* set the rules.

Like the rule about no fighting.

I heard the back door open. A minute later Alan joined me, carrying my purse, which he set on the counter near the prep sink. "I stopped in at the Pub and you're covered for the night. Why were you still working? You quit at ten."

"I was getting ready to turn over my shift when Guy came in. Then I saw Rob come in and I figured I should hang around, just in case. Why are you here so late?"

He leaned his back against the counter so he could face me. With me seated and him standing, we were about the same height. Alan had wiry gray hair, a round face, and a solid frame he kept trim with regular exercise. "I'm testing a new recipe. John brought me some ham and I was fiddling around with an idea for a ham and cheese macaroni."

"I'm happy to be a guinea pig when you're ready for testing," I volunteered.

"You and Owen are always my guinea pigs." The mention of his guy-friend brought Alan's smile, dimples appearing at the corners of his full lips. He and Sheriff Owen Knott kept a very low profile in town, although I suspect most of the townspeople knew they were an Item. Iowa legalized gay marriage a few years earlier, but neither man was willing to test the limits of tolerance, especially where law enforcement was concerned.

I shifted the pea bag on my bruised face. "What did Guy mean when he talked about Rob being a second choice?"

Alan waved a hand. "Old history. Guy and Marianne dated in high school. They broke up when Guy went to college. Marianne turned to Rob. They dated for a long time. I think Marianne finally put her foot down and told him to make it legal or take a hike. Of course, Rob hasn't been able to hold a job long enough to really support a family, so I guess he was waiting for his fortunes to turn around before he popped the question." He shook his head. "I don't think it's a happy marriage."

I moved the bag again to hide my expression. "Well, you never know," I said noncommittally.

"I suppose Marianne wishes now she'd waited for Guy. It's not often your old high school sweetie goes off to the big city, makes a million or two bucks, then comes back to town to retire. Compared to poor old Rob . . ." Alan shrugged. "I wouldn't be surprised if Marianne is having second thoughts. Rob's job as manager at the chicken factory can't pay much." He tilted his head, concern evident in his brown eyes while he regarded me. "You should go to the eye doctor tomorrow."

I pulled the bag away. "You think so?"

Alan nodded. "Can you move your eye? How's your vision?" He held up two fingers. "How many?"

"Six." I dropped the bag on the counter. "Just kidding. I'll see how it is in the morning."

He straightened up. "Can you drive?"

I yawned. "I could get home on autopilot, I think." I patted his shoulder and slid off the stool. "Thanks for the worry. I'll be fine. All I need is a good night's sleep and some aspirin."

"Sure?"

"Sure." I picked up my purse and extracted my car keys from the outer pocket. "You'll close up for me?"

"Yep, no problem." He grinned. "You'd do the same for me if I was in a brawl."

I winced at the mental image of a barroom brawl, the beautiful oak floors of the Acorn strewn with drunks. "If Guy Gibson comes in tomorrow, I'm tempted to snatch his arm off and beat him with the stump."

Alan laughed. "You're the woman to do it. Good night, Tucker."

I waved good-bye and headed out the back door, making for my dark red sedan under the streetlight on the east side of the parking lot. I glanced at the cat alcove when I passed, but saw no movement. Poor critter. I was willing to help find her and her kittens a home, but I couldn't get close enough to make the attempt.

"Maybe tomorrow." I steered my car through the lot and making a left turn onto Broad Street to go north. I drove past Central Park, the one-block green space in the middle of town then I passed the movie theater, drugstore, clothing store and other establishments that were Barnsdale's downtown.

I saw the hospital sign on my left and turned into the parking lot, reasoning if the E.R. was busy, I'd go home. But the large waiting area was empty and before I knew what was happening, I was whisked into a cubicle where a brown-haired guy too young to be a doctor examined my face.

After asking me to stare here, there, and everywhere, he straightened. "There's no permanent damage to the eye, so keep up the ice and come back if you have any problems with your vision."

I said I would, signed a sheaf of papers probably promising my life away, and was on the road twenty minutes later. I passed the country club on my right and made a left turn into my subdivision, Sherwood Acres. Towering oak and maple trees surrounded me while I navigated a series of left and right turns on streets named after English counties, so-designated by the eccentric developer who created the subdivision half-a-century earlier. I drove along Suffolk Street, Devon Way, and Northants Avenue heading to my driveway on Lincolnshire Lane with my headlights illuminating my small blue three-bedroom home with the back yard sloping to the river below.

I entered through the garage door into the kitchen, a doorway separating my kitchen/dining area from the living room on my right. I dropped my purse and my car keys on the dining table and went to the fridge to get a hot-cold pack I kept frozen for when my aching back acted up. I took it, a dishtowel, and a glass of white wine and went to the living room where I sank onto my dark gold couch.

First I took two big swallows of wine then put my feet up on the hassock and gingerly positioned the ice bag on my right cheek. I lowered the brightness on the lamp next to the couch, which I always left on when I was out. I winced when light angled into my right eye, making it tear.

My vision was blurred, but I think that condition was normal with a black eye in the first few hours of injury. I could Google it to be sure, but my computer was in my home office, two doors down the hallway. I swallowed some more wine and leaned my head against the sofa, the cold pack balanced against my nose.

After another gulp of wine, I tossed the cold pack and towel onto the braided area rug covering the oak floor. So Rob and Marianne were getting divorced? I stared at my pale green ceiling, a contrast to the darker green of the walls and wallpaper. They were married shortly after I moved to town and I think they were maybe happy early on, but it wasn't long before I started getting sob stories from Rob about their wedded not-bliss.

I once again thanked Heaven or my Guardian Angel or whoever watched out for such things that my divorce years earlier was so amiable. Of course, the amiability was due in a large part to the fact we had no children and very little property. We didn't have a lot to argue about. It was odd that I was divorced and Rob and Marianne were married within a few months of each other. *Funny how things work out. I was busy separating myself from my husband while Marianne and Rob were busy intertwining themselves.* I yawned, my eyes closing.

I woke once and realized groggily I was snoozing on the couch. My face hurt and I shifted position, tucking a pillow under my ear so my bruised cheek wasn't pressed against the fabric. I drifted back into sleep, lulled by the sound of the air conditioner.

The brisk ringing of my phone woke me. I propped myself up on my elbow and fumbled for the receiver on the end table near my head. "What?" I mumbled when I managed to find it.

"Tuck, I need help."

I sat up straighter and rubbed my left eye. Luckily, I remembered in time and didn't touch my right one. "Rob? Is that you?" I asked around a yawn.

"I need help. Can you come here? Can you come to the cabin?"

"The cabin? Why are you there?" Rob had a cabin which his family owned for generations. It was north of town near the river in the middle of a tract of forest and not far from the flood plain. "You were going home, weren't you?"

"I had John bring me here. I need help, Tuck. Can you come out?"

I blinked at the clock on the wall over the dining room table. One-ten. Damn. One o'clock in the morning and Rob was calling me. "Why?" I snapped, waking up more fully.

"It's Guy."

"Guy? Guy Gibson? What about him?"

"I think I killed him."

Chapter 2

"What? What do you mean, you killed him?" I got up and stepped on the squishy, still-cold gel pack lying on the floor. I jumped and almost did a header onto the braided rug. I avoided it by running into the coffee table and banging my shin on it. "Shit!"

"What's going on? Are you okay?"

I sank back on the couch, rubbing my leg. "I'm fine." I gritted my teeth when my shinbone started to throb, keeping time with the headache pulsing above my right eye. "What are you saying, Rob? Why do you think you killed Guy? The last time I saw him, he was mad as hell and driving away in that fancy car of his." I got up cautiously and made my way to the fridge, where I refilled my wine glass.

". . . and we argued. I told him Marianne and I talked but he . . ."

"Rob, you're fading out. Are you using your cell phone? Reception is crappy around the river." I sipped the wine, trying to rinse the taste of a too-short nap from my mouth. It felt like sweaters covered my teeth.

". . . come and help me. I wasn't sure who to call. I can't call her because . . . alone here. She and I aren't talking and . . ."

I downed more wine. "Go to bed and sleep it off. Guy was at the bar, alive and well and being an asshole an hour or so ago. He's not dead. You're dreaming."

"Hold on."

"What? Hold on? It's one in the morning, why—" Silence. There was no indication Rob was still on the line. I considered hanging up, but my momma drilled politeness into me as a child and it was hard to kick the habit. Besides, if I hung up, he'd probably just call again.

I kept the portable phone pinned to my ear while I went to my bedroom at the back of the house. I peeled off my shirt, tossing it near the laundry basket before going into the small half-bath attached to my bedroom, flicking on the light while I went.

"Holy Mother of God," I muttered when I saw myself in the mirror. My right eye and cheek were dark blue-red streaked with yellow at the edges. The discoloration went up my face from my cheek to my eyebrow, but my eye appeared to be okay. The white part was white and the green part was green, which I guess was a good thing. Some blood had trickled along the side of my face and I dabbed at the crusty patch with a washcloth.

"Tucker, I heard something. Can you come out? I really need help. I don't know what to do. Please." His words tumbled over each other so much I could barely understand him.

I glanced to my left, at the inviting bed. "What can I do?"

"Please." He sounded desperate.

I sighed. "Okay. I'll drive out soon as I get dressed."

"Thanks."

A click on the line told me he'd disconnected. "Why me, Lord?" I asked the air around me. I went to the closet in my bedroom and drew on a loose blue cotton shirt. Then I shucked off my jeans, replacing them with a clean pair from the dresser. When I headed back to the kitchen, a deep rumble overhead made me pause. A second later the sound of rain hit my roof.

I hurried to the front window and pulled aside the curtain to peer past my small porch at rain pelting through the trees in the front yard and bouncing off the driveway. Well, thank God it finally rained, but did it have to start right before I needed to drive into the country on a twisting road that was about thirty feet from the river? I'd gone to Rob's cabin many times because he and Marianne often threw parties, but I usually was with someone and we didn't drive at night in a rainstorm.

I started to turn from the window but movement outside made me lean forward. A person leaned toward me on the other side of the glass. "Holy crap!" I skittered back, bounced off my recliner, and landed in a heap on the floor when a booming knock sounded on my front door.

I checked the clock again to confirm what I saw earlier. "It is one-fucking-thirty in the morning," I said, crawling to the recliner and using it to pull myself up. "This had better be the second coming of Christ for you to come to my door." I went to the peep hole, flipped on the switch for the outside light, and stared out.

My nephew, Will Redman, gestured frantically at the light, hunching his shoulders and turning so his face was in the shadows.

"What the hell?" I threw the bolt and opened the door. Will pushed past me, bringing with him rain and the heady aroma of wet earth and grass. I closed the door behind him and turned off the outside light. "What are you doing here at this time of night?" I demanded. "Is everything okay?"

"I don't want to be seen. It might get you in trouble." Will ran his hands over his head, shaking off the raindrops. He wore all black—a black T-shirt, black denims, and black sneakers. "I was hoping you were still awake. Aunt Tuck, I need your help."

Well, shit. This was my night to be the knight in shining armor, no pun intended. "Help with what?" I asked.

"This." He dug in his jeans pocket and held out a small gray rectangle. A USB disk gadget. "I need you to keep it safe." His dark gold hair, thick and short, sparkled with raindrops in the light. He'd been an angelic child with his tousled curls, big blue eyes, and his dimpled, engaging smile. Will was still a handsome young man, now in his thirties with the slender build of his momma and the long legs of his daddy.

"Why can't you keep it?" I moved to the couch and into the circle of light cast by the lamp on the end table.

"Wow, what happened to you?" He touched my shoulder gently, turning me so the light illuminated my face. "Are you okay? Who hit you?"

I gestured at the easy chair for him to sit. "It was a bar fight I broke up. I'm fine. It looks worse than it is."

"It looks pretty bad." He set the USB stick on the coffee table before taking a seat.

"You want a drink? A glass of water?" I went to the kitchen, getting the pitcher of water from the fridge and filling a glass.

"No, I have to get back before I'm missed. I told the guys at the apartment I was going for smokes. Hold on to the files for a day or two, until I'm sure it's safe to go public."

I took a long swallow of water while I considered that. Will wasn't technically my nephew because my no-good brother didn't breed before he died, thank the good Lord. But given the convoluted family tree from which I sprang, I considered Will my kin. His mother, a cousin to my mother, took refuge with my family when she got pregnant out of wedlock. I ended up helping raise Will and stayed in touch with him when I left Louisiana as a new bride.

Recently, rumors swirled through town about the recall of eggs from the production facility in the nearby town of York, part of the Fitz agribusiness conglomerate. The egg factory (*Buy Your Yolks at York's Yolkshire Farm*) employed a lot of people from Barnsdale and their jobs were on the line if an investigation shut down the plant. Will was an animal rights activist and when he told me he came to town to gather evidence about the factory, I welcomed the chance to help, not only because he was family but because I was pretty damn sure the factory was a little bit of hell on earth.

"What's on the memory stick?" I resumed my seat on the couch. "Why give it to me?" I eyed the little gadget nervously.

"Nobody knows we're related. It'll be safe with you."

That made sense in a way. "But what's on it?" I asked again.

"You read about the new law? The Ag-Gag law?" He leaned forward, his tanned forearms resting on his thighs. Will appeared exhausted, with dark circles under his sky blue eyes and his oval face creased with lines that didn't belong on the face of a thirty-three-year-old.

"Yep. I can't believe those sons-a-bitches did it." My headache thrummed unmercifully against my noggin, but I think it was anger more than my injury that made it so painful. The Iowa legislature recently passed a law making it illegal to film or to record the goings-on in a factory farm operation without permission of the owners.

Of course, 'permission' was laughable because the factory farms in question were hotbeds of inhumane treatment of animals and poultry. It almost made my head explode to consider it. "The whole damned legislature is in the pocket of agribusiness lobbyists. I swear, politicians are so crooked they could hide behind corkscrews," I fumed. "They're setting out to punish whistleblowers."

"They worded it so it only pertains to those of us who take jobs in order to gather evidence," Will corrected. "So-called 'true whistleblowers' can still report." He shot me a cynical glance. "Like anybody would now."

"I read the Humane Society and some other groups are organizing to get it overturned."

"They are, but until they do, I can be arrested for working there and gathering evidence like that." He nodded at the memory stick. "What I've found could close the place. And it'll implicate the Fitz family in almost seventy deaths, including all those kids at the day care."

"Oh, Lord." A salmonella outbreak in eggs killed dozens of people around the country and was linked to the Yoke, as the factory was facetiously known. "Who knew about it?"

"Everyone in management," Will said. "I'm sure of it. I have copies of fudged safety reports, all signed by the supervisors. If the Feds come in to investigate, it's all over for Fitz Ag."

I sat back, my stomach twisting into knots. "Rob Huntington? He knew?" Rob was the Chief of Operations at the production plant, a job he took several years earlier when he sold the hardware store he inherited from his father.

"He had to know. The cover-up goes all the way to the top."

How could Rob do it? How could he deliberately put lives in danger? Damn. I was going to Rob's house. How could I face him knowing this? "Are you sure?"

Will pointed to the USB stick. "It's all there. Pictures, videos, copies of documents." He got to his feet. "Keep it for me, okay? I don't dare keep a copy on me. I emailed a copy to my contact in The Group but I want a backup. I think I've been followed."

The Group was the humane organization Will worked for. I couldn't remember the name. Farm Humane, or Farm Freedom, or something like that. He showed me some of their literature and it sickened me so much I immediately tossed it away, probably *not* the marketing strategy the graphic images of caged and injured farm animals was meant to evoke.

My cell phone, buried somewhere in my purse, blared George Thorogood's "I Drink Alone," one of my bar-themed ringtones telling me someone was calling. "I'll keep it for you, Will." I went to the entryway table to retrieve my bag. "I'll put it in my safe at the bank."

"No, keep it with you, please." He picked up the USB stick and followed me to the door leading to the garage. "I'll let myself out this way and go around back."

A crack of thunder sounded overhead. "It's pouring rain. At least take a jacket or umbrella."

"Nope. It'll be better if I come home soaked. I don't know if I trust the other guys in the apartment. They're company men, I'm sure of it." He pressed the memory stick into my hand.

I would've laughed at his somber accusation but he seemed so damn serious. I reached for my purse, but George had stopped singing. I dropped the memory stick into an interior pocket, zipping it inside and making sure Will saw me do it. "Take care, sugar." I stood on tiptoes to tug his shoulder to my level.

He stooped and I put a kiss on his whisker-stubbled cheek. He was so tall and grown-up but when I peered into his pretty blue eyes, I still saw a little toddler I chased around our house. "You take care. Don't go getting into any more fights."

"You know me. I can't walk away from 'em." I opened the door to the garage, swinging it wide so the motion light came on to show the three short steps. "Be careful," I said when he slipped past my car and headed for the back door leading into the yard.

He raised a hand. "Love you, Auntie."

"Love you, too," I said, but he was already gone, the door opening and closing so fast I might have imagined it.

I stepped back into the house when my phone blared "I Drink Alone" again. This time I managed to find the phone before the caller hung up. "Who is this and what do you want at—" I checked the clock, "—at two damn o'clock in the morning?" A crackling noise on the line garbled whoever was talking. It was either static or the person was talking around marbles. "Slow down, slow down. Who is this?"

"It's me. It's Rob." He laughed shakily. "You don't have to come. I was wrong. I didn't . . . God, I guess I'm too drunk to know . . . going on."

I longed to fling the phone against the wall. *Why me, Jesus?* I stared at the ceiling and took a steadying breath. "I was getting ready to leave. Are you saying I don't have to?"

"Oh, good . . .you might be on the road . . . drunk or . . . passed . . . and when I came to . . . gone. I think I saw him walking …."

"You think you saw him? You mean Guy?"

"I was kinda fading in and out."

Another burst of thunder crashed overhead and static swelled, drowning out whatever else he said. "Are you sure you don't want me to come out?"

"No, no, don't come out. It's a mess. I'm a mess." Rob talked so fast his words tumbled over each other. "It's terrible. I mean, the house is a mess, and I'm a mess and I cut my head and there's blood. Don't come. Please."

He sounded desperate. I remembered how drunk he'd been. "Are you sure? Are you okay? What do you mean, you cut your head?"

"I'm fine. Really. Please. I'm sorry I called you. I shouldn't have done it. Go to sleep. Everything is—" A burst of static punctuated his final words.

I waited but he didn't come back on the line. I clicked the phone off and dropped it back in my purse.

My Good Samaritan personality warred with my Don't Give A Shit personality. If Rob was injured, someone should check on him. He was there by the river, alone.

I turned off the light next to the couch and walked to my bedroom. Rob was a grown man and he was married. If his wife didn't care, why should I?

My Don't Give A Shit personality won. I peeled off my clothes, dropped into bed, and was asleep before my head touched the pillow.

****

I slept the sleep of the innocent, deep and without dreams and awoke refreshed and ready to face the day. I sauntered to the mailbox across the street to retrieve the morning paper and yesterday's mail, delivered late in the afternoon when I was at work.

It was a beautiful summer day, the cool breeze contrasting with the bright sunlight dancing off puddles from last night's rain. I drew in a deep breath of grass, flowers, and warmth then sneezed, a reminder I needed to take my allergy pills. My lawn needed mowing and my hedge needed trimming, but my ineptitude with power tools had convinced me to hire a landscape service to handle it. Now that the heat wave was broken, they would probably be coming to work their usual magic.

Mine was one of the oldest neighborhoods in Barnsdale, with many mature trees providing me with privacy and shade. Through one of the breaks in the trees, I spied my neighbor on the right puttering in his flower garden and across the street I saw a couple walking their dog. Other than those folks, it was all quiet in Sherwood Acres. I sometimes felt like I'd been transported to Beaver Cleaver Land. All that was lacking was the Beav himself, riding by on his bicycle.

I returned to the house and opened the windows, anxious to let in fresh air. When I examined myself in the bathroom mirror, I decided my eye wasn't really so bad. My vision was no longer blurry and the color had morphed into a decidedly bluish-gray. Therefore I was on the mend and didn't need a visit to the optometrist.

While I sat on the couch nursing my second cup of coffee, the phone rang. "It's your dime, so start talking," I said around a sip of dark roast Columbian.

"Tucker, this is Marianne Archer. Could you come to the office before you open the bar today? I need to talk with you."

I longed to slap myself upside the head. Why, oh why, couldn't I learn to check caller ID before picking up a phone? "I'm not sure, Marianne. I'm kinda busy. Why? Is this about Rob?"

She laughed, a sad, soft noise. "Yes and no. Can you stop by?"

I could easily imagine Marianne at her desk in the Barnsdale Bugle newspaper office, the phone almost hidden under her mane of white-gold hair that tumbled along her back in curls. Most women in mid-life sported short hair-dos, but Marianne still was like a throwback to the Sixties, with loose clothing, long, flowing hair and a kind of breathlessness that reminded me of the Hippy Movement. Everything Marianne did had a brittle quality to it, like she was made of porcelain and would break if touched too roughly.

I eyed the clock. It was now ten in the morning. I alternated as head bartender on the weekends with Miller, the head brew master, and this was my weekend to work. I had a firm rule that the Acorn didn't open to the public until two p.m. even though the Parlor opened at eleven in the morning. As far as I was concerned, no one had any business drinking before two in the afternoon.

"I'm surprised you're in the office on Saturday," I said, stalling for time. "Don't newspaper people get a day off?"

"I'm working on a special insert for Wednesday's paper about the Founders' celebration. Can you drop by? I usually eat lunch at my desk, so any time would be fine with me."

"I suppose." I mentally tallied the errands I needed to run. "I'll drop by before I go to the Acorn."

"Thank you. I appreciate it." She hung up before I could say *I can't stay for long, though.*

I heaved myself off the couch and went downstairs to my partially unfinished basement, which housed the laundry room and my exercise equipment. I set my television to home improvement shows, hopped on the treadmill and did a forty-minute fast walk followed by twenty minutes of free weights. I was dripping with sweat by the time I finished, so I toddled off to the get ready for the day. If I timed it right, I could drop by the newspaper office a few minutes before I was scheduled to open the Acorn for the afternoon. That way I had a built-in excuse to not stay long.

Cheered by my plan, I showered then toweled my hair and finger-curled it into place where it would dry eventually. Next, I examined myself in the mirror. My face had returned to its normal shape and I no longer looked like the Old Me, praise Jesus. I kept few reminders around me of The Fat Days, but I did hold on to a pair of jeans which used to be snug. I used those pants to remind me whenever Dairy Queen or fast food called to me.

I dabbed on tinted moisturizer but didn't try to cover the shiner. No amount of foundation would cover it. I passed on the eye makeup and went to my home office. I got the memory stick from my purse and without stopping to consider the consequences I opened the contents on my computer screen.

A Read-Me file caught my attention. I opened it and saw a detailed list of dates, times, and what appeared to be file names. There were also some notations I didn't understand and a cryptic note: *Make sure this information doesn't fall into the wrong hands. It might mean your life.*

Good heavens. Surely Will didn't mean . . . I wasn't sure what he meant. I turned my attention to the other files, many with .doc extensions and many with .jpg or .vid extensions. I clicked on one of the .jpg files and leaned back, stunned.

I knew factory farming was inhumane. Anyone who knew anything about agriculture knew you couldn't mass produce animals without some suffering. But this? Holy God in Heaven, someone should smite the people who did this. Will's files showed pictures of hens so confined they couldn't move, couldn't flap their wings, let alone do the things that chickens do: build a nest, perch, or simply breathe without another animal nearby.

I skimmed through the documents he copied, some of which were probably taken with a cell phone or another less-than-perfect camera. Yes, I saw Rob's signature on bills of lading, on safety reports, on production reports. He had to know what was going on, had to know those animals were being so tortured, so confined that disease was inevitable.

I opened one video file and it was my undoing. What I saw sickened me. Animals so jammed together they were like bundles of feathers, the din of their screaming like something from hell. Small chicks were mowed down by machinery, mangled by metal while the hens screamed and flapped, terror so evident in their motions I wondered how anyone could stand there and film it. I jerked the memory stick from my USB port and dropped it in my purse with shaking hands.

I took steadying breaths and focused on my desktop. This kind of barbaric behavior was going on right now, seven miles from me in York, Iowa. No wonder the workers called the place The Yoke. They must feel as dehumanized as the creatures confined there. In many ways, the human workers were also confined, kept there by relatively good pay for simple manual labor. How could they do it? How could they go there, day after day, knowing what was happening?

I've heard people dismiss chickens or pigs or cows as lesser creatures, without feelings, without knowledge of pain. Were they being dismissive because they didn't dare think about what was done to provide them with a cheap food source?

I pushed away from the desk, the images of those terrorized creatures flashing through my mind. They knew pain. I'd stake my life on it. Someone had to pay, not only for this brutality, but also for putting humans at risk in order to save money and maximize profits by shipping unsafe food. If Rob didn't pay, someone would.

I'd see to it.

I was getting ready to leave the house when my home phone rang. I checked the caller ID this time and when I saw the name, I was primed to give him a piece of my mind. "What the hell do you want, Rob?"

He laughed shakily. "I'm sorry, Tuck. I can't blame you for being pissed off at me."

"You have no idea." I struggled to remind myself that the information on the USB stick was private, confidential and dangerous. I couldn't mention it to anyone. Will trusted me and I would honor his trust.

"Did I keep you awake last night? I'm sorry. I should never have called you. I was upset and I couldn't call Marianne again because she was mad at me."

"Don't ever come to my bar drunk again. I won't have the Oak's Acorn getting a reputation for serving lushes, do you understand me?"

"That's a bit rough, isn't it? I mean, it's only a bar. People expect that kind of thing now and again."

I felt like the top of my head might blow off. "Don't you dare say the Acorn is only a bar. Alan and I worked hard to make it more than that. We didn't have anybody helping us to do it, either."

There was a pause. "What's that mean?"

"You heard me. I scraped together every penny I could to go in with Miller on the Pub and when Alan joined us with the restaurant, we had to dig deep to renovate the building. None of us had a father or a friend to give us a job. We worked to make the Oak's Acorn a success. We have nothing to fall back on if it doesn't succeed."

"And you think I do have something to fall back on?"

"You have a wife."

"Not for long. I don't know what I'll do if Marianne leaves." Rob's voice morphed from anger to morose.

Several answers popped into my head. *Quite well, Rob.* Or maybe, *Easier than you think, Rob.* Or how about, *You're better off without her?* I restrained myself admirably. "I'm sure you'll find a way."

"And what if I lose my job?" he continued. "What will I do?"

The same as most people, I longed to say. *You'll make do.* "What do you mean?"

"Richard is coming to town next week. The investigation isn't going well. The Feds are trying to pin the salmonella outbreak on us."

"Of course the investigation isn't going well. Your factory is hell on earth. Why should it go well?"

"That's not true." He said it automatically, with no passion behind it.

"We can argue until we're blue in the face. You know and I know factory farming is wrong, it's unethical, and it should be banned."

"Yeah? Well, I'll bet you'd be the first to yell if your food prices went up. What would happen to your precious restaurant? You'd have to raise prices and then what would happen?"

"We use all organic food now," I retorted. "No one has complained about our prices. John Smalley charges a fair price for his food."

"John." Rob almost snarled the name. "Did you know he's sponsoring egg-free Friday?"

"Good for him." A local consortium of vegetarians were advocating for Meatless Mondays and Egg-Free Fridays as a way to educate the public about the costs of a carnivorous lifestyle. "Why shouldn't he sponsor it?"

"It's hypocritical, don't you think? After all, John raises animals for slaughter and chickens for their eggs."

"You're missing the point, Rob. John's operation is natural and organic, the kind of thing which doesn't require large sales to stay in business. Unlike a factory which has millions of dollars tied up in the operation. If more people used meat or eggs as an option, not a main course—"

Either Rob didn't understand or he didn't care. "If everyone tried to go organic, prices would shoot up. That's what would happen if we didn't have large-scale meat and poultry processing."

"Rob, you're so full of shit I'm surprised you can walk without farting chunks." I slammed the phone so hard the end table wobbled. I slung my purse over my shoulder, more resolved than ever to see the damned Yoke shut down. If Rob lost his job, so be it. That asshole could figure out something else to do with his life. He wasn't my problem.

I stalked from the room, a woman on a mission.

Chapter 3

I drove into town, still shaking with anger from my argument with Rob. I don't normally air my viewpoints, but I was a proponent of the locavore movement long before there was a movement. Alice Waters and Frances Moore Lappé were, in my not so humble opinion, Goddesses of American cuisine and their insistence on using in-season foods for freshness and quality was an epiphany for me.

I studied their philosophies and their recipes, seeing in the locavore movement a return to home cooking in its simplest, most basic form. When I met Alan, whose culinary talents were centered in organics, I knew I found a business partner I could trust. My dream of opening a pub expanded to include the kind of restaurant I never thought I could own.

I took several calming breaths while I drove through the Sherwood neighborhood, noting how last night's downpour perked up the grass, flowers, and trees. Prior to the rain, everything had a dusty, tired feel, which came from too long in heat with too little water. But now the red and gold marigolds in the flowerbeds seemed especially vibrant, the oak and maple trees glistened with health, and the grass of lawns appeared almost lush and soft again.

It's June in Iowa. If I stood long enough near a field, I could probably hear the corn grow. My jangled nerves relaxed while I drove past tidy home gardens, with fields of green corn and soybeans in the distance.

I parked on Main Street and first dropped by Barnsdale Hardware to pick up a new screwdriver to replace the one I lost outside. A *Closed* sign was on the door and when I peeked through the glass window, I saw the goods were off the shelves and someone was in the middle of painting, evidenced by drop cloths on the floor. I made a mental note to drop by the Weed and Feed Store on the outskirts of town and get the screwdriver.

I walked across the street to my next stop, the Nature's Corner Flower Shop, to buy a pot of geraniums to hang on my front porch. I am usually incapable of keeping flowers alive for any length of time, but I had hopes this summer I wouldn't forget to water the poor things. I discussed the weather with the two ladies in the store, agreeing it was probably a perfect summer day. I accepted commiserations from the staff, all of whom expressed amazement at my shiner. It was, we decided, a real beaut.

Next I dropped in at the Fourth Street Coffee Shop which relocated to Main Street twenty years earlier but kept the name because all their glassware and paper goods were imprinted with the old name. This tended to confuse anyone new to town but it didn't faze the old-timers. Once again, I was the topic of conversation, this time about the best way to treat a black eye. The consensus of opinion finally concluded I probably did the right thing using ice, although Art Blandish, John Smalley's cousin, felt a good steak would have been better.

By the time I picked up my iced coffee and left the debate behind me, it was close to one o'clock. I figured I stalled enough so I wouldn't be trapped too long by Marianne. I went to the Barnsdale Bugle office, which sat between the Millworks Antique Store and Friar's BBQ on Third Avenue. The bell on the door tinkled when I entered. "Marianne?" I called when I saw the receptionist desk was empty.

"In here," a voice sounded from a doorway behind the desk. "I'm in the layout room."

Well, where the hell is that? I wondered grumpily, walking past the desk and through an open door. A hallway peppered with closed doorways was in front of me, the overhead lights illuminating every other one.

"I'm here." Marianne poked her head from one doorway, her blonde-gold hair catching the light and glittering like someone tossed sparkles in her curls. When I neared her, she examined my face. "Tucker, that looks terrible. I heard you got hurt last night in a fight between Rob and Guy. I'm so sorry."

"It wasn't your fault. It was Guy who hit me."

"Oh, I'm sure he didn't mean to. He would never hurt a woman. You know Guy. He wouldn't hurt a fly." She went back into the room and I followed.

A fly? I remember how he pounded Rob the night before and leveled a kick at the cat. *He might not hurt a fly but he'd kick a mother cat.* "Right," I said skeptically. I glanced around the small room which barely contained the three desks it held. On each sat a large computer display showing a different depiction of a newspaper page. "If you're busy, I can come back later."

Marianne went to the center display and sat in the office chair there to peer at the screen. "Did you know Richard is coming to town on Thursday?"

I drew in a calming breath. Trust Marianne to keep me standing here while she considered coming to the point. "Rob mentioned something about it. Richard who?" I leaned against the doorframe and tapped one foot.

"Richard Fitz. He's CEO of Fitz Agri-Industries. Haven't you ever met him?" She swiveled her office chair to regard me with wide blue eyes. Apparently Richard Fitz was such a fact of life that surely everyone knew him.

"I haven't met Richard Fitz. I know PJ, of course." Patrick John Fitz was the Fitz son who was left in charge of the Fitz agribusiness concerns in Barnsdale when his older brother Richard went to Chicago to dabble in real estate. "Every bartender in town knows PJ."

Marianne's lips curved, the pink of her lipstick exactly matching a pink peony on her blouse, the same way her eye shadow matched the palest of pale blue of the background on the blouse. "PJ does enjoy himself. He always has." She wore dark beige capris and white sandals with big pink flowers near her toes, which were also painted pale pink. On any other fifty-year-old woman, it would seem like an attempt to recreate youth. On her, it was like the style was created for her. "That's Richard." She tapped the monitor.

I took a step closer and saw the screen. A man stared at me, his dark eyes direct and unwavering and with a slight smile on his full lips, as though to say, *Here I am, honey.* His red-brown hair was long and swept back from his high forehead with streaks of gray giving him a mature, upper-executive appearance accentuated by the broad line of his shoulders in a dark business suit. Richard Fitz wasn't handsome but he was a man who would always get a second and maybe third glance. "He and PJ don't look like brothers," I commented.

"When we were growing up, we called Richard 'Leo,' because he was the king of the Lions. Our football team," she added, like I was unaware of that fact after living for decades in town. "Richard was a standout quarterback. He went to the University of Iowa on a full scholarship. He probably could have played in the pros but his father wanted him to work in the company."

The mention of Fitz Agri-Industries made me think of Will and the information I carried in my purse. Richard Fitz was CEO of the company which owned the Yoke. I pressed the bag harder against my side like I could keep data from leaking out. "I think Richard Fitz was in town a few years ago, but I never met him. He doesn't often leave Chicago. Why's he coming? Checking up on things?"

She turned back to the screen, frowning at this glib dismissal on my part. "He's coming to speak at Founding Family Day. It's a special celebration this year."

"Why special this year?" When I first moved to town, the annual town-creation anniversary was called Founding Fathers' Day. I pointed out that the fathers probably needed a few mothers to found a town. The council at the time, most of whom were women, agreed and the name was changed to its current title. A few people in subsequent city councils tried to change it back, but the name stuck.

"It's the town's Dodransbicentennial."

I blinked at her, my mouth agape. "The what?"

"Our 175th anniversary. Richard is going to speak at the town picnic. After all, the Fitz family had a great deal to do with the settling of the town."

Settling of the town and enslaving most of the people. The sour thought surfaced and vanished. Old Henry Fitz, the patriarch of the Fitz conglomerate, used to have a reputation as a tight-fisted, narrow-minded autocrat who ran his companies like an Army. I'd heard stories about Old Henry from townspeople who worked for one of his many business concerns.

"Richard is also coming to put to rest any fears about the salmonella outbreak and to reassure the townspeople their jobs are secure," Marianne continued, her face placid.

"And that's the story you'll print." I crossed my arms and shot a glare at her computer screen. "Everything is hunky dory and life can go on as usual."

For an instant, her sweet, careful veneer slipped. Her baby blue eyes narrowed. "A lot of people in town have jobs tied to the factory. If it dies, the town dies."

"My cow died last week, so I don't need your bull. The town isn't that reliant on the Fitz family for its survival."

Her face relaxed, the girl-mask back in place. "You Southerners. You have such colorful expressions." Marianne straightened a piece of paper on her desk. "You don't know what it was like in town before the factory opened. We don't want to go back to how it was."

I ground my teeth. Marianne always brought out my Southern side, even though I shook the dust of Catahoula Parish from my feet half-a-lifetime earlier. All that remained of my Southern roots were two graves in a mournful rural cemetery and an alcoholic brother who was knifed to death and buried somewhere outside New Orleans. I left that life behind me when I married Ron Church, but there were times when the past crept up and grabbed me by the ankle.

"I expect Guy will be back by then," she continued, oblivious to my annoyance or, more likely, uncaring about it.

"Back? Where'd he go?"

She blushed prettily. "He left me a note. We were going antiquing but he had to leave town on business." Her eyes went to a folded square of paper on the corner of the desk. "Guy loves to shop for things for his new house and he likes to have me along, to give him my opinion."

Guy's so-called new house was a McMansion in Nottingham Court, a subdivision west of town. Homes there cost about half-a-million and sat on two and three acre lots. Guy's house was so big it seemed like a motel from the road. I wondered if Marianne regretted pushing Rob into marriage when she saw Guy's Porsche and his fancy house. *Water under the bridge. No use thinking about woulds*, as my Mama said. *Coulda shoulda woulda*. "Speaking of Guy, how is Rob today?" I asked brusquely.

Marianne sighed. "I have no idea. He stayed at his man cave last night. He's such a river rat."

"Man cave? The cabin?" I considered the small house on a bluff over the river, rustic but pleasant. "I don't know. It doesn't seem cave-like to me."

Marianne nudged something on the desk. It was an ad for Barnsdale Hardware, the store Rob used to own until he got in trouble with debt and had to sell it to the clerk, Stewart Warman. "That place on the river suits Rob," she said. "He loves it almost as much as he used to love that dusty old hardware store."

I liked that dusty old hardware store. It was crowded with all kinds of nifty things, like a throwback to the Vermont country store days when men sat around a pickle barrel and talked. "I saw a sign on the door that they're closed."

Marianne straightened the ad. "Temporarily. Stewart's remodeling. He told me it will be completely modernized and with the latest inventory, like at Home Depot in Des Moines."

"I didn't know hardware went out of style."

"Of course there are innovations and changes." Marianne tilted her head to one side, her blonde curls slipping over her shoulder. "I suppose it was for the best that Rob sold the store. Stewart has a lot of innovative ideas."

I doubted Rob would have agreed, but I nodded then made a show of checking my watch. "You said you needed to talk to me about something?"

Marianne faced me. "I want you to refuse to serve Rob alcohol when he comes to your bar." She kept her hands folded in her lap. Unlike my hands, which were chapped and red from the dish soap at the bar, hers appeared smooth and pale with long nails painted with dark pink polish. She wore two rings, one a single band on her left ring finger and the other a large heart-shaped ruby on her right hand. I didn't remember ever seeing the ruby before. It was certainly large enough to be noticeable.

"It's not that easy," I replied. "I have to have a reason to refuse to serve him."

"He's an alcoholic. Isn't that reason enough?" Her harsh tone of voice was at odds with her pretty-girl appearance. "Look at what happened last night. His drinking impairs his judgment and he makes stupid mistakes."

"Hitting Guy wasn't a stupid mistake. Letting Guy hit him back was stupid."

Marianne stood slowly, a graceful maneuver reminding me of a cat unwinding herself from a sleeping position, sinuous, effortless, and totally unself-conscious. She towered over me even though I wore platform sandals and she wore flats. "Rob has been ill and his medication doesn't mix well with alcohol. If he's harmed by his drinking, it will reflect badly on your bar."

"If he's harmed, it will be his own damn fault," I retorted. "Don't make threats about my business, Marianne." I turned to leave.

"I'm not threatening. I'm telling you. Rob is an alcoholic. If you serve him alcohol, it may have bad consequences."

I bit back the retort I longed to hurl at her. *Why the hell don't you talk to him about it and lay down the law with him, not me?* "Okay. I'll discuss it with Rob if he comes in again."

"Good Lord, don't do that! He'll hate it that I interfered."

Marianne appeared so appalled by the idea I resolved there and then to make sure to mention it to Rob the first chance I got. "Rob is a grown man. He can make his own decisions." I started for the door.

"I'm not sure Rob remembers how to make decisions. He won't do anything unless Richard approves of it."

I stopped. Marianne stared at the picture on the computer screen, her face thoughtful. "Really?"

Marianne's mask settled back into place. "He respects Richard so much. We all do."

"Uh-huh," I said doubtfully. "I have to get to work now."

"I'll make sure you get a chance to meet Richard when he's here." She followed me to the door. "I'm certain he'll want to meet the owner of our successful little restaurant."

Little restaurant? The Oak's Acorn reservation list was full every night. We had reviews in *Midwest Living, Our Iowa, The Iowan,* the *Des Moines Register* and the *Kansas City Star.* Little restaurant? I longed to strangle Marianne with her own curls but I settled for a brief and insincere smile. "Can't wait to meet him, too, and hear what he has to say about the egg contamination." *The King returns. Let's hope his subjects welcome him.*

"Yes, it will be good to get the facts." Marianne paused, hanging back in the hallway doorway while I went to the front door. "I hope you'll reconsider, Tucker. Rob really shouldn't be drinking."

"See you later," I said breezily, stepping onto the sidewalk. "And good riddance," I added when I heard the door close behind me. I strode to my car, anxious

43

for fresh air. A conversation with Marianne always left me feeling like I stepped out of Willy Wonka's Chocolate Factory due to the surfeit of artificial sweetener.

I drove six blocks to the old glove factory and parked on the west side of the lot. At this time of day it was in full sun, but come nightfall the trees separating the parking lot from the neighborhood park would provide shade and relief from the heat. When I neared the back door of the Acorn, my keys in hand, Alan emerged from the Parlor and headed straight for me.

"What's up?" I asked when I saw his uncharacteristically grim expression. "What's wrong?"

He met me in the parking lot, blocking my way to the path leading to the Acorn. "It's the mother cat. She got hit by a car this morning."

"What?" I glanced automatically at the arbor near the back door where pink clematis climbed over the wooden trellis. "When?"

"I'm not sure. One of the bus boys told me about it. He found her on the grass near the roadside when he came in to work. She wasn't there when I came in earlier. I, uh, I took care of the body."

I didn't want to ask what he meant. "Oh, damn." Sudden tears made my eyes hot. "Son of a bitch. Some idiot was probably driving too fast and hit her." I moved to the arbor. "What about the babies?" I'd seen four small furry critters previously, staggering around, but the black-and-white mother kept a protective eye on them and didn't let them stray far.

"They're fine. They were either weaned or close to it, because when we found them, they let us get close and they drank some milk I put out." Alan followed me and watched me peek through the tangle of vines and boxes. "One of the waitresses' roommate came and got them. She said her roommate's mom wanted two kittens, but that leaves two kittens who need a home. She can't have pets in her apartment. So either we find them a home or they have to go to the pound." Alan peered expectantly at me.

"Oh, no." I held up my hands, backing up. "After Scooter died, I swore I'd never have a pet again." Two years earlier I held my beloved little tuxedo cat when she was euthanized after the vet discovered she had liver cancer.

"Well, maybe we can find them a home. I can check with John Smalley. Maybe he needs some barn cats." Alan pulled out his cell phone. "I snapped some pictures. Here they are."

I stared down at four adorable piles of fur. Two were gray-and-black tabby cats, one with longer, fluffier fur. One was orange striped and one was white, gray, and orange, like a paint-splotched mixture of all the other ones. "Which ones did the roommate's mother take?" I stared at the picture.

"The orange one and the short-haired tabby." Alan tucked the phone back in his shirt pocket. "I'll check with John. Maybe he knows someone who might want them."

"They're so little. They'll be lucky if some crow doesn't swoop in and get them if they're taken to a farm."

"We'll see. I talked to John earlier when he dropped off the pork chops. You should see the radishes he brought in. They're big but they're really sweet, too. Usually big radishes are too sharp, but these are amazing." Alan patted my shoulder. "I'm sorry about the cat, Tuck. Sometimes it's a crappy world."

"Yeah, no kidding." I shook my head wearily. He went with me to the back door, opening it by tapping in the security code on the door lock.

"Are you okay to work tonight?" he asked as we entered the hallway leading to the Acorn. "How's your eye? Has the swelling gone down?"

I flicked on the lights, inhaling the scent of floor polish and beer which characterized the place. "I'm fine. No headaches, no eye blurring. All I needed was a good night's sleep." I did all my usual opening chores on autopilot: unlocked the back access door to the restrooms, unlocked the staff break room, and verified the overhead fans and lights were working.

I walked around the main room, giving it a cursory check to make sure the overnight cleaning crew did their usual excellent job. Alan went to the front door and unlocked it. "I stocked the bar an hour ago," he said. "And the till is loaded."

I knew he'd handle those details, but I still went behind the counter and verified the contents in the dishes of lemons, limes, and other perishable supplies we shared with the restaurant. I checked behind me, through windows that used to be above the factory but which now looked over the brewing operation. I waved to Miller, our brew master, who walked around the vats and kettles in the attached brewery. I turned back to the bar and entered my access code to the cash register which was also linked to our inventory system. "Thanks, Alan, for taking care of the momma cat. I appreciate it."

He paused near the door which led to the Parlor. "You can't save 'em all, Tuck." He unlocked the door and went into the restaurant, closing the door behind him.

"Maybe not, but I'd like to save one now and again," I said to the empty room. I moved from behind the bar and surveyed the Acorn. The front windows faced north so the sun was muted, casting a glow over the front tables. The east side shared a wall with the Parlor and the west side faced into the brewery with mirrors behind liquor bottles on the wall between the windows. The south side of the room faced the parking lot, so there were no windows there. I designed the space to be a refuge from the world, not a reflection of it, so there were no televisions and no music. Forty, maybe fifty people could squeeze into the room, and frequently did. It was small, cozy, and exactly what I wanted when I thought of a pub.

The back door opened and voices called out, one female and one male, telling me the afternoon shift was starting. I went to the front door and flipped the light to illuminate the front *Open* sign.

It was time to go to work.

****

By four o'clock the pub was three-fourths full. Alan stopped in, letting me know the Parlor was fully booked for the evening. "It really paid to put an ad in the newspapers. I had the waitresses do an informal poll. Almost a third of the tables in the Parlor for lunch were from out-of-towners and half of the dinner reservations are, too."

I took a sip of water from the thermos bottle I kept under the bar. "All those city folks must be bored with the fine restaurants they have in their towns."

"Good prices, excellent food, nice atmosphere. It's worth a drive." He leaned closer. "Owen and I were going to get together tonight, but something came up and he can't make it. Let me know if you want me to take over for you later."

I nodded my understanding and turned to help a customer while Alan returned to his duties in the kitchen. Alan and Sheriff Owen Knott's discrete affair was going on now for almost five years. I think they were happy with their easy-going relationship and neither was anxious to formalize it or advertise it.

I walked carefully on the two-foot wide platform behind the bar which allowed me to reach the beer pulls and the counter. There are disadvantages to being only five feet tall, but there are always ways to cope, too. I made sure my Pullers Platform was installed when we built the bar so I could work the counter, a job I loved.

After Alan left, I scooped up empty glasses from bar patrons and filled orders from the two barmaids. I turned to set drinks on their trays when the front door opened. When I saw who entered, I almost dropped the glass of Deacon's Downfall, our house lager. Isabel Fitz stood in the doorway, sweeping the crowded room with an imperious gaze.

PJ Fitz's wife was tall and slender with shoulder-length dark brown hair hanging in an unbroken line to frame her face. Isabel was in her mid-forties but appeared at least a decade younger, unlike her husband who looked every year, if not more, of his fifty-five on God's earth.

Like Marianne, Isabel was beautiful, but unlike Marianne's ethereal prettiness, Isabel projected a svelte, smoldering sexuality. It wasn't garish or blatant but it was there nonetheless. I seldom interacted with her because Isabel was on the Haute social ladder while I was on the unHaute one but I golfed with her a few times and played bridge with her now and again. She was a merciless adversary and a generous playing partner.

Isabel caught sight of me and headed for the seat at the end of the bar. Her navy skirt, blue-and-white striped silk blouse under the matching navy jacket and her navy pumps made her perfect for an advertisement for Bobby Brooks. She laid her navy blue leather handbag on the oak counter and slid onto the seat. "I see the rumors are true. That's a terrible black eye."

"It looks worse than it is. How can I help you?" I set a bar coaster in front of her, one decorated with the logo of our Friar's Folly Imperial Stout, featuring a fat and jolly Friar Tuck, laughing.

"Have you seen my husband yet?"

Hmm. Yet? "Nope." I busied myself with the bar pulls. "He doesn't come in every night." *Not a lie,* I reasoned. *PJ comes in often in the afternoon, too.*

"Very discreet of you." She rested her hands in her lap and regarded me with a calm, somewhat exasperated expression. "Will you tell him to meet me at the country club? We were scheduled to go there for dinner tonight."

"I don't take messages." I held up my hands when she opened her mouth to speak. "It's a house rule. We don't act as a messenger service. If you need to contact him, call his cell phone."

"That won't get his attention." Her dark brown eyes held mine in a steady gaze. "I know he comes here to meet his girlfriend. It's irrelevant to me. We have an obligation to be at the dinner and it's important he attend." She stated this with no hint of anger, self-pity, or reproach, but as a statement of fact.

I grudgingly admired her calmness in the face of her husband's blatant infidelity. My mother used to say *Cream rises to the top, but so does the scum*, and that was certainly the case with Isabel Fitz and her no-good husband. I nudged a clean napkin toward her. "You can leave him a note and if I see him, I'll make sure he gets it."

Isabel tilted her head to one side. "Thank you." She spoke while she jotted words on the paper. "We're scheduled to go to the Sherwood Faire to benefit the Food Bank. PJ is supposed to hand out the prizes for the raffle after dinner."

"What prizes?" I drew a draft of Vicar's Vengeance, our house pilsner, and set it on the bar maid's tray.

"Archery lessons, a gift certificate to the Forest Spa, and the dinner coupon you provided." Isabel finished writing and folded the napkin in half, creasing it with one pink-painted fingernail. She glanced around the room. "This is very nice. You did a good job on the restoration and decorating. Very tasteful." She touched the napkin, edging it in my direction.

"Thanks." I put the napkin on the back bar, propped next to the bottle of Maker's Mark, which was PJ's drink of choice most nights.

She watched my actions. "Can I ask you something?"

"You can ask. I may not answer." I leaned over to clean a glass before running it through the hot sanitizing water. I'd done this for so many years I barely felt the heat any more.

"Is Tucker your real name?"

I set the glass on the drying rack. "Yep. My momma thought it would give me an edge in a man's world."

Isabel's nodded thoughtfully. "Did it work? Did it give you an edge?"

I drew a glass of The Archbishop's Ardor, our India Pale Ale, and held it up, the golden liquid molten in the light. "You tell me. I own a bar and a restaurant. Well, I partly own them. Miller owns half of the Pub and Alan owns half of the Parlor. I worked hard all my life to save up the money and when the chance came, I didn't look back."

"Good for you. You found your path and you took it." She examined the coaster and the laughing Friar Tuck. "Why did you name your beers after religious figures?"

I grinned. "It was Miller's idea. You see, I love a dark beer. So we thought we'd use a play on my name. Our stout became Friar's Folly. Tucker Frye, you see. From there, we brainstormed some other ideas and before you knew it, we had names."

Isabel touched the coaster with a pale pink fingernail. "I always wanted . . ." She shook her head and frowned.

"Wanted what?" I asked.

Isabel glanced to her left, but the nearest customer wasn't interested in our conversation. "I always wanted to be a chef," she confided. "In fact, I took classes in

France. But my father fell on hard times, and we didn't have any money, and PJ came along." She shrugged, her beautiful linen jacket sliding over her silk blouse with a whisper. "And here I am."

I glimpsed the glitter of tears in her eyes but a moment later, she slid off the bar chair, her poise in place once again. "If I see PJ, I'll give him the note," I promised.

Her eyes went to the bottle of Maker's Mark. "Thank you, Tucker. I appreciate it. It was good talking with you. You've given me some things to think about."

I started to reply but the bar phone rang, the long jangle easily heard over the low buzz of conversation. I picked up the receiver while Isabel left, brushing past some newly entered customers. "Oak's Acorn, Tucker talking."

"Aunt Tuck, it's me, it's Will."

I turned my back on the bar and hunkered over the phone. "I can barely hear you."

He spoke in a whispered rush, his words tumbling together. "I'm being followed, chased. Be careful, Aunt Tuck. They might know I gave you something. I'm sure they're after me. Somebody called me and threatened me."

"Where are you?" He sounded frightened out of his wits. I checked the window. It was still light outside, but clouds were rolling in again, piling up above the trees. "What do you mean, someone called you?"

"I'm at the factory. Something's wrong. Make sure you take care of the information I gave you. If you have to, get it to—"

The line went dead.

Chapter 4

I set the phone back in its cradle then went to my purse stored under the bar. A call to Will on my cell phone just bounced immediately to voice mail. I wiggled my fingers into the snug little inner purse pocket and checked. Yep, the USB stick was still in there. I debated calling the police but immediately nixed the idea. If Will was at the factory after hours, it was probably best the police not know about it. I jammed my purse back into the drawer and returned to work, not sure what else to do.

About an hour later, John Smalley came into the bar. "You've got a good crowd in the restaurant." He glanced over his shoulder at the glass doors leading to the Parlor while he took a seat at the bar.

"Alan said we had a full house reserved for tonight. What can I get you?" I set a coaster in front of him.

John rested his tanned forearms on the dark oak counter. Like the rest of him, his arms were big, with dark wiry hair and clearly defined muscle showing under his rolled-up pale brown shirtsleeves. "A club soda. I really stopped in to see how you were doing. I felt bad leaving you last night. Did you go to the doctor?"

I tossed some ice cubes into a glass and filled it with soda from the spigot then set it in front of him, nudging the dish of lemon and lime wedges his way.

"I'm fine. A bit sore from the fall I took. You've got nothing to feel bad about. I'm glad you were there to break up the fight."

His coarse black hair, cropped short and curly, bounced gently when he shook his head. "You'd think Rob would know better. He and Guy have been fighting most of their lives. I wonder what set Rob off last night."

"Probably Marianne." I glanced at him while I leaned over the sink to wash glasses. "Guy has the hots for her and I suppose Rob takes exception to it."

John gasped, choking on his drink. "You don't pull any punches, do you?"

"It doesn't take a rocket scientist to see what's going on. I have to admit, though, I'm surprised Guy isn't making a play for a younger trophy woman. That seems more his style."

John's dark eyes narrowed with laughter, giving him the appearance of a mischievous young boy. "I think it has more to do with Rob than it does with Marianne. Guy always resented Rob."

"Seriously?" I held up a finger when I was summoned from the far end of the bar. "Hold that thought. I'll be back." I took care of my other customers, returning in five minutes or so to resume our conversation. "So you think Guy is making a play for Marianne as payback at Rob?"

John stirred his drink with the swizzle stick. "I wouldn't be surprised. Rob was always popular in high school, more than Guy was. Guy's family had money, but Rob was always the first one chosen for sports, the king of the prom, Homecoming king. You know how it goes."

I smiled wryly. "I spent most of my high school days pretending to be a Goth. We weren't exactly part of the In Crowd."

John grinned, small white lines crinkling in the dark tan skin around his eyes. His neatly trimmed beard, like his hair, was liberally streaked with gray and it seemed to twinkle in the light coming in from the windows. "Yeah, I didn't fit in, either. My parents were organic farmers."

"Really? So you were part of the Green Movement years ahead of your time?"

His eyes narrowed. "Not really. It was before there were the new refined organic products. We used raw manure. I stunk all the time. I smelled like, well, you know, like manure. It got in our clothes and our hair. It followed me wherever I went. I was teased unmercifully."

The raw bitterness in his voice made me wince. "I can only imagine," I murmured.

He didn't hear me. John was on a roll. "Marianne never made fun of me. You should have seen her in high school. You think she's beautiful now, you should have seen her then. She had waist-long, gold-white hair, pale skin. You know how it was. Everybody thought they needed a tan. But not Marianne. She was pale as snow. Untouched and beautiful."

Pale like snow and cold like snow. I felt the little twist of jealousy I always felt around Marianne, so beautiful, so perfect.

Unaware of my thoughts, John continued. "She never laughed at me. Marianne was the only one who didn't."

"Well, I guess you showed them," I said, trying to toss lightness into an otherwise bleak conversation. "You're a success now and Rob is stuck managing an awful factory." I scowled, remembering the images on the USB stick in my purse. "That place should be shut down."

"I won't argue with your sentiment. I wish some animal rights activists could get in there and get pictures. What they do there is ethically wrong," John said in a low voice, glancing to his left where another customer sat. "It should be morally wrong, too, but it isn't."

I paused in the act of reaching for a beer glass. "What's the difference?"

"Ethics are a personal belief system. Morals are the belief system of a society."

"Really? I always thought it was the other way around."

John shook his head. "Nope. I have a minor in philosophy from the U. That's one of the few things I'm sure of."

"You went to the University of Iowa?" I put the glass under the spout of Friar's Folly and drew a glass of the dark stout.

He grinned. "Moo U. Iowa State University. I have a B.S. degree in Agribusiness."

"And a minor in philosophy." I shook my head. "A well-rounded farmer."

"I guess. I don't know how Rob can work there. The right thing to do is to close the damn factory."

"I don't know if it's black and white," I temporized, setting the glass on the serving tray and drawing another. "It affects so many jobs, not only here but in York. If it's closed, the town will suffer."

"The town will evolve," John said confidently. "It's not right that a population should profit from the exploitation of a weaker species."

He was repeating the arguments I presented to Marianne and Rob earlier. Images from the memory stick drifted across my mind. I always prided myself on my eco-friendly lifestyle. I always bought organic (where possible), I recycled (when convenient), and I tried to reduce and reuse (when I could).

But now I was confronted with a moral dilemma—and an ethical dilemma—which wasn't convenient or timely. That awful factory did produce low cost food, but at what price? "I'm sure it's only a matter of time until someone checked how they run the factory. The egg recall threw the spotlight on the Yoke."

"And Richard will come to town and cover it all up." John's voice resumed its bitter quality. He tilted the glass up and drained the club soda, his throat surprisingly pale compared to the tan of his arms and bit of chest I saw at the top of his shirt. "It's what he does so well." He reached for his back pocket but I held up a hand.

"It's on the house, John." I leaned forward, my elbows resting on the counter. John obligingly leaned forward, too. "Richard may find there's evidence even he can't cover up."

Our faces were so close I clearly saw his beard quiver when a muscle twitched in his jaw. He nodded slowly, his eyes intent on mine. "Good to know. If I could help in any way, I'm be happy to do it."

I started to brush him off with an airy, *thanks but no thanks.* Then I remembered Will's frightened voice on the phone earlier. "I may take you up on that, John."

He touched my work-chapped hand with his equally rough and chapped hand. "My home phone will bounce to my cell phone if I'm not there to answer." He squeezed my hand gently when he straightened. "I mean it."

I nodded gratefully. "Thanks." I didn't know if I'd ever call on him, but it made me feel better knowing I could if needed. He headed toward the door, pausing to chat with a couple of customers on his way out. Well, it was nice to know I had reinforcements. Then I wondered where that idea came from. This wasn't a war and I wasn't on the defensive. Was I?

There were no answer to my rhetorical question, so I turned my attention to waiting on customers. The Acorn wasn't extremely busy, which was usual for an early summer evening. Many people preferred to be outside taking advantage of the good weather. Our real evening rush wouldn't start until the sun went down, at eight or nine o'clock.

I took a break at seven and tried calling Will again, but once again the line bounced immediately to voice mail. I called my home answering machine but there were no messages there. Where was he? What was happening? All I could do was hope he was okay. I went to the back of the pub and walked through the back restroom access hallway to the Parlor, which was full of patrons. It was just a few steps to the kitchen where I dined on a sandwich at a table in the corner while Alan and his assistant chefs bustled around me.

I loved watching the kitchen staff at work. They were like a machine composed of human parts, one which danced and wove its way around an obstacle course of hot stoves, a pastry chef applying the finishing touches to a dessert plate, a salad maker who chopped and diced with elegant flourishes of a knife, a saucier who applied exactly the right amount of rich burgundy gravy to a steak.

At the heart of the machine was Alan. He usually hummed and sometimes he sang while he cooked, his choice of music consistent with his mood of the moment. Alan had formal musical training and was in demand at weddings and funerals and other public events. His rendition of "Memories" from the musical *Cats,* could move a roomful of mourners to sighs and cathartic tears.

The kitchen staff all knew to listen closely to his repertoire because it gave excellent insight into his temperament. When he sang various songs from *Showboat*, things were going well. I had never heard him raise his voice to any employee, but when he sang Neil Young's "Barstool Blues" his staff knew they needed to pick up the pace.

Alan paused near me, a giant metal mixing bowl in his arms. His white chef's coat was spotless and crisp, fitted to his lean frame by tucks in the back. Alan always changed his coat whenever it got splattered because he said a clean coat meant a clean kitchen. He eyed me while he briskly whisked the batter in the bowl. "Still feeling okay?"

I nodded. "I'm fine, but . . ." I hesitated, not sure if I should confide in him. "I'm worried about a friend of mine. He called earlier and he sounded upset."

Alan arched one dark brown eyebrow. "Upset? About what?"

I bit my lip, not sure what to say. "I can't really tell you. But if you talk to Owen and he says there are some problems at the Yoke, would you tell me?"

"The Yoke?" Alan withdrew the whisk and eyed the consistency of the batter when it dribbled back into the bowl before resuming his beating. "Do you know someone who works there?"

I stood and gathered up my dinnerware. "Forget it. I shouldn't have said anything." I went to the dishwashing station at the back of the kitchen and handed my dishes to the boy.

Alan watched me traverse my way through the busy kitchen. When I reached the door leading to the Parlor he called out, "If I hear anything, I'll let you know."

I nodded and beat a retreat, happy I didn't spill the beans about Will. I didn't want to get Alan in trouble with his boyfriend, but if anyone knew about problems brewing, it would be the Sheriff.

I went back to the Acorn, which was busier than when I left. I checked the clock over the door. It was after eight, which meant golf matches were wrapping up, baseball games were finishing, and the swimming pool was closed for the night. We'd probably have a good crowd from now until closing.

"Somebody said you had a shiner, but I didn't know it was such a beauty."

I turned at the bantering voice behind me. PJ Fitz was coming through the back door, bringing with him a gust of hot moist air. "Hey, PJ." I brushed by him to get to the drop-gate into the bar area. "Is it raining?"

"Not yet." He put a hand on my arm, pulling me to a halt. "Somebody told me Guy Gibson threw a punch at you."

I tugged my arm. "He was aiming for Rob Huntington but I got in the way."

"I heard John Smalley decked Guy. I'm surprised he helped Rob," PJ said. "You'd think John might hold a grudge."

I paused on my way to the bar. "Hold a grudge? For what?"

"Rob's been a fuckup since high school and John's always worked hard all his life. He probably doesn't think it's fair Rob has so much and he has so little."

I remembered John's bitter comment about the teasing in high school. "John is an independent businessman and Rob has a job managing your chicken factory." I grimaced. "That's not so great."

PJ leveled a glare at me. "Don't knock it. The factory keeps a lot of people working."

I swear, if I heard that argument one more time I was going to take a swing at the person who said it. "At what price? Why would John resent Rob?"

"Rob got the girl."

I turned to stare at him. "Was John in love with Marianne?"

PJ nodded. "Just about every guy in school was in love with the Ice Princess."

I shook my head. "I don't get it. What is it about her that makes men go google-eyed?"

PJ grinned. "If you've got to ask, you don't get it."

Well, that was probably right. I continued walking, weaving my way between two groups of drinkers who congregated near the end of the bar. I ducked under the gate and jumped up on the Puller's Platform while PJ elbowed his way through the crowd to stand at the counter.

"Give me a Maker's Mark," he barked over the noise of the people around him.

I nodded to indicate I heard him then I checked in with our brew master's son, Mike, who worked the late shift. His evening eight-to-two shift meant he could go immediately from the bar to the bakery where he worked from two until six in the morning. We often overlapped our shifts when it was busy, like tonight.

We divvied up the workload with him taking the north end of the bar and me taking the south end in addition to any orders from the staff. That meant I was stuck with PJ. I filled a highball glass with two fingers of Maker's Mark, grabbed the napkin with the note on it and set both in front of PJ where he stood at the bar, elbows planted on the edge to give himself some space. It also let one arm press against the boob of the blonde in the bar chair next to him. The babe giggled when he raised his arm, the action giving him a good feel.

"Your wife left you a note," I said loudly, tapping the napkin on the bar counter.

The blonde eyed PJ. She often came in on weekends with girlfriends, sometimes leaving with a guy, sometimes leaving with the girls. I think she waitressed at the cafe downtown and had a mean boyfriend who worked weekends at the John Deere factory in Des Moines, which probably explained why she came to the bar on the weekend.

PJ glowered at me. Although he and John Smalley were both darkly colored and bearded, that was where the resemblance ended. PJ was like a dark thundercloud, only a minute or two away from lightning and disaster. John was like a big carnival panda bear, comforting despite his size. "I've already talked to my wife." He took a gulp of his whisky.

I frowned at his lack of respect for fine Kentucky bourbon. "Fine. I'll pitch it." I crumpled the napkin in my fist.

PJ's hand snaked out and grasped my wrist. "I'll take it."

I dropped the wad of paper on the counter and yanked my arm away from him before moving to the right to answer a question from another customer. I watched PJ covertly when he read the note before wadding it into a tight little ball and tossing it at the wastebasket near the bottle wall opposite the counter. I waited until he was diverted by conversation with the blonde, then I retrieved the napkin and opened it under the cover of the counter.

Patrick: uncouple yourself from your whore and keep your promise to appear at the club.

I grinned then tossed the napkin in the wastebasket. *You go, girl.*

"I suppose you know what's in the note," PJ mumbled when I was near him again a few minutes later.

"I talked to Isabel earlier. She was worried you'd forget you were supposed to go to some dinner or other." I couldn't resist a little dig. "She said you were probably busy."

PJ leered at me. "Yeah, I was. I'm a man with appetites and my wife doesn't always satisfy them." He took another slug of bourbon like it proved how much of a man he was.

I rolled my eyes. "You may have appetites but you've got no taste. Your wife is a class act."

PJ shrugged. "It was an arranged marriage."

I laughed aloud. "In this day and age? Please."

"Her family owned a company my brother wanted. It was easier for me to marry her for it." PJ swirled the amber liquor in his glass, one corner of his mouth twisted in a wry smile. "It worked out fine for both of us. She wanted security and I wanted the company."

"So you lived happily ever after." I considered Rob and Marianne, who waited for years to get married only to have the marriage be so unhappy. Then there was John Smalley, who was married years earlier only to divorce a few years later. And Alan, who bounced from relationship to relationship. Was their graduating class all cursed?

"Where's Guy?" PJ twisted so he leaned back against the blonde while he surveyed the bar. "He missed the dinner. He always goes to all those charity fund raisers."

"Marianne mentioned he was gone." I edged to the left, heading for the group of drinkers at the end of the bar, some of whom were holding up empty glasses.

"Well, Marianne would know what Guy's doing. She's got him tied to her apron the same she's got Rob tied." PJ turned, his torso pressed against the side of the blonde so he almost enveloped her with his plump body. "How come I've never met you before?" he asked her.

I left him to his games and focused on my other customers, not anxious to see duplicity in action. My own divorce was amiable and based on a mutual decision, but as a bartender, I saw too many spouses who used my bar like their private playground. I disliked it but couldn't do much about it.

I fielded more good-natured kidding about my black eye, with several people expressing disapproval of either Rob, Guy, or both. I chose not to take sides, but it was interesting to see who sided with who. I kept a mental tally and came to the conclusion that most of the customers were split fifty-fifty, with blame on each man equally.

It was almost ten o'clock and nearing the end of my shift when I made my way back to PJ's end of the bar in time to hear him say to the blonde, ". . . over my dead body."

I grinned when I picked up the woman's empty glass. "That's tempting."

"You don't mean that, Tuck," PJ said in the wheedling voice he used when he drank a tad too much. "We'd be lost without you. Everybody loves Tucker Frye, the Mistress Mixologist at the best brewpub in Barnsdale, Iowa."

"It's the only brewpub in Barnsdale, Iowa." I smoothed my bar cloth over the counter. "And even if I off you, it doesn't mean I'd get caught. I'm smarter than that."

He raised the remains of his Maker's Mark to me in salute. "True. No one would believe such a horrible thing from someone so perky."

"Perky?" I started to seriously consider ways I could kill him without risk to myself or my business.

PJ nodded, the dark shadows of the bar making his pudgy face seem almost thin. "Since you lost all your weight, you're definitely perky." He took another swallow while I considered a biting retort. "Besides, you're clever enough to escape detection."

Trust PJ to give me a backhanded compliment. "I didn't know that a large weight loss would transfer me to the category of perky. What was I before?"

"You were robust." He burped softly. "I meant what I said. Those protesters will stage an egg-out over my dead body."

As usual, the subject of conversation was yanked back to PJ who always acted like a drama queen, or in his case, a drama prince. I was told that his mother, Eleanor, was the true drama queen in the family. The "egg-out" was the upcoming Egg-Free Friday, planned to draw attention to the deplorable conditions the chickens endured in order to provide us with our eggs.

That thought made me consider Will again. I would be off-shift in a few minutes. I could drive by the Yoke and see what, if anything, was happening. If it was quiet, I could go home and hopefully have a worry-free night.

"I don't expect you to sympathize," PJ continued, his plump fingers smoothing his dark goatee which successfully hid his sagging chin. PJ had gained and lost weight throughout the fifteen years I knew him. As a recent weight-loss victor myself, I could commiserate with his battle, but PJ was losing his fight.

"Of course I don't sympathize. The chicken farm is one of the most inhumane places on earth."

"Factory farming keeps prices low." PJ smiled smugly at me, his dark eyes cold. "And it helps the local economy."

"At what cost?" I demanded. "Chickens are kept confined in a tiny space, they never see the light of day, it's hot in the summer and cold in the winter, and they're forced to lay eggs until they're used up. Chicks are mangled if they aren't wanted." I drew in a deep breath, forcing myself to calmness. Arguing with PJ Fitz wouldn't get the damn chicken factory closed. Only cold, hard evidence might do that.

I left him, sure if I stayed I'd either hit him or say something wrong, something which would get Will in more trouble than he already was. I stayed busy for a few minutes when a women's softball team came in, followed by an influx of people attending a family reunion. Once I handled those customers, I consulted with Mike and turned the till over to him.

I grabbed my purse and ducked under the bar gate in time to see Alan working his way through the clumps of customers toward me. He'd shed his white chef's coat and wore a dark brown polo shirt and pale khaki shorts. He appeared cool and crisp, not at all like a man who just spent an eight hour stint in a kitchen, cooking.

"We were wrapping up in the kitchen when I heard a bus boy talking to the kid at the dishwasher. The bus boy said there's trouble at the Yoke. His girlfriend called him about it. She lives near there." Alan spoke in a low voice, his gaze darting to PJ, focused on the blonde.

"What kind of trouble?" I longed to check my cell phone for messages but I restrained myself.

"He said squad cars were all around the place and a bunch of the chickens got out. The police blocked off the road leading to York."

"Holy crap," I breathed. "PJ's sitting right over there. I wonder why he hasn't left. Wouldn't the police call him if there were problems there?"

Alan nodded. "They should. Or they'd call Rob, since he's the manager there."

"I talked to Rob this morning. His number is probably still on my phone." Without giving myself a minute to consider it, I found the number and dialed it. I moved from the crowds into the back hallway where it was quieter, Alan following me.

Rob answered on the second ring. "What?" he demanded brusquely.

"Rob, it's Tucker Frye. I heard there were problems at the Yoke. Is everything okay?"

"I'm on my way there right now," he replied. "I'm on the County Home road to York, I just left my cabin. Are you at the Acorn? Have you seen PJ? I've been trying to get hold of him for the last hour but his cell phone must be off."

"He's sitting at the bar. Shall I have him call you?" I gestured to Alan and nodded at the busy pub, full of patrons. He hurried away.

"Have him meet me. The police called me and told me there were intruders on the premises. They shot someone."

"What?" I almost dropped the phone. "Who? Where?"

"I'm not sure. I don't have the details. But Sheriff Knott said one of the trespassers was shot. An ambulance was on the way but Knott sounded pretty shook up. I have to go, Tucker. I need to concentrate on my driving. You know how the road is here."

I did know. The County Home road was twisty and winding, going up and down hills with very limited visibility in spots. Woods lined each side of the road and deer or other critters were apt to leap at you at any time. Most people who drove to York from Barnsdale went to Highway 63, east of town, which was a straighter route. But for Rob, leaving from his cabin near the river, the twisting road would be fastest. "I'll tell PJ to meet you. Be careful."

"Thanks. Oh, and Tuck, call Marianne, would you? I didn't have a chance to talk to her." He clicked the phone off before I could say 'yea' or 'nay.'

I clicked the End button on my phone and lowered it, leaning over to peer into the bar. PJ and Alan were in conversation, PJ staring at the cell phone in his hand. A sudden shiver shook me. *Someone's walking on a grave,* my mama used to say when a shiver like that came out of nowhere.

I hoped she was wrong.

Chapter 5

I ducked into the staff break room at the back of the bar and extracted the battered phone book from a pile of magazines on the table. I found Marianne's home phone number and dialed it on my cell phone. When she answered, I said in a rush, "This is Tucker Frye. I talked to Rob. He's on his way to the factory in York. There's been trouble."

"Really? What kind of trouble?" She sounded almost bored, not like an eager newspaperwoman. Of course, she didn't need to be eager with people calling her with the news. I noticed she didn't ask why Rob asked me to call her or ask why I was talking to Rob. *Ice Princess. Apt name.* "I'm not sure. He was driving there to find out."

"Funny. I didn't hear anything on the police scanner." She sounded curious, not worried. "Where are you? Did Rob call you or did you talk to him in person?"

Police scanner? Then I remembered: Marianne owned the local newspaper. Presumably she'd cover any news stories and thus might have a scanner close at hand. "I called him. Somebody said there were problems at the Yoke and I was wondering what was happening. You might want to get over there. They've blocked the roads and there's a real mess."

"Thanks, Tucker. I'll call our photographer. We may need pictures to go with the story. I'll call Rob on his mobile phone while I drive. Maybe he can tell me what's going on." She hung up without so much as a thank-you or sorry-to-inconvenience-you-again.

I stowed my phone in my purse. Marianne sounded more worried about getting a news story than she did about her husband. Was it more evidence of their deteriorating relationship? Or was it a sign of Marianne's professionalism? I realized I wanted something negative to blame on her and I mentally chastised myself. Just because I didn't like Marianne, it didn't mean she was a cold-hearted bitch. Did it?

Alan appeared in the doorway. "PJ is on his way to the factory."

I glimpsed PJ bobbing through the crowd. "Is he sober enough to drive?" The last thing I needed was a lawsuit because that asshole got into an accident. It was a constant worry of mine despite the fact we carried a hefty insurance policy to protect ourselves and I trained all personnel to alert me to any drunks. That was one reason I followed Rob out of the Acorn the night before, to make sure he didn't try to drive. Well, that and to try to circumvent any fighting, of course.

"He called his son. Three will pick him up and they'll go together."

"Good. I served PJ two drinks. I'm sure he's relatively sober but I'd rather not take the chance." I started for the back door, relieved to know Henry the Third, PJ's son, would be handling his father. Three was a likeable young man in his mid-twenties who was more like Isabel than PJ, thanks be to God for him. He was being groomed to take over PJ's place in the Fitz business empire and from the rumors around town, he was doing very well.

"Is your friend involved in whatever is happening at the Yoke?" Alan asked in a low voice, keeping pace beside me when I went outside.

I looked automatically to my left, at the spot where the mother cat used to live. Then I remembered. It was empty now, with no mama or babies there. For some reason, I felt a pall of depression settle over me. Poor momma cat, killed on the street and her babies all scattered here and there. She lived a crappy life except for the small scraps of kindness she got from me and the other staff. It was unfair for her to die like that, probably in pain, and probably trying to crawl back to her kittens before she died. It seemed like every place I turned, I saw evidence of humans dealing shit to animals. I shook my head, trying to shake away the gloom.

"I don't know if he's involved or not. He was scared." I stopped at the edge of the parking lot, breathing in the smell of damp pavement and the earthy odor from the park nearby. Lightning bugs glimmered in the distance, little dancing motes of light hovering and skimming erratically through the air.

I thought about the momma cat and I remembered Will as a young boy, playing with kitties on our farm, laughing when they all tumbled together in the grass. My worry combined with my depression and I blurted, "He's not a friend. He's family."

Alan batted at the night bugs buzzing around us, frowning in bewilderment. "I didn't know you had any family around here. Who is it?"

"It's a long story. Trust me, by Southern rules, he's blood kin. He's a nephew, or as near as makes no never-mind."

He blinked. "I can't believe I understood what you said. I've hung out too long with you. Is he working at the factory?"

"He was. I can't tell you any more about it. Will swore me to secrecy. Don't tell Owen, okay?" I put a hand on Alan's arm, his skin warm under my touch. "Promise."

"I'm not sure," Alan said slowly. "If he's involved in what's happened, I might need to tell Owen. I mean, if your nephew did something—"

I tightened my hand on his arm. "I helped raise Will, Alan. He's like my own child. Please. Don't tell Owen unless I give you the go-ahead. Please?"

Alan nodded reluctantly. "I won't make any promises, but I won't volunteer any information."

"Thank you." I didn't want to press him about it. Alan was very protective about his relationship with Owen and I respected that. But I also wanted to protect Will, at least as much as I could. "I'll keep trying to call Will tonight. Maybe it's got nothing to do with him."

"Yeah, who knows?" Alan walked with me to my dusty red Chevy, which was an ugly stepsister parked next to his polished gray Acura, glittering like Cinderella in her finery at the ball. "I'm sure he's fine."

I slipped into my car and started it, getting the windows opened to let in cooler air. The oppressive heat of the day was lessening but it was still humid, the air so damp it was like a sponge when I inhaled. "I have to open tomorrow," I said through my window. "I should know by then if there're any problems."

"I'll be in early, too. You know how Sundays are." Alan walked around his car to the driver side.

I waved and backed out of my spot. I knew how Sundays were, for sure. On Sunday the Parlor only served a brunch, opening at eleven and closing at three. We usually had a line of people waiting to get in to sample Alan's amazing brunch buffet.

I drove through town, past the movie theater where a crowd was getting out. Downtown was relatively busy for ten o'clock on a Saturday, with cars in front of the theater, the Huntsman's Grill, the Barnsdale Bar on B Avenue, and the Old Grove Inn, a restaurant whose bar was open late. There were two other bars in Barnsdale, one north of town and one south, bringing our drinking total to six. The number of bars and churches were equal, a fact my daddy would've said was a balance between light and dark, with the church being the dark entity in that analogy. I smiled when I remembered him saying such a thing just to annoy his mother-in-law, my granny, who was a devout church-going woman and a teetotaler to boot.

"How she must be spinning in her grave," I mused, pulling into my driveway. "Here she wanted me to be the first lady preacher in the parish and I end up running a bar. I guess she was right." My grandmother predicted a dire end for me if I married a Yankee. I suppose, according to her morals, I fulfilled her prediction.

I entered my quiet house and turned on the couch light. The silence of the building surrounded me. Normally I welcomed the quiet after the busy noise of the bar, but tonight it was oppressive. I poured myself a glass of wine and sipped while watching reruns on television, my cell phone next to me on the couch.

My inactivity lasted for about fifteen minutes, then I got up and paced, refilling my glass now and again while I walked in a steady circle from my kitchen, through the living room to the front door to peek through the window. Then back to the kitchen to glare at the clock and pace again.

I debated calling the hospital but I hesitated. I wasn't listed as kin to Will, so I couldn't expect anyone to give information to me if he was there. Besides, if he was injured, he might not be in the Barnsdale hospital. Des Moines was less than an hour's drive away and oftentimes patients were transported straight to one of their emergency centers if tricky surgery was needed.

I stepped onto the front porch, staring into the dark night of the park across the street. The deep rumbling of a toad echoed from the pond in the nearby woods, echoed by another, deeper rumbling. The air was still humid but cooler now and a faint breeze eddied toward me, something fresher than the moist breath which blew earlier. Maybe the weather was breaking.

I went inside and stared at the phone, considering my options. That's when I decided I had none. With a sigh, I went to bed knowing I wouldn't sleep but would lie there, tossing, until morning came. I made a promise to myself: if I didn't hear from Will by nine in the morning, I'd call Rob. Maybe I could get some details from him without revealing I knew Will.

Satisfied with my logic, I dropped into bed and fell into a fitful doze.

****

I tossed and turned for a few hours then got up before dawn and did my morning workout in record time. I dressed in capris and my dark red Oaks golf shirt and was savoring my second cup of coffee when my doorbell rang at seven-thirty. I sagged with relief. It was probably Will. Who else would be visiting so early? I raced to the door and jerked it open, ready to give my errant nephew a piece of my mind for scaring me half to death.

What I found was a young woman in ragged denim cut-offs, pink flip flops and a bright pink T-shirt holding a brown cardboard box with quarter-sized holes spaced evenly along its sides. It was roughly two-feet square with *Florida Oranges* on the side and a logo with a big smiling orange on stocky legs holding a glass of juice, which struck me as somewhat cannibalistic.

"Hey." She thrust the box at me.

I set my coffee cup on the table near the door. "What's this? Who are you?"

"Sorry it's early, but we're going to the lake today. Jen said you'll take care of them." She turned and left, striding down the front walk, her flip-flops snapping a sharp cadence on the pavement. A blue Honda sat in the drive, a patchwork apparition of faded paint, duct tape, and wire which snorted and gurgled while it idled in the early morning sunlight.

"Wait, what?" The box tilted in my hands. It wasn't heavy but it was awkward, with weight inside shifting from one side to another. I heard a pitiful *mew* and glanced down to see a white paw wiggling through one of the holes. Oh, shit. I shifted my gaze to the girl getting in the car. She must be the roommate who took in the kittens.

"Wait!" I hurried after her but the car was already belching down my drive. A young man waved while they drove off, the girl staring intently at the screen of her phone, her bare feet propped up on the dashboard.

The box upended in my hands, all the weight going to one end. "Whoa. Wait a minute." I scurried back to my living room and closed the door as the bottom gave way. Two kittens tumbled out, bodies twisting so they landed somewhat flat on their feet. For an instant we all stared at each other then they scampered under the couch, the upholstered skirt fluttering behind them. "Oh, for cryin' out loud."

I couldn't take care of kittens. For one thing, I didn't have pet supplies. When Scooter died, I resolutely got rid of all cat toys, litter boxes, beds, blankets, and reminders of my sweet little companion. For another thing, my house was cat-proof but it definitely was not kitten-proof. I could easily visualize small bodies disappearing under the washing machine or getting stuck behind the air conditioning unit in the utility room.

I got down on my hands and knees and lifted the couch skirt. Two sets of baleful eyes stared back at me. The kittens were so small the five-inch space gave them ample room to hunker. "Hey, guys, come out. No need to hide." I wiggled my fingers near them, but they promptly turned their backs on me, showing me a good view of furry butts, one mostly solid gray and one gray-and-black tabby. I let the skirt drop back into place. "Fine. Be that way."

I sat back and crossed my legs, draping one arm over the coffee table and tapping a staccato rhythm on the wood. I was stuck here. I couldn't leave with the kittens under the couch. God knows what mischief they'd get into if I left them free to roam. There was no easy way to block off the kitchen from the living room. It was all one large space. If I wanted to block off the hallway to the bedrooms I'd need to manhandle furniture to cover the doorway. Even if I did move it, I couldn't stop them from climbing. They were cats. That's what they did.

I remembered what Alan said the night before. Maybe John could use a barn cat or two. I nodded. That was the thing to do. I worked long hours. I couldn't have pets. I started to stand, but when I did, a striped paw inched from under the gold fabric of the couch, tiny claws clicking on the oak floor, questing to and fro.

I picked up a pencil from the coffee table and rapped the paw lightly. It withdrew but re-emerged almost immediately, tapping for the pencil. I ran the pencil along the floor and the paw stabbed eagerly for it, more and more frantic and stretching further and further. Finally a pink nose dotted with dark gray peeked from under the skirt fabric.

"Gotcha." I swept my arm under the couch. A kitten was scooped into the crook of my elbow and emerged from its hiding place, so comically startled I laughed. The kitten—a fluffy tabby with a white chest—bolted across the room, small legs churning for balance on the braided rug. The kitten ran into the corner near the front door, caught sight of the box I dropped, hissed and backed up, raced to the kitchen, bounced off a wall there, then ran back toward me, all in the space of a few seconds.

I blocked its entrance to the couch underworld by flattening myself onto the floor. The kitten ran up and over my body and landed on the couch, tiny claws digging in for stability. I twisted to peer over the cushion at it. The kitten turned, saw me, puffed up its fur, then sank down, obviously exhausted. "Good Lord. I forgot how energetic you young-uns are."

The fluffy one regarded me with bright gray-blue eyes, purring so loudly I expected the couch to shake. It must have been a signal to its sibling because the other kitten poked its head from under the couch and regarded me where I was sprawled on the floor. It slinked forward and clambered up on my knee. This one was mostly gray with a lighter gray-white tummy and dark brown paws. A bright splotch of dark brown-and-calico fur across its cheeks gave it a mask-like appearance, contrasting with the tabby markings on its forehead and around the eyes.

I picked it up gently around the tummy, depositing it next to its sibling, taking advantage of the moment to lift up the kitten's tail and examine its posterior. Yep, I saw a slight bulge near the smaller, lower dot-like opening. "Boy," I said, nudging him.

He collapsed on top of the fluffy one, who rolled over and yawned. I gently lifted the tabby-striped tail and checked. This one was harder to figure because of all the fur, but a bit of careful prodding showed me 'the landing stripe,' what my father used to call that distinctive dark bit of fur on a tabby leading to a female cat's vulva.

I leaned back against the coffee table and regarded the two newcomers, who returned the look with sleepy eyes. They appeared healthy, although they seemed so very tiny. My previous cat was petite, but she was gigantic compared to these guys. The female could easily fit in one of my shoes and the male was only slightly bigger. "I can't keep you." I rubbed a finger over the mixed-one's forehead.

He purred louder and sagged even more against his sister. His eyes were golden brown, and the thin black stripes on his head mixed in with blotches of black, gray, white, and even dark orange. "You've got some cayenne there, don't you?" I touched a dark red-orange spot on his nose.

The female, sensing my attention to her brother, emerged from under his weight and plopped near my hand, rolling slightly on her side to show me her plump pale tummy. "And you." I rubbed the soft fur under her chin. "You're like café au lait, aren't you?" The creamy beige and brown of her markings altered when I ran my hand over her fur, the same way coffee changed color when swirled in a cup. A sudden memory of beignets and café on the porch of our house seemed to fill my senses, a warm Louisiana breeze eddying through the curtains behind me.

The male mimicked his sister and rolled on his back, colliding with her in a tangle of paws. That set her off again. She righted herself and took off. He chased her, both of them racing down the hallway. I ran after them only to see them disappear into the hallway bathroom. "Gotcha!" I jumped in behind them and tugged the door closed.

The boy-cat was already behind the stool and the girl-cat pawed at the narrow linen closet. I satisfied myself they couldn't get into any trouble then I carefully backed from the room and closed the door securely. Well, they were safely locked up for now.

What to do? I checked my watch. Eight o'clock on a Sunday morning. I needed a cat carrier and maybe a few items of cat equipment, in case I needed to hold on to the little critters for a day or two. I started making a mental list while I strode through the kitchen, grabbed my purse, and headed for that Bastion of All-Night Shopping, Wal-Mart.

An hour later I returned, dumped all of my purchases on or near the kitchen table, and tip-toed to the bathroom. I pressed my ear against the wood paneling of the door. All quiet. I proceeded to my bedroom, the guest bedroom, and my den, closing doors while I went. I returned to the bathroom and listened again. Still quiet. That was ominous. I opened the door cautiously and peeked inside.

Two woebegone faces peeked up at me over the rim of the bathtub, barely visible over the edge. I saw immediately what happened. They probably slid in and couldn't get out because of the slanted and slippery sides. The upper doors, which enclosed the tub when it was used as a shower didn't provide any climbing traction, so they couldn't get a grip on anything.

I picked them up and set them on the rug. They took off in a flash, gamboling along the hall only to encounter closed doors. They whirled and set off for the living room, tripping over paws in their haste. Laughing, I followed, keeping an eye on them while I unpacked my purchases, many of which were loaded into the cat carrier.

I unwrapped what was billed as 'teething toys,' hard oblongs of cloth that the male kitten, Cayenne, immediately began to gnaw on. He abandoned it for the small sponge ball I tossed his way, pausing once to watch his sister Café chase a crinkly, sparkly ball enclosed in a plastic frame. The two disappeared, romping after their toys.

Satisfied they were diverted, I quickly filled a water dish and emptied some canned kitten food into two dishes, which I set inside the small pantry closet near my back door. Then I filled another dish with kitten kibble and set it down, too.

The litter box was simple to set up. When Scooter was alive, she used a cat door to go to the enclosed back stoop, which was big enough for her litter box, a watering can, her cat carrier, and a few other oddments. I filled up the covered litter box and cleared a space for it on the porch. All I need do was introduce the kittens to the pet door, and voila—bathroom problem solved. I also purchased another, much smaller litter box. That and the kittens would go into the spare bedroom while I was at work, at least until I found them a permanent home.

It was now past nine o'clock. I put a scratching post near the couch before I unpackaged the other toys I bought and put them into an old wicker picnic basket, storing it in my den. I need to be at the Acorn by one to open at two, but it gave me plenty of time to scout around for my lost nephew and still come back here, check on the kittens, and go to work. Maybe I could even drive by John Smalley's house and talk to him about a possible adoption.

I grabbed the smaller litter pan and started for the back of the house. Before I went two steps, though, the doorbell rang again, startling the kittens into racing ahead of me and disappearing back into the bathroom. I left the feline equipment near the kitchen table and approached the door cautiously. The last time my doorbell rang, I was one hundred dollars richer and didn't have two rambunctious animals racing around my house.

I stared through the peephole but drew back, startled, when I saw Alan looking expectantly at me. He wore khaki shorts, a navy polo shirt, and sneakers, his usual "going to the restaurant" attire.

"What are you doing here?" I asked, pulling open the door. I ushered him in, glancing back over my shoulder to make sure the kittens weren't making a run for freedom.

He came in, stepping to one side so I could close the door. As he did, Cayenne thundered along the hallway, raced to the couch, and jumped up, teetering on the back cushion before bouncing to the seat, pushing off, and tearing back to the hall.

"What the hell was that?" Alan followed me to the kitchen and gazed after the vanishing kitten.

"Cayenne. Male kitten. His sister is probably—yep, there she goes." I took a step back when a fluffy furball zoomed past me into the living room to pounce on a catnip mouse.

Alan's gaze bounced from me to the kitten to the hallway. "Sister? Cayenne?"

"The kittens. Jen's roommate came over today and dropped them off. I named them. Temporarily."

"Right." Alan moved to one side when the small multi-colored male cat stalked down the hallway, eyes fixed on a rubber ball. "Which one is which?"

"Cayenne. His sister is Café."

Alan grinned. "I've never heard it pronounced like that. Ki-ya-an. It's like it has three syllables."

"It does." I went back to the kitchen table and picked up the receipt. "I figured it might take a while to find them a home, so I bought a few things. I'm glad Wal-Mart was open early on Sunday. So many places aren't open until noon, Hey, wait a minute. It's Sunday. You should be at the restaurant." I turned to regard Alan. "You're usually doing . . ." *prep work* died on my tongue when I saw the sad look he leveled at me. "What?"

Alan swallowed hard, his Adam's apple bobbing. "Owen is going to call you." The words came all in a rush. "I mean, I think he will."

"Damn it, Alan. You said you wouldn't tell Owen about me and Will." I shook my head angrily. "I told you, I wanted you to keep it private."

"He died." Alan's face, normally so relaxed and happy, was settled into a hard mask of grief and pity.

My knees started to shake. I sank onto a kitchen chair. "Who?"

"The man they shot." Alan took the seat next to me, his eyes pinned to my face. "Early thirties, blond curly hair, blue eyes, oval face, slim build. About six feet tall. A scar under his chin."

I was okay until he said the last bit. "Sweet Jesus." I started to tremble. "Will fell off the porch when he was ten and split open his jaw. They stitched it up but it left a scar from one side of his jaw to the other. Oh, Lord Jesus, no, don't let it be Will." Even while I said it, I knew my entreaties would be futile. I knew it was Will.

Someone walked on a grave.

"They had his cell phone." Alan put his hand on mine. "They're going to call some of the last numbers he received calls from. I told Owen I wanted to be here, just in case."

I swallowed, hard. "In case one was me?"

Alan nodded. "I didn't mean to tell him, Tucker. But I didn't want you to be alone."

Garth Brooks' "Friends in Low Places" rang loudly in the depths of my purse, sitting on the chair next to me.

Chapter 6

"Oh, God." I picked up my purse and dumped the contents on the kitchen table, sifting through it all for my cell phone. I answered it, my hands trembling. "It's Tucker," I whispered.

"I'm sorry, Tucker. This is Sheriff Knott. I have the phone of a man who was shot today. Can you tell me . . .?"

His voice faded when I lowered the phone, staring blankly at the window over my sink where sunlight brightened the room. Images of Will danced through my head. Years with him as a baby, a toddler, a young boy, a young man. All of those mental images blended, swirled and flashed through my brain. I was barely aware of Alan gently prying the phone from my hand or my tears, which streamed down my face and splashed onto the oak table.

"I'm sorry, Tuck." Alan's hand covered mine. It was the human contact more than the words that awakened me from my trance. "Owen asked—he needs someone to identify the body." I wasn't able to speak. He correctly interpreted my stunned silence. "Can you do it?"

"Lord help me. I don't know if I can." I swallowed hard, remembering Will's terrified voice on the phone. "How did he die? What happened?" I snatched my phone away from him. "Owen, what happened? Who killed him?"

"I can't discuss it, Tucker." Owen's deep voice sounded hushed and I wondered if he was trying to be covert. "It's an ongoing investigation."

"Will was killed because of what he knew," I said, my grief segueing into anger. "He told me he was scared for his life."

"Don't jump to conclusions. What do you mean? When did you talk to him?"

I remembered the memory stick, zipped securely into the pocket of my purse. "I'm not sure I can talk about it. I'm not sure who to trust." Alan's shocked expression told me I may have overstepped my bounds, but I barreled ahead, not caring. "Will was as good as murdered, I'm sure of it."

"Do you have information about it?" Owen's voice was still low but I heard intensity in it. "Do you know who was after him?" Before I could answer, he said, "Don't say anything. Hold on. Let me think." There was a long pause. "Was he ever arrested?"

"What?" Why would it matter if Will had been arrested? I shook my head, not sure I understood the question.

"Was he arrested? Would his fingerprints be on file somewhere?"

"Oh." I thought frantically. "Yes, he was in a protest in South Caroline last year at a factory farm there. Will and some others were arrested."

"Okay. You stay put. Don't tell anyone you know the man who was killed. I'm going to see if I can identify him by his fingerprints. Put Alan on the phone."

"What? Wait a minute, whatever you tell Alan, I want to know." I pressed the *speaker* button on my phone. "Go ahead. Talk."

"Who died and put you in charge?" Owen sounded half-angry, half-amused. "I'm thinking we want to keep Tucker out of this, Alan. If this young man was killed because of something he knew and if someone knows she's related to him, she might be in danger."

"What do you mean he was killed because of something he knew?" I demanded. "You killed him, didn't you?"

I heard Owen take a deep breath. "He was shot, yes. But it wasn't my bullet that killed him."

I stared at my phone, open-mouthed. "Holy crap in a bucket. Someone shot him and then you hit him?"

"I shot *at* him," Owen corrected quickly. "I aimed over his head, to slow him down. But another shot was fired. I think it came from him."

"Well, that's bullshit. He'd never carry a gun. Will was a pacifist and he'd never do anything like—"

"Would you let me get in a word edgewise?" Owen interrupted. "I can't go into details. You keep quiet about knowing him. I'll come over and see you later."

"That won't work, Owen," Alan said. "She has to go to work. Either she goes to work or she calls in sick."

"He's right," I agreed reluctantly. I glanced to my right where the two kittens were tussling with something. Damn, it was a sock. How did they get in my bedroom? I pushed that worry aside. "I have to go in and open the bar. Alan needs to get to the restaurant and get ready for brunch. Otherwise people will know something's up."

"Do you have any information which might shed light on what happened last night?" Owen persisted. "Anything at all?"

Who could I trust? I didn't dare focus on Alan's evaluating eyes. I was an adept liar, but Alan had the uncanny knack of ferreting out the truth when I least expected it. "I don't even know what happened last night," I said, stalling for time. "How do I know if I— hey, wait a minute, you guys!" I leapt from my chair and headed for the hallway, chasing the two kittens, one of whom was dragging a sock and the other who was dragging a pair of undies.

Yes, it was the coward's way out, but I couldn't think of anything else to do. I needed time to think. The kittens raced ahead of me, stumbling now and again when a paw got tangled in an article of clothing. The bedroom door was wide open and when I entered, the first thing I saw was my wicker laundry hamper, lying on its side near the bathroom door. "You little poops." I wrestled the sock and the underpants from the thieves.

They promptly disappeared under my double bed. I took advantage of their absence to stuff the laundry basket into the attached bathroom, closing the door firmly. I turned to leave the room and caught sight of a stack of scrapbooks sitting on the chair in the corner. One of my summer projects was to scan my old photos and other memorabilia into my computer, hoping to preserve memories against the ravages of time. I touched the top album, one of those dime store books with black pages and pictures spilling from the sides.

I took up a stack of photos and leafed through them. Pictures of Will at home in Louisiana, pictures of my daddy and momma, granny, and my no-good brother. Each one held a wealth of memories. I wiped at a tear while I shuffled through the images. All of them dead now. All of them gone.

"Tuck?"

I turned at the sound of Alan's sympathetic voice. "I'm okay," I said, sniffling.

"Sure you are." He smiled. "I'm going to the restaurant. Owen thinks you'll be fine for now, and I agree. Nobody knows you were related to—" He hurried on. "As far as anybody knows, you've got nothing to do with what went on at the factory. We'll keep it quiet that you—you knew—" He ground to a halt again. "Owen wants us to meet him later this afternoon. You can come to my place and we'll talk to him there. That will keep it private. You can leave work early, right?" He watched me expectantly.

I nodded. "I'll see if I can get Miller to fill in." Our brew master often stopped in on Sunday anyway. I was pretty sure I could talk him into doing a couple of hours behind the bar. I met Alan at the bedroom doorway, pictures still in my hand.

"Is there anything I can do?" he asked.

I dropped the pictures on the bed. "Not unless you can turn back time." I shook my head, swiping tears while we walked. "I was so worried about him. Will never cared much for his own safety. I suppose that's how it is when you're young. You never think you can be hurt."

Alan squeezed my shoulder in sympathy. "Owen will find out who did this. It won't bring your nephew back, but it's something."

"It's not fair. Will was a sweet, kind young man with his life ahead of him. He died for a bunch of fucking chickens! Sweet Jesus God in Heaven, what a waste!"

Alan put a hand on my arm. "That's not true."

I turned on him. I needed to rage at someone. The grief, the anger, and the unfairness churned inside me, aching to bust out. "How can you say that? He died at a god-damned chicken factory. Poor Will was killed because of some damn birds." Tears splashed off my face.

"He didn't die just because of a bunch of birds," Alan said, his voice soft with sadness. "Will died for what he believed in, which was the humane treatment of all creatures. If you say he died for a bunch of dumb birds, you belittle him. That isn't fair, Tucker."

Alan was right but I didn't want to hear it. I paced into the living room, wishing I could vent my rage somehow. "I'm sorry if you think I don't trust Owen, but I'm not sure I can trust him. After all, he *says* he didn't hit Will, but how do I know for sure?"

"You're wrong." Alan stopped in the middle of the room, his face drained of color.

"Well, of course you'd say that."

For an instant, I was sure he'd yell back at me. Instead he shook his head. "You're overreacting."

I struggled to hold back a new flood of tears. "Will was scared when he called me and he wasn't overreacting. Lo-oo-ok wha-wha-what happened." I stammered, grief making me trip over my words.

Alan gently enfolded me in his arms and I let loose with my tears, burying my face in his chest and crying like a baby. It felt damn good to let him hold me, to feel safe, loved and protected. I blubbered for a minute or so then I pushed away, brushing at his shirt. "I got you wet," I mumbled. "I'm sorry."

He pulled a hanky from his back pocket and I took it gratefully, mopping my face. "My shirt will dry by the time I get to the kitchen. You can trust Owen. I know you can."

I nodded. "I guess you're right."

"Give him a chance to explain what happened. Hang in there, Tuck. If you need anything before you go in to open up, you call me. I'll check in on you this afternoon." He smoothed back my disheveled hair. "Lock up behind me."

I led the way to the front door, jamming his hanky into my pocket. "I'll call Miller and see if he can cover for me."

"I'll handle it," Alan said. "I'll tell him I talked to you and you weren't feeling well. I'll ask him to stand by in case he's needed. Don't worry about it."

"Thanks, Alan." I stopped at the front door, my hand on the doorknob. "I'll get to the Acorn in an hour or two. I need time to—" Time to what? Absorb the pain? No amount of time would dull my grief at the thought of a sweet young man, cut down in a farm field at night.

Once again, a kitten came to my rescue. The two little wild things tore into the living room, chasing each other and landing in a tumbling pile under the coffee table. Both Alan and I laughed at their antics. "I need time to get them corralled." I pulled the front door.

"Don't worry about it. If you can't get there by two, I'll open for you." He bent to put a light kiss on my cheek. "I'm here if you need me."

I could only nod, not trusting myself to speak. I closed the door and leaned my head against it, inhaling the wood odor mixed with the sharp tang of the outside air. I felt like my chest would burst from anger and grief. I twisted and sank to the floor with my back against the door, propped my head on my upturned knees, and wept.

I don't know how long I sat there, my head lowered and tears dampening my shirt. I didn't stir until I sensed the tentative questing head butts from my tiny feline companions. I raised my tear-burning eyes and saw two kittens sitting next to me, heads tilted in obvious confusion. *What happened? How come you're not playing? What's going on?* I could almost see the thought bubbles above their heads.

I wiped my face and tilted over slowly, coming to rest a foot or so from them. For an instant they were poised to flee, regarding me suspiciously. Then they approached, sniffing and patting and prancing near my head, like Lilliputians around some Gulliver. I held my breath when they snuffled my face and tangled with my hair. With a soft laugh, I righted myself and they scampered away.

Their youthful curiosity reminded me of Will as a child. He would get into scrapes, tangling with trees when he sought hidden places where animals holed up, or falling into the river when he chased after a bird that lured him from her nest. I got to my feet, realizing his curiosity probably killed him this time.

But Alan was right. I did Will a disservice if I dismissed his death as the result of youthful foolishness. Will cared passionately about animal rights. I should respect that.

I blotted up the last of my tears and headed for the kitchen. If Will was right, the information in my possession might hold the key to his killer. I needed to make a copy of it and stash it somewhere safe. After I did that, I could focus on who killed him. Someone associated with the factory murdered my nephew and I was damned well going to discover who it was.

Despite my assurances to Alan, I wasn't at all sure I could trust Owen Knott. Fitz Agri-Industries had its fingers deep in the financial pockets of Barnsdale and York. What if Owen was charged with covering up what happened to Will in order to make sure the Fitz family wasn't compromised?

I wasn't going to let this get swept under a rug the way the egg recall was. I went into the bathroom attached to my bedroom and examined myself in the mirror. My black eye had morphed to purple, encompassing most of my eye socket and my cheek. At least some of my red-rimmed eyes could be attributed to my wound. I ran cold water over a cloth and pressed it against my face, then I dabbed on makeup, going heavy with the foundation. I figured people would be so focused on my bruises they might not notice my bloodshot eyes.

I grabbed the scrapbook from the bed and went into the hall. I heard the telltale sound of cat paws digging in litter. I hurried to the kitchen in time to see Cayenne assiduously covering his pee in the litter pan I set there earlier, being supervised by his sister. "Well, good. At least I don't have to train you." I left my scrapbook on the coffee table and went to corral them.

Easier said than done. Forty-five minutes later, I gave up on the idea. The kittens easily eluded me on a chase through the house and were firmly ensconced under my double bed. Nothing I did, no treats I presented, would get them out. I decided to admit defeat and put the used litter box in my attached bathroom. I put a water dish under the sink and closed them in the bedroom, making sure the door was pulled tightly shut.

I fished Will's memory stick from my purse and went to my den, inserting the device into the slot on my desktop computer. I skimmed through the list of files then on impulse I printed a copy of the directory so I'd have a record of the contents along with the dates the files were saved.

I debated putting a copy of the files on my own computer but decided it might be risky. I found the memory stick I used as backup for my home computer and buried a copy of Will's files deep within a file folder on the stick, tucking it into a location where even I would be hard pressed to find it. I put it into a plastic bag then I put it and the folded-up printout of the directory into my flour canister in the kitchen. Maybe I was being paranoid, but I could laugh about it later. Right now I didn't feel like laughing at all.

I came back to the office and to enhance my paranoia further, I dug into a desk drawer and found a fat round Angry Birds memory stick I bought on a whim while standing in the checkout line at an office supply store. I copied the contents of Will's memory stick to the little red USB device which served as Red Bird's butt. Where to hide it?

I considered and discarded several ideas. That's when I spied the wicker basket where I tossed the various kitty toys. I tossed Red Bird in with the other canvas mice, plastic balls, and sponge fish, tucking it under a pink fluffy snake. It was right at home with all the other brightly colored objects.

That gave me three copies of the information. I zipped Will's original memory stick into the inner pocket of my purse and considered my next move. I needed to find out what happened last night. Who would know?

I considered and discarded the idea of trying to find Will's roommates and talk to them. The story of the shooting was probably all over town by now. Maybe Marianne. No, wait. Rob. I could talk to Rob. He was at the factory last night.

"That's it." I went to the bedroom to check on the resident escapees. I opened the door and peeked inside. They were curled around each other, tucked into a compact ball on my pillow. Small puckers in my chenille bedspread showed me where tiny cat claws dug in and pulled. "Okay, guys. You're on your own."

Cayenne opened one eye, regarded me with a sigh and closed it again. His sister purred. I closed the door softly and headed out.

It promised to be another warm day, with dampness in the air accenting the dense odor of flowers and trees. Fat white clouds lazily perambulated across the pale blue sky and for an instant I was suffused with happy warmth, enjoying the pristine day.

Then I remembered.

I drove east then south for a block or two, driving past Rob and Marianne's house on Forest View Drive. I glimpsed Marianne's sedan in the open garage but Rob's green pickup wasn't there. I drove through town, checked Fitz's headquarters on Prince Street, and even drove past a couple of bars, trying to spy Rob's truck.

I finally gave up on town and headed onto the river road. If Rob wasn't at his cabin, I could continue on and go to the factory in York. Maybe he was there. The road followed the river with all its twists and turns. On my right side was a ditch with the river ten or twenty feet below. On my left was often woodland, sometimes farmland, and sometimes swamp, depending on the terrain.

About three miles north I crossed over a bridge and now the river was on my left with swampland on my right. Twisted tree trunks stuck out of the muck, evidence of last year's heavy flooding which pushed the river right up to the roadside.

I slowed along a tricky series of S-curves, grimacing when I saw the mangled remains of a coon on the side of the road, only identifiable by the black mask around what remained of its face. Road kill was a common occurrence on any highway, but this piece of county blacktop always seemed to have more than its fair share.

The turnoff for Rob's cabin was on the right, paved for about a hundred yards before changing to gravel. A farm in the distance was like something from a Grant Wood painting with its white farmhouse and bright red barn. In my opinion, this was the prettiest time of the year in the Midwest. A haze of green hovered over the fields, but there were still dark ribbons showing through the sprouting seedlings. The corn was only a few inches high and the soybeans were still nubbins. This gave the viewer a chance to see the curves and contours of the hills and the intricate details of the plantings, whereas later in the season, when everything grew in, all you'd see was the crops themselves. The fields were broken up by greening meadows where cows grazed, black and white dots on the horizon.

I slowed to go over rutted railroad tracks then I was back on a twisting bit of road, heavily shadowed by trees on either side, the river on my left in the distance. The road climbed steeply here with a hairpin curve at the top where I made the left turn into Rob's lane. The cabin was situated on a bluff over the river with verdant green woodland all around it. I drove the short distance to the house, but I didn't see a pickup truck in the drive.

I parked near the garage and got out, taking the path around the enclosed porch on the side of the house. Rob sometimes parked his truck in town or here at the cabin and took his boat to and fro. I walked past the supports for his redwood deck, going downhill until the deck loomed above me. I walked along the cleared slope of grass leading to the bank near the river where I spied the dock and his boat tied up there.

"Well, shit. I guess I have to go to the factory." I didn't have that much time. Of course, from the factory I could take the highway home, which would be faster. I started to walk back uphill when I glimpsed something dark in the shrubbery down the hill on my right.

I moved a few steps but lost sight of it. I moved again and there it was, a jacket or a lump of clothing. I hesitated. If it wasn't moving and it was an animal, it was probably ill or hurt. I considered checking it, but time was wasting and to be honest, I wasn't sure I could face another dose of animal misery after seeing what was in Will's files.

I'd tell Rob about it, I decided. Let him deal with it. I hurried past the deck supports, grabbing hold of one to give me momentum up the hill.

I froze. The wood felt cold and wet and it was discolored, darkly soaked with what looked like blood.

I sprang back, eyeing my hand while I laughed shakily. There were no telltale red splotches, only flecks of paint or grease. I scrubbed my palm on my denim capris and kept going, sliding on the grass which was soggy and torn up a bit. My sneakers couldn't get much traction on the trampled turf. Rob must have dropped something heavy there, or maybe dragged something because a distinct trail led along the underside of the porch to the drop-off to the river.

Well, whatever. I shook my head at my own nervousness. I peered once again at the shrubbery but couldn't see the dark lump anymore. Maybe it was an animal and maybe it moved.

"Not my problem," I said, coming around the end of the deck. I paused to peer over my shoulder at the river and the dark shape under the bushes . . .

. . . and screamed when someone grabbed my arm.

Chapter 7

"Let go of me!" I pulled back and promptly slipped when my grabber released his hold.

John Smalley reached me in time, preventing me from falling. "Sorry, Tucker. I didn't mean to startle you. I wasn't sure who it was. I'm looking for Rob."

I tried to get a breath around the shocked cacophony of my heart, which was going a mile a minute. "I didn't hear your car."

"I left my car and boat at the public launch and came up the path. I was going to do some fishing today. Is Rob around?"

The boat ramp was downriver from Rob's cabin, a few hundred yards as the crow flew or a half-mile by road. "I haven't seen him. Maybe he's at the factory."

"Why would he be there today? Office staff doesn't work there on weekends." John peered past me to the cabin. "Must be important for you to drive here." His gaze returned to me, his dark eyes inquisitive.

My brother always said the best way to tell a lie was to twist the truth. I decided to follow his advice because he'd been a proficient liar, God rest his devious soul. "I was trying to find out what happened at the factory last night. You know, about the shooting."

"Shooting?"

I resumed walking up the hill to my car and John fell into place beside me. "Yeah, there was a shooting at the factory last night. I figured Rob might know something. PJ was at the bar last night and he took off after he talked to Rob."

"That's crazy. Why would anyone break in? Was it trespassing? Theft?"

"That's why I'm trying to find Rob." I managed a shaky laugh. "I suppose I'm a nosy old busybody, but I was curious." I paused in the drive and checked my watch. "I need to get back to town now and open the Acorn. Rob must be at the factory."

John held my car door open for me while I slipped behind the wheel. "You said you had a friend who worked there. Does this have anything to do with it?"

I bit my lip to keep from revealing my surprise. "I didn't say anything like that, did I?"

"I guess I assumed it. Is everything okay?"

"I suppose." I tugged the door closed and decided to lay the groundwork for my later illness. "I'm not feeling good today. I have a headache that won't quit."

"It could be an aftereffect from that punch you took," John said sympathetically. "You really should go to the doctor. You might have a concussion."

He seemed so worried I felt guilty for planting the idea in his head. "I'm sure it's nothing. Probably allergies or something." I sniffed mightily and dabbed at my right eye. "If you see Rob, tell him I was being a nosy neighbor."

"Will do. And if I hear anything of interest, I'll make sure to let you know. After all, we have to make sure our bartenders know all the good gossip in town."

I nodded agreement before backing up carefully in Rob's narrow drive, almost running into the big rhododendron near the porch. It took me two or three twists and turns, but no way was I going to back my car onto the road with its blind turn. When I was finally pointed at the road, I checked my rear view mirror and saw John stride off toward the trees, but not on the path leading to the river and the boat launch. He went around the deck the same way I did.

What was he doing? He paused at the spot where I stopped to examine the damp deck post. Then he straightened and turned. I waved and pulled onto the road.

Go left, to the factory? Even while I considered it, I knew I wouldn't go there. There was no way I could pull off a casual, "Hey, Rob, how's it going?" by showing up at the factory on a Sunday afternoon. I shook my head and turned right, heading back to town. I was lucky John chalked up my inquisitiveness to inherent nosiness. Otherwise my clumsy attempts at detecting might be suspicious.

Something John said resonated with me while I navigated the twisting road. He was right. Bartenders were truly at the hub of gossip in town. That gave me another idea. I might stop in and visit a few fellow bartenders and see if anybody knew what happened. I needed to do something, damn it. Anything.

I spent the next hour dropping in at the three different bars in Barnsdale which opened on Sunday at noon. The 'doings at the Yoke' were a hot topic among the regulars. Most of the stories I gathered were the same. Someone vandalized one of the factory buildings, destroying property and opening the doors so the chickens could escape. Night workers called the police and the Sheriff arrived, his office having jurisdiction because York was too small to have a police force of its own. Two factory workers were injured in the resulting confusion and one person was shot, but no one was quite sure who it was or why.

I did learn one surprising tidbit of information at the last place I stopped. "Richard Fitz is in town," Lee Knight mentioned. Lee owned Knight's Title and Abstract Company, which handled most of the real estate transactions in town. He and some cronies were in the Huntsman's Grill, having a few drinks after a round of golf.

"I heard he was coming later in the week," I commented. "For the town picnic."

Lee toyed with his mixed drink, twirling the swizzle stick around in the glass. "I saw him and PJ at PJ's house. They were standing in the drive when we came up the fifteenth fairway to the green. I'd recognize Richard anywhere, that arrogant son of a bitch."

I sat up straighter in surprise. Lee was normally a laid-back kind of guy who didn't have an enemy in the world. "I don't think I've ever met him."

"No loss for you." Lee's mouth twisted sourly, distorting his thin face. "From what I could see, PJ wasn't too happy to have big brother in town." Lee's thin brown hair lay in damp waves on his high forehead, feathering over the tan line where his hat had rested. "Richard has a way of managing things which can sometimes be tough to handle."

"Really?" I sipped my tonic water, stealing a glance at my watch. I needed to get going but this was juicy gossip. "I didn't know that."

"Yeah. I did some legal work for them a long, long time ago." Lee scowled at the bar counter, a deep flush mottling his cheeks. "Richard always adheres to the letter of the law, but just barely." He started to say something more, then he stopped, shaking his head slightly.

"Do you think he came here because of what happened at the factory?"

"You mean the shooting?" Lee didn't wait for my reply. "Yeah, I doubt Richard would let PJ handle something like that."

"Like what?"

"Lawsuits. Let's face it, if somebody was injured and lived, they'll probably figure a way to file a lawsuit. Everybody files lawsuits nowadays. And if somebody was shot and died, the next of kin will probably file a lawsuit."

Next of kin? Was I Will's next of kin? For an instant I contemplated a wrongful death lawsuit against the Fitz family. I probably wouldn't win but the thought of being a thorn in PJ's side was delightful.

Unmindful of my notion, Lee continued. "And Richard probably needs to talk to PJ about the salmonella lawsuit."

"Is one going to be filed?" A lawsuit was threatened, but I didn't realize one was imminent.

"Already filed." Lee leaned closer. "I was at the courthouse filing the title deed for Rob Huntington's property and I overheard."

"Rob? What property?"

Lee straightened. "If Rob doesn't want folks to know . . . ." He shrugged.

"I'm surprised, that's all. Rob hasn't mentioned anything." I touched my black eye. "I've seen him a lot lately."

Lee's pale green eyes narrowed in thought then he appeared to come to some decision. "I guess it's not surprising he and Guy got into a fight, what with Guy buying up Rob's river land. Of course, if he didn't do it, Rob would be belly-up with debt."

"From what?" I slid off the barstool. "Rob sold the hardware store and probably got good money for it. Did he do some bad stock investing or something? He loves that old cabin of his. No way would he sell it."

"I'm not sure. All I know is from what Guy said, Rob needed the money." Lee frowned. "No, I take that back. From what Guy said, Marianne needed the money. I guess I assumed it meant Rob needed the money." Lee turned to his right when one of his friends nudged him.

I put my money on the counter. "Poor Rob must be desperate if he's selling off his cabin." I felt a pang of sympathy for him.

"He's still got it for thirty days. I filed the paperwork but unless Guy comes in and signs it, nothing will be processed." Lee returned his attention to his golfing buddies, our conversation forgotten.

I waved goodbye to the bartender and left, emerging into brilliant mid-day sunlight. I considered Lee's information while I drove the six blocks to the pub and found a spot in our crowded parking lot, testament to the lure of the Sunday brunch at the Parlor. What could Rob possibly have done which would cause him to sell the cabin and its land? He loved that place. If he was gambling or drinking, I would know about it. Any kind of bad gossip eventually found its way to my ears, but I hadn't heard a word about Rob except for his occasional bouts of alcoholic over-indulgence.

I went inside to start my opening routine. Alan, bless his heart, left me a sandwich which I munched while I worked and mulled over everything that happened. By the time I opened for business, I'd run through all possibilities in my head but I was still stumped.

Why did Rob need money? I flipped on the *Open* sign, unlocked the door, and began my usual routine of doling out beer, my mind half focused on my customers and the rest of it focused on everything else, on Will, Rob, animal cruelty, lawsuits. They all ran together in my brain like a revolving door, cycling and circling endlessly.

At four in the afternoon, Alan came in and took a seat at the far end of the bar, the side nearest the back door. "Parlor's closed," he said when I paused near him. "I called Miller. He'll come in at five to relieve you. I said you got a bitch of a headache from the hit you took."

"I do have a headache." I clamped my lips tight for a second to hold in the grief which threatened to tumble out. "Every time I think about what happened, I think I might explode."

"Don't think about it. At least not for now. Give me a pint of the Reverend's Revenge." He nodded at the beer taps. "I'll stick with you until Miller comes in. We can leave together and nobody will be the wiser. You can come over to my house and Owen will meet us there."

I drew a glass of the dark amber lager and set it in front of him. As I did, the front door opened and PJ entered with another man, both talking so heatedly they barely noticed where they walked. The man with him had to be Richard Fitz. He wore light colored khaki slacks, a navy blue golf shirt, and loafers. He reminded me of Guy Gibson with his expensive sartorial taste. Fitz's hair was mostly steel gray, swept back from his round, tanned face. His eyebrows were dark lines across his forehead and underneath his dark eyes flickered here and there, missing nothing. Where PJ was rotund and soft, Richard was stocky and hard, muscled and fit.

"Well, well," Alan said. "The King returns."

"You know him?" I turned slightly so I could keep the two men in sight while appearing to be busy washing glasses.

"Yep." Alan sipped his beer, his eyes fixed on the arrivals. "He's a few years older than us. He was a senior in high school when we were freshmen." Alan's face seemed to stiffen, his expressive brown eyes cold. "I haven't seen him in years. I heard he finally married but there aren't any kids." Alan's smile was bitter. "I'd be surprised if there were."

I tidied up the counter, nodding to a new customer who took a stool three seats from Alan. "Really? Why?"

"He's gay."

I almost fell off the Puller's Platform. "Seriously?"

"He's not out of the closet but he's gay." Alan lifted his glass. "I know." His eyes met mine and I saw a deep abiding hatred glow in their brown depths. "His wife is a socialite in Chicago. They're seldom seen together."

"So I guess that means PJ really will inherit, if Richard has no children." I went to fill some orders but was soon back with Alan. "Why do you think he's in town?" I peered over my shoulder at the corner of the room where PJ and Richard lounged, sipping drinks the waitress brought them. They ignored the crowded room, intent on their conversation. I noticed the other patrons in the bar shoot glances their way and a couple of people nodded at Richard, who nodded in return.

"It doesn't matter about the children," Alan said. "Old Henry divvied up his assets so each kid got a share."

"Each kid? It's only PJ and Richard, right? Those are the only kids who people mention."

Alan shook his head. "The oldest was William, but he died when he was little. I think it was a fever or measles. Young Henry died right after he graduated from college. I think he got food poisoning or an infection. He and his father fought tooth and nail over the business, and I heard a rumor Old Henry disinherited Young Henry right before Young Henry got sick. Old Henry had a fit of remorse but it was too late. His kid was dead." Alan recited this with a faint air of satisfaction, as if pleased the old man got his comeuppance.

"That's a tragedy. So young."

"Good riddance," Alan said blithely. "Young Henry was an asshole. Richard and John both wanted a part of the business. I don't think anybody else cared. Geoff was younger than us. He got as far away from the family as he could. He's breeding dogs, Brittany spaniels, I think, in California. The girls all married and moved out of state. I think Matilda is in Indiana and Eleanor married somebody who owns a soap company. Poor Joan, the youngest, was married to Cecil Somebody, who died. She married someone else who was a nasty S.O.B. When he died, she joined a nunnery."

I blinked in surprise. "A nunnery. Heavens, she and my ex would be a match made in heaven."

Alan almost choked on his beer. "I always forget Ron joined the church."

"It's hard to argue with God," I said with a straight face. "When God calls, a man must answer." I started grinning. "At least he finally lived up to his name." When Ronald Charles Church and I divorced, we all said how apt it was that he joined a monastery.

Alan's grin faded when his gaze went past me. I turned to see Richard Fitz heading our way. I moved back to the center of the bar as Fitz said, "Alan Dale, is that you? It's good to see you. How long has it been?"

From the look on Alan's face, I think the appropriate answer would be *not long enough.* I busied myself with customers at the far end of the bar, but soon rejoined Alan in order to wait on some new arrivals.

"Tucker, this is Richard Fitz." Alan leaned back on his bar stool to tacitly include the other man in our conversation. "PJ's brother," he added.

Richard's face hardened momentarily, his lips twisting slightly in distaste. It must have rankled to have his claim to fame to be PJ's brother. "I've heard great things about this pub and the restaurant," Richard said, his gaze going from Alan to me. "It's what Barnsdale needed, an upscale sort of establishment."

He was right, but something in his supercilious attitude grated on my nerves. "We're pleased with our success," I said noncommittally. "Marianne Archer mentioned you were visiting for the town celebration."

"That's one reason." He leaned a tanned forearm on the counter and edged closer to Alan, who sat back slightly, avoiding contact. Fitz was crowding him, almost leaning on him. But then Fitz spoke in a low voice and I decided it was his way of being conspiratorial. "Did you hear about the problem at the factory last night?"

"Problem?" I kept my voice steady, but it was hard. Fitz was equating death with something as mundane as *a problem?*

Alan's eyes narrowed and he shook his head slightly, warning me to keep my temper under control. "Can you talk about it? Do you know what happened?"

Richard shot him a speculative gaze. "Don't you know all about it? Aren't you and the Sheriff friends?" His voice was carefully neutral but I detected curiosity and maybe distaste or censure.

"Despite what you may have heard, the Sheriff has always acted in a totally professional manner. If there is an ongoing investigation, he wouldn't jeopardize it by speaking out of turn." Alan started to stand. "Tuck, I hope you're feeling better. I'll talk to you later."

"I'm sorry, Alan. I didn't mean to offend you." Richard put a restraining hand on Alan's forearm. There was something strangely intimate about the gesture, something almost, I don't know, something obscene.

Alan shook off his hand. "Sorry, but I'm busy, Richard." He left, moving so quickly he almost knocked over the man who sat next to him at the bar.

"I think I must have irritated him." Richard smiled at me like he was inviting me to share his bemusement. "I suppose I should apologize."

"Well, that would be about as useful as a football bat." I caught a glimpse of PJ, who stood near the back doorway, talking to a woman with her back turned to me. I recognized her plump butt in skin-tight denim short shorts and the mop of *three-T* hair—teased, tangled, and tumbling down her back. I shook my head in disgust. What did PJ want with some tramp when he had such a classy wife at home?

Richard looked over his shoulder at the pair and sighed. "My brother has questionable taste in women." He turned back to me, dark eyes amused, inviting me to once again share in his jokes.

"If brains were leather, he couldn't saddle a flea." PJ chose that moment to shift his attention, his eyes meeting mine over the crowd. His gaze shifted from me to his brother and one corner of his mouth turned up in a sour grimace. The woman tugged on his arm and they vanished through the back door.

His brother, unaware of PJ's exit, laughed softly. "Colorful phrasing, but true. I don't know why Isabel married him."

Well, duh. For the money. I *almost* said it aloud, but I restrained myself. "Nice to meet you." I moved away on pretense of helping one of the waitresses.

As I filled orders, I wondered how I was going to meet Alan. The plan was for me to go to his house with him, but I was supposed to be ill, so it might seem odd if I left the bar and went to his place. Of course, maybe nobody was watching me. Maybe this was all a lot of paranoia for nothing.

I mentally reviewed the files on Will's memory stick while I worked. From what I could remember, it was all copies of invoices, bills, and those disgusting photographs. Thinking about the pictures made my stomach twist. I considered the laughing people around me and I could imagine their horror if they knew how their eggs were produced.

And I could easily imagine how quickly they would forget when it came time to compare prices in the grocery store. Rob and PJ were right. Factory farming produced cheap food. Whether it was ethical, moral, or good for you was another story. Many people couldn't afford to make the distinction, especially given the economy.

"So are Alan and Owen Knott involved?"

I raised my head. Richard Fitz was in front of me, having sat while I was woolgathering. "That's really no one's concern, is it?" I said in an *I'm not talking about it* tone of voice.

He took the hint. "I'll have a glass of your dark stout. What is it?" He eyed the framed advertisements over the mirrored back of the bar. "A glass of the Friar's Folly. Named for you, I presume?"

I carefully poured a glass and knifed the suds from the top before setting it in front of him. "I don't know if I can be accused of a lot of follies in my day."

"Oh, I'm sure there are depths to you which might be surprising." He took a sip. "Very nice. Who's your brew master?"

"Miller Muchson. You probably don't know him. He came here from Des Moines. He owned a brewpub there." I started to walk away.

"Ah, yes. The Ploughman's Pub." Fitz set his glass down, centering it on the coaster. "It was unfortunate what happened to him. He was probably happy to have a second chance here."

I stopped in my tracks. "If you knew who the brew master was, why did you ask?"

"I was curious to see if you'd answer."

"Since his name is on the plaque outside, it's not really a secret." My hands trembled when I wiped the counter. "I'm surprised you know what happened."

"I did some research." Fitz's smile didn't reach his eyes, which flickered past me to the booze wall, the beer pulls, and the back bar, probably estimating the cost of everything. "I was curious about your establishment. It's done very well."

"We've worked hard," I said, keeping my voice neutral. "Miller is a fine brew master."

"Except for that small problem in Des Moines, when a batch of the beer was tainted and so many people got sick." Fitz's gaze came back to rest on me.

I leaned forward, meeting his gaze. "Just like the eggs in your factory, I guess." We stared at one another for a few long seconds before he nodded.

"True. Of course, the egg problem is nationwide. It wasn't limited to one neighborhood in one town. And it's received so much attention. Unlike the problem Mr. Muchson had."

My mind raced while I considered and discarded several retorts. I knew about the lawsuit which forced Miller into bankruptcy but it happened decades earlier and brewing techniques and equipment had changed radically since that time. I trusted Miller and I knew he was a conscientious, careful man. We were forced to get hefty insurance policies because of what happened to him, but I didn't mind. Well, not much anyway.

"What happened with Miller happened years ago," I said. "And no one died. Unlike those children at the day care who died when they ate scrambled eggs."

"Eggs which probably were undercooked," Fitz said immediately.

I raised an eyebrow. "Good defense. Blame it on the underpaid cooks at the school."

"A school shouldn't blame a food supplier if they can't afford to hire competent staff." He said this with such glib assurance I realized I was hearing a line the defense would take.

"I'm sure it will be consolation to the parents whose children died." I walked to the far end of the bar, relieved to see Miller coming in the back door. He was a small, wizened man with a shock of dark hair sprinkled with white and strong arms, muscled from years of lifting heavy equipment.

"I talked to Alan and he said you needed help." He ducked under the bar divider. "That's one heck of a black eye."

I forgot all about it. I touched my cheek and winced. "Yeah, it still hurts. Thanks for coming in. I'm beat." I smiled shakily but I didn't have to fake it that I felt sick. My little conversation with Richard Fitz set my stomach to churning and my head to pounding. "I think I'll go home and take a nap."

"Don't worry about anything here. I'll close 'er up later on. Anything I need to know?"

"No, not really. I'm running a tab for the bourbon and coke at the far end and the guy in the middle with the beer hasn't paid. Other than them, we're mostly current."

"Sounds good." He moved to the center of the bar where Richard Fitz was seated. I headed for the staff room and my purse, anxious to leave before I got into any more verbal fistfights with Fitz.

The alliteration of the thought made me grin. Fist Fights with Fitz. It sounded like a movie. I slung my purse strap over my shoulder and had my hand on the knob when the back door was flung open. Bright afternoon sunlight momentarily blinded me. A woman took a step inside, stopped, bumped into me and yelled, "Is a doctor here? I need help!"

"Call 911, Miller," I yelled over my shoulder.

He nodded and picked up the phone.

"What's up?" I turned to the woman. It was PJ's girlfriend, the short-short girl with big hair. Her blouse was only half-buttoned, revealing a large amount of her white right breast and her shorts were unbuttoned, sagging on her hips. I stepped back. "What's going on?"

"He's dying. I don't know what's wrong. He's dying."

"What?"

She grabbed my arm and pulled me to the door. "It's PJ. He's dying."

Chapter 8

"What the hell?" I tried to pull away from the woman, but I was pushed from behind by Richard Fitz, who put his hands on my shoulders and propelled me through the door. Fitz almost ran over me as we hurried along the back sidewalk to the parking lot.

The woman—Marsha? Marcie?—I couldn't remember her name, dithered ahead of us, stopping so we almost collided before racing ahead only to stop again a few steps from a black SUV parked at the southeast end, as far as you could get and still be in the lot. It was set off from the other cars by the simple method of parking at a diagonal and taking up extra space.

"Asshole. What right does he have to take up three parking spaces?"

"Probably worried about dents," Richard said. "It's an eighty-thousand dollar car."

"What is it, made of gold?" The idea of a car costing almost as much as my house was mind-boggling. I expected it of sleek BMWs or sports cars, but an SUV?

"There," the woman sobbed, her pointing arm wobbling up and down. "He's there."

"That doesn't give him the right to use three parking slots. What did you do?" I asked the woman, venting my anger on her.

"I didn't do any-any-anything," she stammered, tears streaming off her face. She seemed oblivious to the mascara-streaked tears or her breast which was clearly visible now. "We were fooling around and-and—" A new gush of tears obliterated anything she tried to say.

"Get a grip. Tuck yourself in. Button your pants. Your mother must be spinning in her grave to see you like this."

My harsh words seemed to have the effect I intended. "My mother isn't dead," she protested, fumbling with her pants snap.

"Well, if she isn't dead, you'd give her a heart attack, acting like this. What happened?" I took a couple of steps nearer the SUV where Richard stood, staring through one dark gray-tinted window into the back seat.

"We decided to have fun," the woman said, tears mingled with makeup dribbling onto her blouse. She must have felt their contact with her skin, because she gasped at the sight of her breast, bobbing free for all to see. She stuffed it back in her blouse while she babbled her tale. "PJ was hot to trot, so we got in the back seat. I told him he had to use a condom, so we got the condom on."

I held up a hand. "Too much information. Cut to the chase, what happened?"

"You can't see in," Marcie-Marsha said to Richard, who was trying to peer into the back of the SUV. "PJ said it's special glass, you can't see anything. Did you call a doctor?" she asked, swinging to me and almost overbalancing in her high-heeled sandals.

"Somebody inside did." I saw a few pub patrons grouped around the door. I waved them back inside. "Nothing to see!" I called out. They waved in response and meandered away, curiosity satisfied.

Richard threw open the SUV's door and I got a clear view into the back seat. PJ Fitz sprawled on the leather upholstery, his feet pointing at me and his head lolling near the far foot well. He was twitching, his hands jerking and his tongue flapping around like a beached fish gulping for air. His pants were wadded around his knees, revealing a surprising glimpse of chubby white thighs, his flaccid belly and something I didn't want to identify.

I hastily averted my eyes. "Holy hell. What happened? What did you do?"

Marsha-Marcie took a step toward the SUV and her eyes widened. She seemed to crumple, her knees buckling like all her bones dissolved. I caught her when she went past me, but she was at least six inches taller than me and heftier.

I landed on my right side when her dead weight descended on top of me, the injured side of my face making contact with the pavement and her body colliding with my purse and pushing it into my stomach. I heard a tearing sound then my elbow cracked against the asphalt and I saw stars.

For one panicked second I lost all the breath in my lungs. I heaved in a gasp, almost choking in my anxiety to get oxygen. "Get off of me!" I poked and prodded at the female flesh on me but I was pinned to the sweltering pavement, enveloped by mixed odors of cloying perfume, tar, and sweat. If the weight didn't kill me, the smells would.

I floundered, finally managing to get an elbow into her waist to roll her off of me. My purse went with her, but I grabbed it and tugged, dragging it from under her inert body. Sirens wailed in the distance, getting closer. The firehouse and EMTs were only three blocks to the south and the police station was eight blocks north, so I expected to see an ambulance, but instead it was a patrol car that pulled in first, screeching to a halt between rows of parked cars, lights flashing.

I sat up and rested my bleeding elbows on my knees, my head ringing and my stomach heaving. Two police officers emerged from the car and one headed for me. "I'm fine," I called out. "Go help in the car there!" I waved them to the SUV. The door nearest me was closed, with Richard on the other side, as was the patrol car. One of the officers joined Richard and the other continued on to me.

"I'm okay." I wiped sweat from my face with one grimy forearm. When I lowered the arm, I saw the blood. "Oh, cripes, now what?"

"You got a cut on your cheek." The young officer knelt next to Marsha-Marcie, who was starting to stir. "Ma'am, are you okay?"

She rolled over and her boobs nearly escaped her blouse again. "What happened? Where am I?" she asked in true fainting damsel-in-distress fashion.

The guy's eyes bugged at the sight of all her female flesh. I used his distraction to get on my feet, starting on all fours before pushing upward off my knees, my purse dangling off my shoulder. I groaned aloud when my hands made contact with new bruises and I was pretty sure the warmth on my cheek was trickling blood. I retrieved Alan's hanky which was still in my pocket and dabbed at my face. It came away dotted with blood but not saturated, so apparently I escaped serious injury.

I edged past the distressed damsel and her rescuer and rounded the rear of the SUV. The police officer and Richard were staring inside. "What happened?" I asked, still patting my face with the once-white hanky.

"I don't know." Richard's voice was tremulous. His face seemed odd and I realized it was leeched of color, his tan skin mottled and mixed with an ashy gray. He appeared ten years older than he was minutes earlier.

I looked past him into the SUV. PJ Fitz's head drooped over the window, his tongue swollen and protruding and his eyes—Lordy, his eyes were like a doll's eyes, all bulging and glassy in his beet red face. I took an involuntary step back when the smell reached me, a stench of feces and sweat. "Is he—?" *Stupid question. Of course he's dead. Or damn close to it.*

I backed up again, right into another car. A screeching siren went off, a discordant blast which made me jump, almost scaring the crap out of me. PJ dangled in the SUV like a lump of dough. Was that what happened to him? Was he scared to death?

People started emerging from the pub and I was shunted to one side when the police officers hurried to intercept the curious gawkers. Two other police cars arrived, the screeching car was silenced, another car alarm went off, an ambulance pulled in to the lot, and suddenly the street was full of people, cars, and noise.

I sat on the curb near the back door of the pub. Trees on the far west side of the park kept the ground relatively cool, although the pavement still radiated heat from earlier in the day. A couple of bar patrons paused to ask if I needed help, but I shook my head, not anxious to speculate on what was happening. I was going to have a hard time putting that last glimpse of PJ from my mind.

I spied Richard Fitz sticking close to the SUV, watching the white-coated people from the ambulance work around the back seat, maneuvering a wheeled gurney into place. Everyone else was kept back by five police officers who formed a loose cordon, their presence enough of a deterrent to hold the crowd at bay.

I resolutely stared at my purse resting on the pavement in front of me while my stomach did little flip flops. Whatever happened to PJ, it happened fast and was horrible. I'd never seen the aftereffects of poisoning, but for some reason that had to be what happened. The few mystery books I read talked about protruding tongues and glassy stares.

I gulped, struggling to retain the remnants of the potato chips I ate a few hours earlier. I felt like a weight was pressing me, bending me over until I was hunched in anticipation of a blow from behind.

I didn't get a blow, but I did get a surprise. A hand touched my shoulder and I bolted upright, tipping forward when I lost my balance. I landed on my already-skinned knee and kept myself from tumbling face-first into the asphalt by flinging out one hand—a hand already bruised and scraped. "What the hell?"

Marianne Archer regarded me with wide blue eyes, her pale blonde hair pulled back from her face with a dark blue ribbon which matched the blue of the flowers on her gauzy blouse. Her faded blue denim capris were decorated with dark blue flowers, too, as were her sandals. *She looks like a damn hydrangea bush.* I struggled to my feet. *How does she do it? It's a thousand degrees in the shade and weeping with humidity and she looks like she stepped out of the walk-in fridge.*

"I'm sorry, Tuck, did I startle you?" She gestured vaguely behind her. "I cut through the park. The street is all blocked off."

I brushed dirt and gravel from my capris. "No, I always make a nosedive for the pavement when someone comes up behind me."

My sarcasm appeared to bewilder rather than anger her. Her pale brown eyebrows drew together like little caterpillars touching noses on her forehead. "Were you a witness?"

"To what?"

"To PJ Fitz's murder." She gazed at the parking lot and the authorities gathered around the big SUV.

"Murder? Who said it was murder?" I tucked in my shirt, noting there were bloodstains on the front where my elbows got tangled with the fabric.

"I overheard the emergency technician tell Officer Peel that PJ's Cadillac was a crime scene and it should be taped off so they can examine the ground around it."

"It's a bit late for taping off. I don't know if a comment like that means that it's murder."

She nodded wisely, wisps of golden hair shining in the sun around her face, giving her a haloed angelic appearance. "I think it does. Did you see it?"

"I didn't see a damn thing." I pushed my tangled hair back from my forehead, brushing over the new wound on my face. "Shit, that hurts."

"It looks bad, too. But it matches your black eye, at least. Can I interview you?" She held up a cell phone.

"Hell, no. I didn't see anything so there's nothing to interview me about."

"It's interesting how your pub seems to be a place where all sort of tragic activities happen." She regarded me with polite curiosity, head tilted slightly to one side.

"Tragic? What's that supposed to mean?"

"Well, a fight happened here the other night and now this." She gestured with the phone at the ambulance.

"The fight wasn't exactly tragic."

Her cheeks darkened, turning a becoming shade of deep pink. "It was for the people involved."

"And what is *that* supposed to mean?" I demanded. "Quit pussyfooting around, Marianne. Spit out whatever is stickin' in your craw."

"The fight the other night solidified my decision to divorce Rob, which is perhaps not a tragedy, but which does affect us negatively. And poor PJ has died, which means the factory is without a CEO. We're lucky Richard Fitz is in town so he can step in and help."

"Why can't Rob step in and help?" Her coolness was more than irritating. It was unnerving, like listening to Mr. Spock intone to Captain Kirk about how an emotional decision was illogical. It was unnerving because presumably Marianne wasn't a Vulcan and presumably she did have emotions. Presumably.

She smiled pityingly at me. "Rob isn't capable of such management responsibilities. He can barely manage day to day operations."

"And see what happened." I seized on this chance to pump her for information for a change. "Someone died."

"Well, it certainly wasn't his fault. It was one of those undercover animal rights people, trying to smear the factory's reputation."

"How do you know? Did someone tell you?"

"I'm a reporter, Tucker. It's my job to investigate and research facts. The man who was killed was here under an assumed name and they're trying to find his family even now." Her gaze went back to the ambulance. "The Sheriff will probably handle that investigation because it occurred at York, although our police department will handle PJ's investigation."

"Maybe he had a heart attack," I suggested. "Maybe there's nothing to investigate."

"Maybe. Excuse me, I need to talk to the officer in charge and get a statement for the paper." Marianne moved past me, aiming for the cordon of police personnel.

"Where's Rob? Rumor has it he's selling his cabin." The words popped out of me of their own volition.

She turned like a marionette on strings, arms and legs disjointed but moving in harmony. "What did you say?"

I shrugged. "Just a rumor I heard. You know how it is in a bar, all kinds of talk goes around. I'm surprised he's selling it."

Marianne regarded me for a long moment, her shoulders stiff. Then she sighed deeply, shaking off her momentary paralysis. "I don't think his real estate affairs are any of your business." She stalked away, cutting through the crowd like a hot knife through butter.

"Bitch." I surprised her when I mentioned knowing about Rob selling his cabin. Apparently it wasn't common knowledge. But was it even known to her?

"You okay, Tuck?"

Sheriff Owen Knott was making his way to me from the right, skirting the parked cars now trapped in the lot by the ambulance and the police cars. "I'm fine. A bit bruised, that's all." Owen was an outdoorsy kind of guy with cropped gray-blond hair, a stocky and solid physique, and the prettiest gray-blue eyes like smoke on water. He reminded me of Lee Majors, a movie star who was my biggest crush in high school, evoking a feeling of nostalgia whenever I saw Owen.

He moved so his back was to the ambulance scene, effectively preventing anyone from seeing me. Tonight he wore his uniform with the pale brown shirt, black trousers, and gun belt with all kinds of gadgets hanging off of it. "Why don't you come to the station and talk to me about what you saw here?"

"Huh?" I gaped at him. "Don't you mean talk to you about, about, you know?"

"I told the police I'd get your statement." He put a hand under my arm and started to steer me to the exit. I hastily grabbed my purse and let him lead me along the perimeter of the lot. "Come to the station and we'll talk. I'll bring you back to your car." His hand tightened. "We'll stop at the hospital first and have the cut examined."

He stopped next to one of the officers and they exchanged a few words. I eyed the huddle of people around the expensive SUV. The ambulance people were moving something onto the cart, angling it from the car. That's when I realized the something was PJ, zipped into a black plastic bag.

"You okay?" Owen asked while I swayed, held upright by his grip on my forearm.

I blinked. "Think I'm gonna puke," I mumbled.

He pulled me off to one side and gently pushed on my neck. "Lean over, take a deep breath," he commanded. "I've got you, you won't fall."

I did like he said, bracing my hands on my knees and sucking in shaky gasps of air.

"You've been hurt." One of his hands squeezed my neck and the other gripped my arm, firmly but gently. "You'll be fine. Take a breath now, relax."

Sweat pooled on my forehead, dribbling into my hairline. I don't know how long I leaned there, gasping. "I'm okay," I finally whispered. "It's past. I'm okay."

He steadied me while I straightened, his hands on my shoulders. "Hospital first, then the station. By then all this—" and he jerked a thumb over his shoulder, "will be finished and you can get your car, go home, and get some sleep."

"I don't think I need the hospital."

He bundled me out of the parking lot and stuffed me into a dark blue sedan sitting at the curb, several cars removed from the action. "Don't touch anything," he said before he hurried around to the driver's side and got in.

I didn't even glance at anything, much less consider touching it. I leaned my head back against the cloth seat and closed my eyes. He settled in his seat with a faint clatter of noise from the stuff on his belt then he started the car. "What happened?" I asked, still keeping my eyes closed. "What happens now?"

Owen was probably accustomed to dealing with people who were largely incoherent with shock, because he answered without hesitation. "PJ's dead. There will be an autopsy to determine cause of death. I saw the body. I'm not sure what it was. The police will impound his car and check it to see if it was tampered with in any way."

Well, score one for Marianne and her crime scene comment. "The woman wasn't hurt, though." I opened my eyes, surprised to see we were almost to the hospital on the east side of town. Did I pass out? I saw a reflection of our car in a passing storefront. Owen had put on the lights, which blinked from the front grill of the sedan. That explained our speed, I guess. "Thanks for not putting on the siren," I said.

"You're welcome. Are you sure you're okay, Tuck? You've had a few shocks today."

The sympathy in his voice made me turn to stare through my window. "I'll be okay."

"That wasn't what I asked."

I sighed. "It's all the answer I have."

There were four people sitting in the Emergency Room waiting area at the hospital, but I got in immediately to see a doctor. I suppose the fact I showed up with the Sheriff accounted for it. The doctor did a double-take when he saw me. "You again?"

It was the same doctor who had examined my black eye. "We've got to stop meeting like this," I joked, sitting in the same cubicle I was in on Friday night.

He shook his head and proceeded to check my various bruises with gentle fingers, touching the side of my head and making me wince. When he rotated my right arm, it made me wince even more. Next he bandaged the cut on my cheek with those little butterfly suture things before he made me walk around for him, balancing on one leg and touching my finger to my nose.

"What was it this time?" he asked while he worked.

"A woman fell on top of me. I hit the pavement."

"Lucky for her you were there to break the fall. Not so lucky for you." He straightened. "There's no sign of concussion and the cut on the cheek isn't deep. But make sure to keep the scrapes on your elbows clean and if the bruising on your knee swells, ice it."

"I'll try to avoid any more confrontations," I promised. I once again signed a million forms and was soon leaving under my own power, Owen by my side.

I plopped into the sedan and we drove six blocks east to the courthouse, a brick four-story structure occupying a city block. Owen parked in front in the slot labeled *Sheriff* and we went to the west side of the building, entering into an open area where two deputies sat at desks, separated from the public by a high counter.

The two men looked up when we entered. "Go on in and sit down, Tuck." Owen piloted me through a locked gate which buzzed when we neared it. He pointed to a door on the right with his name on it. "I'll be there in a minute."

Owen's office was a crowded room with a faux wood desk, a computer on a side table nearby, three uncomfortable guest chairs, and a wall of dark gray metal file cabinets on the left. Two tall windows were behind the desk, blinds lowered so I couldn't see the west side of the courthouse lawn, which I knew was outside the office. Several framed pictures and documents were on the walls but I was too tired to examine them. I sat in one of the chairs, confirming that yes, it was uncomfortable.

I set my purse on the floor at my feet. The top gaped open and I glimpsed my cell phone inside, blinking a red light at me. I wasn't completely trained yet on this phone, but I knew it meant a missed message. I got the phone and clicked my way to the menu and the *Recent Calls* option. I clicked the *Missing* option, but *No Missed Calls* showed on the tiny screen.

I frowned at it. I tried a few other options, clicking one thing and another before I found *Messaging.* I clicked *Messages* and saw a phone number listed I didn't recognize. Of course, I never memorized phone numbers anymore now that speed dial had the role of my memory.

I clicked the message and the words formed on the screen:

Stay quiet about what you know or you'll be next.

Chapter 9

I stared blankly at the phone in my hand.

Owen came in behind me and closed the door. He crossed to the desk to sit in the black mesh desk chair and pulled a folder from a drawer. "Thank you for telling me about that arrest a few years ago. I'm sorry, Tuck, but we've positively identified the man who died as William Redman, formerly of Leland City, Catahoula Parish, Louisiana."

I barely heard what he said while I tried to process the threatening words on my cell phone. "What?"

He slid a picture across the desk to me. I leaned forward. Will stared into the camera, his lips twitched upward in an almost-smile, with a hint of mischief in his eyes. I saw that look enough times in the past when I accused him of something like filching a piece of pie or teasing Old Man Moody at the barbershop. But this wasn't a picture from misspent youth. This was a booking photo, with the height and inch markings next to his right ear.

I slid the photo back to Owen. "I guess I'm not surprised. I didn't hold much hope you were wrong."

"We recovered his cell phone but there was no other identification on the body. No wallet. We're lucky his fingerprints were on file." He leaned back in his chair. "You seem awfully calm about this."

I checked my phone. The screen was black now, one of the power-saver features which caused it to darken and lock itself so I couldn't butt-dial anybody. I considered showing it to Owen, but could I trust him? I didn't know so I wasn't going to chance it.

I raised my eyes to his then I dropped my phone back in my purse. "It won't do any good to pitch a fit. He's dead and it's up to you to find who did it. Right?"

Owen seemed to be making his mind up about something, because he stared at me for a long minute before he said, "Alan mentioned you weren't sure if you could trust me."

"I'm not sure I can trust anybody," I retorted. "That goddamned chicken factory and the Fitz family have a stranglehold on this town. I don't know who's in whose pocket."

"Fair enough. I'm not at liberty to discuss an ongoing investigation with you, but because you're related to the victim, I feel I owe you what explanation I can give." He paused and I nodded once, which was all I could do after hearing the word *victim*.

"Redman was employed at the factory and apparently was also working undercover for an animal rights group, gathering data about the conditions in the factory." Owen's stormy gray eyes were cold as winter for a second. "Such activities are against the law."

"The law was just passed. It wouldn't have applied to Will. He'd be grandfathered in." I tapped the edge of Owen's desk, making my point.

"That's still up for debate." He raised a hand when I tried to speak. "A tip was called in to our office last night. Someone was seen prowling around the grounds at the factory."

"Don't they have security?"

"Very minimal. They rely mainly on locked gates to prevent access." Owen slid Will's picture back into a manila folder. "I doubt anyone seriously threatened plant operations."

"Maybe it wasn't Will. There are a lot of people who are angry with them after so many people got sick. Maybe it was someone else, maybe somebody with a grudge."

Owen nodded. "We're considering it. But regardless of who else was there, Will Redman was there. Like I said, our office got a tip and I went with a deputy to check it out."

"A tip? What kind?"

"An anonymous call."

"Can you trace it?" I demanded. "Why call you? Why not call the police in Barnsdale? I mean, did somebody call 911 and it was relayed to you, or was it called directly to you?"

He settled back in his chair, regarding me thoughtfully. One corner of his mouth quirked up. "You should be a cop. They called here directly and they used your nephew's phone. You're right, if someone called 911, there's a good chance the Barnsdale police would be notified. They sometimes handle calls in York. We split up the duty since York doesn't have a full-time police force."

"So somebody wanted the sheriff's people there." My mind was spinning, considering and tossing aside ideas. "Why? What's special about the Sheriff's office? What would you do that a police officer wouldn't?"

Owen once again held up a hand. "We're working on it. I have an idea but it's just that. An idea." When I tried to speak again, he leveled his gaze at me and gave a short shake of his head. I got the hint.

"I was short-handed last night because one of my deputies is in Des Moines, getting special training. So I went on the call with the deputy on duty. We got to the factory and saw immediately there was a problem. All the exterior lights were lit, chickens were running everywhere, and the doors to the factory were open. Some animals were trampled or . . . I don't know. It was a mess." He stared at his desk, his mouth grim. "The whole place is a mess. Anyway, Rob Huntington pulled in about the same time we did. He went into the office building while we checked the area. I was coming around the corner of one of the machine sheds when I saw someone running."

He stopped, his eyes still fixed on the desk. "And?" I prompted.

Owen continued, his voice so neutral it was almost robotic. "I called to the person to stop, but they kept running. A gunshot was fired. I ducked behind one of the tractors. There was another gunshot. I saw something flash in the distance. I fired my weapon. It got quiet. My deputy came up and joined me. We walked into the field and found him."

It was too easy. It was too simple. It should be far, far more complicated to kill someone so young, so vibrant. I leaned forward, staring hard at Owen until he finally met my gaze. "What the hell happened, Owen?"

"The DCI is investigating." When he saw my blank expression, he added, "The state Department of Criminal Investigations. It's standard in cases like this. We have to turn the reconstruction over to another department, and I can't be involved in any way in the investigation. I got the preliminary report this morning. It wasn't my bullet that killed him. Someone else was there."

"Your deputy?"

"He carries the same caliber weapon I carry." Owen regarded me somberly. "Most officer-involved shootings take place in close quarters, a few feet from a suspect. The odds of me or my deputy being able to hit a fleeing man in the dark from several yards away aren't good. I'm telling you this because you're owed an explanation for what happened to a member of your family. This is still confidential because it's an ongoing investigation, but it will be announced soon it was not a member of law enforcement who killed the man."

"Holy crap in a bucket. Will was right to be afraid for his life." That damn factory. It truly was a Heart of Darkness. It made me remember the grim scene I witnessed in the parking lot at my bar. "Does PJ's death have anything to do with this?"

"I'm not sure. We're not even sure how he died."

"It's a tad suspicious when a man is killed at the factory and the factory owner dies within a few hours."

"I know that. I'm sure the Barnsdale officers will share their findings with me." When I looked surprised, he said, "They have jurisdiction. It happened in their back yard, so to speak. Of course, first there will be an autopsy."

"Really? Isn't the widow consulted about that?"

"Not in the cause of an unnatural death." Owen's lips compressed. "And that was a very unnatural death, if you ask me."

I swallowed hard. "No kidding."

"The County Medical Examiner will do the autopsy. Once cause of death is determined, they can start working on the manner of death and whether it was through foul play."

"Whether it was foul play?" I almost sputtered with indignation. "Lord have mercy, Owen. The man strangled on his own tongue. It has to be foul play."

"We have to wait for the evidence." He stared intently at me. "We *all* have to wait for the evidence."

"Well, of course. What do you think I was going to do?" I bent to retrieve my purse, avoiding his assessing gaze. "I want justice for Will. And I guess I have to trust you to do it for me." Before he could answer, my phone rang. I almost dropped my purse, suddenly remembering those hateful words on the tiny screen minutes earlier.

"Are you going to answer that?" Owen asked while I stared at the bag on my lap.

"It's probably not important." I peeked at the phone display then whooshed a big sigh of relief. "Oh, it's Alan." I put the phone to my ear. "Hey, I got delayed. I mean, I'm with Owen now."

"Why didn't you call me?" Alan broke in. "I saw on the news that PJ died at our restaurant. What the hell happened? Are you okay?"

I winced. When he said it that way—*our restaurant*—I saw how terrible it might be for our business reputation to have a man die of what might be food poisoning in our parking lot. "I'm so sorry. It happened really fast. PJ was there with this woman and they went to the parking lot to have a little sex and the next thing you know, PJ was dead."

Alan's sigh of relief was so loud I'm sure Owen must have heard it. "Thank God. Was it a heart attack?"

"Uh, I don't think so." Owen watched me with an unblinking gaze, so I wasn't sure what I could or couldn't say. "I'm not sure if I know what killed him. But I did get a chance to talk to Owen, at least."

"Did you tell him about the threats?"

My jaw sagged open. "What threats?"

Owen sat up straighter. "Threats?"

"Didn't you say your nephew was threatened?" Alan asked.

I rubbed my forehead. Did I tell Alan? I couldn't remember. "I thought you meant the threat about—" I clammed up so fast my teeth snapped together with a click.

Owen eyed me warily. "It's about time you tell me what you know, Tucker. Starting with any threats."

I ignored him to focus on the phone. "I don't think we have anything to worry about with PJ's death because he wasn't in the restaurant. He was in the bar and a dozen people saw him there and he was fine. But maybe you should call Marianne Archer. She was writing up a news story. Maybe you could say you think the owner of the pub should be allowed to make a comment about the death?" I checked Owen, who still stared at me, his pretty gray eyes positively stormy with anger. "I have to go."

"I'll call Marianne. And I'll see if I can find Rob. If PJ is dead, Rob is probably in charge at the factory. Maybe he can shed some more light on what happened last night."

"Rob was manager there, not PJ." I nodded to Owen and smiled tentatively in an *I'm trying, I'm trying* sort of way.

"He's operations manager, but PJ was the overall manager. I don't know if Richard will promote Rob or not. I'll see what I can find out, Tuck. Call me when you can. Tell Owen . . ." He hesitated. "Tell him I'll talk to him later."

"Will do. Later." I clicked the little icon to end the call and lowered the phone. "Alan said he'll talk to you later."

"What threats?" Owen asked, zeroing in on what I wasn't telling.

I regarded my phone screen. "Can you tell who sent a call if I give you the phone number?"

"What?"

I held up my phone. "Can you?"

He nodded, turning to his computer and pulling a keyboard from under the table. "What is it?"

I retrieved the number on the computer screen and recited it for him. He tapped busily on the keyboard. "Guy Gibson called you. So what?"

I sat back, stunned. "Guy?" I don't know what I was expecting, but a threatening text message from Guy Gibson was not it.

"Tucker? What aren't you telling me? If someone is threatening you, I need to know about it."

I stared around the room at anywhere but directly at Owen, struggling to decide what to do. It made no sense. How would Guy know Will gave me information? Maybe it was a prank of some kind.

Or maybe not. With a sigh, I straightened, prepared to hand Owen my cell phone. Before I could do it, though, a knock came on his door. One of the deputies from the outer office stood in the hall, clearly visible through the glass of Owen's office door. Behind him stood Richard Fitz.

Owen waved his hand for the deputy to open the door while he stood up. "This isn't done, Tucker," he said in a low voice as the two men entered.

"I know." I started to stand, but Richard Fitz and the deputy blocked my movements in the cramped office. I subsided back onto the seat.

"What's being done about my brother's death?" Richard demanded.

Owen nodded to the deputy, who left the office, shooting Fitz a baleful glare on the way. I could easily imagine the arrogant son of a bitch striding into the deputy's space, acting like Pharaoh telling Moses to get his ass out of the palace. "Hello, Mr. Fitz. Would you care to have a seat?" Owen nodded at the other unoccupied guest chair in the room.

"No, thank you." Richard assessed the seat with one quick up-down motion of his head, determining its worth and deciding it was unacceptable for his patrician butt. "I'd like to know the progress of the investigation into Patrick's death."

"I'm not sure about the progress," Owen said calmly. "It's being handled by the Barnsdale Police Department."

"That's ridiculous." Richard glared at me. "Why are you here?"

"The police asked me to talk to Miss Frye and get her statement about what occurred at her pub." Owen resumed his seat, his gaze fixed on Fitz.

"What happened to your face?" Richard eyed my new gash warily. "Did you get into a fight again? Were you involved in Patrick's death?"

"Oh, for heaven's sake. You were there with me. Of course I wasn't involved in his death. Besides, I didn't get into a fight the first time. Other people got into a fight and I got in the middle. Like this time. Your brother and his floozy popped out to the car for sex and the next thing you know, he's dead and his floozy collapsed on top of me." I stood, almost toe to toe with Richard, who towered over me. "Excuse me."

He stepped back. "What floozy?"

I rolled my eyes while I inched by him and started for the door. "You know what floozy. You saw him with her in the pub tonight. Marcia or Marcie or whatever her name is."

Richard turned to Owen. "Is that true? Was it a heart attack?"

"I didn't say heart attack," I pointed out.

"It's an obvious conclusion," Richard countered. "PJ wasn't a young man. Perhaps the strain or the excitement caused it."

Owen held up a hand. "All of this is speculation. The County Medical Examiner will do an autopsy to determine the cause of death. I'm sure the police will be in touch with Mrs. Fitz to discuss their findings."

"Mrs. Fitz?" Richard's mouth opened in a slight O of surprise. "Mrs. Fitz? Oh, you mean Patrick's wife. Why aren't you investigating?"

"The Barnsdale police have jurisdiction," Owen said with admirable patience.

Richard shook his head like shaking off a troublesome fly. "I would prefer that you handle the investigation."

I almost laughed aloud. He sounded like a king who was struggling to speak in a reasonable tone to these most unreasonable peons.

"It's not a matter of preference," Owen said.

"But it is a matter of competence," Richard said. "I'm not sure the Barnsdale police department is capable of handling a complicated investigation."

"Why do you think it's complicated?" I put on my best innocent expression when Fitz swung his attention to me. "You said you thought it was a heart attack. That's pretty straightforward. Do you know something about his death?"

Richard cleared his throat busily. "Well, no, of course not. From appearances—I mean, from what I saw of Patrick, it doesn't appear to be—" He clenched his hands, the muscles in his tanned forearms bunching. At the moment he reminded me of a wrestler or football player, a person who exuded barely contained violence.

The moment passed and the suave, confident businessman returned. "I'm sure the police department is capable of handling an investigation. I'm concerned. After all, Patrick was my brother and I want to spare his widow and his children any further grief."

I almost snorted with derision but I caught Owen's cautionary glance. "I'll give Isabel a call and see if she needs anything."

Richard's gaze swept over me. "I'm sure she'll appreciate that," he said, his voice so neutral it was insulting.

"You're probably anxious to plan a memorial service." Owen's calm tone didn't quite defrost the ice in his gray eyes.

Richard took step back from Owen's desk, almost treading on me. "Memorial service?" He blinked rapidly. "Yes, of course. I'll speak to Lee Knight and Marianne Archer."

"What does Lee Knight or Marianne Archer have to do with a memorial service?" I stopped at the doorway.

"Lee is in charge of the town party this week and Marianne is assisting. It's why I'm in town, to speak at the celebration. Perhaps we can combine a memorial service with the celebration." He nodded, lips pursed. "Perhaps by then Guy Gibson will be back. He could speak, as well as some of Patrick's other friends."

I could almost see the gears spinning in Fitz's leonine head. What an arrogant asshole, to think the town would like their festivities combined with a eulogy for his no-good brother. "What a good way to put a damper on fun. Maybe the town won't miss PJ."

Richard's dark eyes narrowed. "Why don't you let me be the judge of that?"

I strode back to him, bumping into the guest chair and adding another bruise to the ones already dotting my shins. I moved close enough so I smelled his cologne. "I trust you about as far as I can spit, and I was raised to be a lady so I don't spit so good." I glanced at Owen, who watched this exchange with a bemused smile. "Isn't there a law or something about using a public gathering to make grandiose statements about an asshole?"

Richard started to speak but Owen beat him to it. "I don't know if there is a law, but I'll check to be sure."

Richard brushed me aside. "I doubt whether anyone in town would object," he said through clenched teeth. "Fitz Agri-Industries has done a lot for the people here. I'm sure they'd like to repay our generosity with a small token of respect for my brother." He paused at the door. "I'm sure all of our elected officials will be happy to oblige." His attention shifted to me. "All of the businesses in town profit from the robust economy provided by the employment opportunities at Fitz Industries. You'd be wise to keep it in mind."

"Is that a threat?" I turned to face him.

"Of course not. I'm just stating an obvious fact." His dark eyes stared beyond me to Owen. "Sheriff, I trust you'll do what's right for the town."

"And what's right for Fitz Agri-Industries?" I demanded.

"Fitz has many holdings, only one of which is the factory in York." Richard shrugged. "We need to assess the factory's status in light of what happened."

"You mean the egg recall?" I was hard pressed not to sound too gleeful. "I'm sure it must put a damper on your profits if you're forced to recall millions of eggs."

Richard regarded me coolly. "I was thinking of questionable and incompetent business practices uncovered in the course of evaluation of the factory management."

"Geez, PJ is dead so it's not very nice, talking about how bad a manager he was." I frowned at Richard, surprised at this breach of etiquette.

"Patrick?" Richard's dark eyebrows drew together in puzzlement. "Rob Huntington is the manager of the plant. I gave him the job a few years ago when he came to me, asking for work." His lips twisted in disdain. "It wasn't the wisest move on my part, but Rob always did need a helping hand. I felt sorry for him."

I opened my mouth to say Rob reported to PJ, who probably really ran things, given Rob's general feckless nature, but Owen spoke first.

"I'll relay your concerns about the investigation to the police chief." Owen rose from behind his desk and came around to stand next to me. "Thanks for stopping." He put a hand on my arm, gently holding me back.

Richard's eyes met mine for a long second. I stared right back at him, daring him to make some comment. He smiled, lines fanning around his eyes. "Thank you, Sheriff." He swept from the room and I could almost hear his kingly robes rustling while he walked.

"When he takes Viagra, do you think he gets taller?"

Owen chuckled. "Richard Fitz is accustomed to having his own way. Don't let him get under your skin."

"I dislike arrogance."

"So do I. But it's something I've learned to handle. Don't forget, Tucker, I'm an elected official. I serve at the whim of the public. The Barnsdale police chief is appointed, but I have to run for office. It's a political job."

"I tend to forget that. I guess I think 'cop' and I assume you're hired willy-nilly, the same as everybody."

"I always have to be careful to avoid the appearance of favoritism. I can't treat the Fitz family or their businesses any different than I treat you or any other business person. You or Alan or anyone, do you understand?"

I nodded. "I think I see where this is going. If it comes out that someone called the sheriff's office directly, it might be construed as—" I frowned. "As what?"

"I don't know. But I'm not going to let anyone imply I'm treating someone unfairly for political gain." When I started to move away, his hand tightened slightly on my arm. "Weren't you going to show me something? Tell me something? Before Richard Fitz arrived?"

Oh, damn. There was a threatening text message from Guy Gibson sitting on my mobile phone. I wavered, not sure what to do. Once again fate intervened, once again in the form of a deputy who appeared in the open doorway.

"Sheriff?" He stopped when he saw me still there. "Sorry. I didn't know you still had someone here."

"I'm leaving," I said.

"I'll have someone drive you back to your car," he said.

"No, no, it's fine." I made a dismissive gesture, using that to gently pry his hand off of me. "It's only a few blocks. I'll walk."

"I'd be happier if someone would drive you."

"No need." I nodded to the deputy, a man who was far too young to be toting a gun, or at least that's how he appeared to me.

Owen kept pace with me while I walked to the door. "Are you sure there isn't anything you'd like to share?" he asked when I paused in the doorway, the deputy moving to one side to let me pass.

"How easy is it for somebody to get my cell phone number?"

Owen's gaze flickered to my purse then back to me. "If you called them, it's recorded on their phone. And it might be listed on some phone registries. Why do you ask?"

"No reason. I'm just curious." I rested my hand on my purse, which was slung over my shoulder. I had never called Guy Gibson, certainly not with my cell phone.

So how did he get my phone number?

Chapter 10

I left the courthouse and headed south. The Acorn was a five-block-long pleasant walk on a summer's evening. I dug my sunglasses from my purse and settled them on my bruised face. It was only seven o'clock and the sun was still bright in the sky on my right, golden rays striking me when I passed from shadows of buildings into clear spaces.

It was quiet on the street with only occasional cars going past. The main downtown shopping district was two blocks over, to the west. This street was mainly repair shops, a branch building for the community college, and a gas station and convenience store two blocks from the pub.

The sidewalks were damp and the air had a heavy, fusty quality to it which told me it rained earlier but not enough to clear the air. *Sort of like my talk with Owen.* I should have told him about the threatening text message, but it seemed ludicrous to think that Guy Gibson—fussy, overly perfect Guy—would send me such a message.

It was probably a prank, but who would do such a thing? Maybe Guy lost his phone. The more I considered it, though, that didn't make sense. If a stranger picked up Guy's phone, why would the stranger send me such a text message? Unless it was one of those "I saw what you did and I know who you are" pranks, which was too much of a coincidence to be real.

Too many facts, too many speculations, were bobbing around in my mind. I finally gave up and plodded onward, happy to let my brain shut down into a fugue of tiredness. The warmth of the day combined with the dense odors from the cooling pavement which combined with occasional bursts of floral scents coming from random containers of flowers.

I spent an enjoyable few blocks trying to analyze what was going on around me and allowed worry, grief, and anxiety to slip away. My headache began to recede but that let the throbbing from my new cut come to the forefront of my attention. I began to frame the rest of my evening in my mind, starting with a nice cold drink.

My car was where I left it, in the Acorn parking lot. I was surprised to see other cars there, almost filling the lot, although none parked near the taped-off area where PJ's car was earlier. Of course, it was only seven and the bar would be open for several hours yet.

I slid into the driver's seat of my car and leaned back wearily, closing my eyes. What happened to PJ's floozy girlfriend? When would they do the autopsy on PJ? Who was the County Medical Examiner? Was it a doctor? I couldn't remember if I ever heard the name. Suddenly an image of PJ's bloated face swam into my memory, and my eyes flew open while I leaned forward, gasping for breath. I wasn't sure if I could get the picture out of my brain.

Unlike the earlier part of my day, my drive home was uneventful, probably because I drove overly cautiously, careful to avoid potholes and bumps lest it make my stomach lurch and set off a chain reaction.

Luckily there was little traffic so there were no impatient tailgaters behind me. When I got to my house, I parked the car in the garage and went to the mailbox, retrieving my Sunday paper and Saturday's mail, both of which I forgot about in the chaos of Will's death.

I entered my house through the kitchen door from the garage and dropped the mail and paper on the table along with my purse. When I took a glass from the cupboard, I glimpsed movement from the corner of my eye. I froze.

Was someone in the house? It was totally quiet, without even the hum of the air conditioner, although the air was cool, so I was sure it was working. I turned slowly, the highball glass slippery in my sweaty hand.

A kitten sat in the hallway, watching me with a solemn expression. For a minute I couldn't remember where it came from. Then it hit me. I locked two kittens in my bedroom.

Didn't I?

Well, apparently I did *not* have two kittens locked in the bedroom. Cayenne bounded over to me before checking the kitty food dishes I set out so many hours earlier. The empty canned food dish attested to their voracious appetites. And the scattered kibble on the floor told me they found and approved of that food, although their table manners were lacking.

He dug into the food with gusto, scattering brown bits all around. I made a hasty inventory of the house, noting the bedroom door was open a sliver, just enough of a sliver for a tiny kitten. I tugged on the door, latching it and waited a second. Sure enough, it popped open again, held almost shut by the area rug in the bedroom.

I made a mental note to see about getting it fixed while I went in search of Cayenne's sister. It took a few minutes, but I soon found her sitting placidly on top of a chair in the living room, peering through the front window.

I checked my office, the spare bedroom, and bathroom, but everything seemed relatively intact, although a few items were knocked around on my desk, which sat in front of the side window. A kitten probably got up there and pushed over the pencil holder while angling for a good viewing spot. I rearranged my desk items to accommodate a kitten (or two) and went back to the kitchen.

The message light blinked on my machine. I pressed the *play* button, and Alan's voice said, "Hey, kid. Let me know if you want some company tonight. I won't bother you unless you call, but I'm here if you need me. Call if you want to."

I really didn't want company. All I wanted was a drink. My stomach grumbled, reminding me I hadn't eaten anything but a snack eight hours earlier. I went to the fridge and found some summer sausage, cheese, and crackers and was sitting down to eat when a muddy green pickup truck pulled into my driveway.

I met Rob at my front door, opening it and gesturing him in when I saw Café eye the open door with a hint of mischievous speculation. "Come in." I tugged him further into the room. "Kittens. I don't want to chase them around the neighborhood."

"I didn't know you had pets." He stood uncertainly in the tiny entryway, his shoulders hunched.

"Are you okay?" His pale hair was mussed and sweat-curled and his clothes—jeans and a pale blue shirt—looked like he may have slept in them. The stubble on his cheeks and his bloodshot eyes all added to the Portrait of a Sleepless Man.

He drew in a long, shuddering breath. "I wanted to apologize, Tuck."

I started back through the living room to the kitchen and my vulnerable food, sitting on the kitchen table. Cayenne hadn't yet made a grab for anything, but he lurked on one of the chairs, his neck stretched to the edge of the table and his inquisitive nose twitching. "Come on in and sit. Can I get you anything? You want a drink? How about a beer or something?"

Rob stopped at the edge of the living room when he saw my small feast on the table. "I'm sorry. I'm interrupting your dinner. I can talk to you later."

"It's a snack. I got so damn busy today I didn't have much time to eat. Come on in. What can I get you?" I went to the fridge. "I have some Friar's Folly here, do you want some?" I held up the glass jug which customers could purchase from the pub, providing them with some of the Acorn's fine beer in their own homes.

"Beer would be great." He pulled out a chair, startling Cayenne, who jumped off and skittered into the living room, dashing at his sister and racing her down the hall. They disappeared into the bedroom in a tangle of paws and legs.

I started to fill a glass for Rob but stopped. "I'm sorry," I stammered. "Marianne said you're taking medication. Are you sure this is okay?"

He was facing away from me. I saw his hands clench on the table and his shoulders tightened, pulling the fabric of his shirt taut. "It's okay. I'm fine."

It's her word against his. When in doubt, the customer is always right. I filled the glass and set it in front of him then got another plate and put it near his elbow. "Help yourself." I pushed my plate toward him. "There's more where this came from." I piled a cracker with a scrap of sausage and cheese and watched him sip his beer. "Are you okay?"

"Sure." He broke off a corner of cracker and fiddled with it. "No, I'm not okay. I wanted to apologize."

"You said that. Don't worry, my eye is fine."

His head jerked upright. "Oh. I didn't mean that." His pale gray eyes evaluated the new bruises on my face. "Did Guy do that to you?"

I touched the bandages. "No, not this one. This is a new accident."

His mouth twisted in distaste. "Accident? Nothing Guy does is by accident."

"What's that mean?" I nibbled some more cheese, followed by a swallow of wine, which was my alcohol of choice when I wasn't working.

Rob didn't answer for a long moment. His long fingers toyed with the cracker. He didn't have a workman's hands. His were well manicured and tanned, with trimmed nails. "Guy set me up."

"How?" I've been a bartender long enough to know it takes very little to get a person to spill their guts. Often a single word here and there will do the trick. Unfortunately, it often takes more than a single word to shut them up again.

"I'm going broke," Rob said in a low voice. "Hell, I am broke."

I stiffened. There is nothing I hate worse than self-pity and I'm quick to squelch it when I hear it. But Rob's next words had my *Grow a spine* die on my lips.

"It's my fault. I got greedy. He knew why I was greedy and he played on it."

"I'm sorry to hear it, Rob. But losing money isn't the worst that can happen to a person. Believe me, I know. You can recover from lost money."

He shook his head, his fine golden hair catching light and sparkling. "Guy took everything I ever wanted, everything I ever loved. There's no recovering from that." He raised his face to mine, his eyes looking haunted. "Marianne and I should probably have never married, but I honestly tried to make it work. I wanted to give her better things. I wanted to make it up to her. That's why I took Guy's advice on the stock market."

I held myself still, knowing what was coming next. In my years as a bartender, I think I've heard just about every twist on the human story of misery.

"I lost my money." He gave a wry, self-deprecating smile. "No big surprise there, right? Now I'm getting divorced and if I'm not careful, I may go to jail."

"Jail?" I almost choked on a cracker. I took a swig of wine and resumed breathing.

"After what happened at the factory last night . . ." His eyes shone with tears. "That poor boy was killed and why? He was killed because of the Fitz family."

I started to speak but he barreled on ahead, his voice rising. "The Fitz family has run the factory like their own private kingdom for years. They've intimidated people and they've bribed people and they've ignored safety and humane regulations. And I turned a blind eye. That's what I wanted to apologize for, Tuck. When we argued about the factory, I knew you were right. I should have stood up to them a long time ago, but I didn't. I needed a job and I talked myself into believing what they did was okay."

"No one can do what they do to animals and call what they do okay."

"I know, I know." He propped his elbows on the table and rested his face in his hands. "I hated it there, Tuck. I needed a job, though. I sold the hardware business to try to pay my debt to Guy, but it wasn't enough. I didn't know what else to do. When Richard offered me the job, it was a lifesaver. Richard has always been like an older brother to me." He peeked at me through red-rimmed eyes then hid his face again. "I always trusted Richard's judgment and when he told me he needed someone to keep an eye on PJ, I believed him."

I touched his shoulder sympathetically. He was hot to the touch. I wondered if he was feverish or sunburnt. "I'm sorry, Rob. It's hard when someone you trust turns out to be different than you believed."

"Richard was always so sure of himself. He told me PJ was running the factory into the ground. He needed me to come in and take care of things. Richard was so ashamed of having PJ as a brother. Maybe that's why he helped me. I think he thought of me like a brother, too. He needed me at the factory to keep an eye on PJ, but the factory . . ." He shuddered. "It's horrible."

"I know, Rob. And other people know, too." I cast around for something to say which might mitigate his guilt. "It won't be long before it's shut down. I'm sure of it."

"I only did what Richard asked me to do." Rob's voice was low and wavering. Unlike a drunk whose world falls apart suddenly, Rob acted like a man who'd watched his world fall apart for decades. This was a slow and strong slide into despair.

"What did he ask, Rob?" I eyed my wine bottle surreptitiously. I could use a refill. I got up as quietly as I could. Rob didn't even stir. He still sat slumped in the chair, his face supported by his hands.

"It was illegal but I did it. I knew it was wrong."

I stopped in my tracks, wine bottle in hand. "What?"

"It won't be a secret much longer. The government is investigating. It will come out."

"What will?" I refilled my glass and moved back to my seat.

Rob let his arms drop to the table. His face was pale except for dark red splotches where his palms rested. "I won't go to jail for the Fitz family."

"What did you get yourself into, Rob?" I put my hand on his forearm, squeezing gently.

He regarded me with wide, solemn, bloodshot eyes. "Richard told PJ to bribe one of the inspectors who checked conditions at the farm. PJ told me all about it. We got reports from a laboratory showing salmonella was there, in the chickens and in the eggs." Rob shuddered slightly. "It was everywhere in that damn factory."

I sat back, my hand sliding off his arm. My stomach lurched at the thought of those animals, all infected, all trapped and tortured. I swallowed hard. "Who did he bribe?"

"He told me to slip a thousand dollars to the inspector when he came for the monthly check. PJ told me to burn the reports." Rob leaned back in his chair, shoulders bunched. "I didn't do it. I told PJ that I wouldn't be the one to do the bribing. He did it. I made copies of the reports and I kept them. They prove PJ knew what was going on. I'm sure Richard knew, too."

"Good Lord," I breathed. "If they knew about it . . . Good Lord, hundreds of people got sick. Those children died. Anyone associated with the factory could be charged with murder."

"Murder?" Rob shook his head. "No, not murder. Negligent homicide, maybe."

I blinked in surprise. He sounded very knowledgeable. *But he's probably been stewing about this for months. Of course he's considered the options.* "Why didn't you go to the authorities?"

"I needed the money. I told you. Marianne wanted—" His lips compressed and he briefly closed his eyes, his expression bleak. "I wanted to give Marianne things. She never complained but I knew how unhappy she was. She doesn't know how broke we really are."

I took a big swallow of wine to banish the cloying film of distaste clogging my throat. If what Lee Knight said was true, Marianne did indeed know how bad off they were. Why else would she tell Guy she needed money?

What a tangled chain of circumstance! Poor Rob, unable to succeed, turned to Guy for advice. Guy gave him exactly the wrong advice, which landed Rob in a job where he ended up abetting a crime. "My daddy always said if you sleep with dogs, you're liable to wake up scratching fleas. I guess that's God's truth in a nutshell."

"You always come up with those sayings. Where was it you grew up? Back Bum, Arkansas or someplace like that?"

"Catahoula Parish, Louisiana." I deliberately laid on my accent so thick it was like molasses rolling off my tongue.

"Catahoula," he repeated. "Sounds so peaceful and easy-going the way you say it."

I raised my glass. "It's peaceful as the grave most days except payday when everybody heads to the nearest bar and gets drunk and acts stupid and mean."

"Is that where you learned to tend bar?" He took a sip of his beer, which up to now sat untouched in the glass.

"There and other spots." I pulled my mind back to the current conversation. "Speaking of Guy, have you talked to him lately?"

Rob tilted his glass, letting the amber liquid slide around the sides. "No. I think he's away. I haven't seen him since the night we got into a fight. I am sorry about it." He leaned forward as if to touch my face.

I leaned back. For a split second he seemed angry then he relaxed, sipping more beer. "Guy called me," I said, trying to cover up the awkwardness. "I wonder how he got my mobile phone number."

Rob eyed me over the rim of his glass. "Why wouldn't he have your number?"

"I don't give it to many people."

Rob shrugged. "Maybe Marianne gave it to him. Why do you care if he called?"

"No reason." Did Marianne have my cell phone number? I tried to remember if I called her using that phone. "I'll bet she's swamped tonight at the paper."

"Why?" Rob took a piece of cheese and held it to the side.

I peeked under the table. Cayenne had his front paws on Rob's leg and was stretched out long, nose questing for the cheese. "Don't feed them from the table, please. I don't want them becoming beggars."

"Spoil sport." Rob popped the cheese in his mouth. "So why is Marianne busy?"

"Richard said he wants to give a memorial speech at the town centennial or whatever it's called. I'm sure Marianne and Lee are busy rearranging schedules."

"Memorial speech?" Rob glanced to his left. "Do you want them on the chairs?"

"For PJ." I followed his gaze, seeing the kittens tussling with each other on the chair next to his. "And no, they shouldn't be on the chairs."

Rob lifted Cayenne off the chair and set him on the floor. Then he straightened, staring at me. "Wait a minute. Richard? Richard Fitz is in town? What about PJ?"

I gaped at him. "Didn't you know? PJ's dead. And yes, Richard is here. I saw him earlier, at the Acorn. He and PJ were there, having a drink."

Rob stared at me, his eyes bulging. "What?"

"PJ died tonight. He was at the pub. He died in the parking lot, not four hours ago. Didn't anyone call you? Richard said he'd get in touch with you."

Rob pushed back his chair so fast it almost toppled. "When did you talk to Richard? Did you talk to him lately?"

"I went to the police station to make a statement. He came in while I was there. Good Lord, Rob, didn't you know about it?"

"I left my cell phone at the cabin and I haven't gone back there today." He made a beeline for my front door, almost treading on Café in his hurry. "Where is Richard staying?"

I hurried after him, scooping up both kittens while I went. "I have no idea. Lee said he saw Richard at PJ's house, so maybe he's staying there."

I was talking to my door. Rob was outside and moving fast down my sidewalk, heading for his truck. I set the kittens on the couch and went to the front window to watch him back the pickup out of my drive and take off so fast he left rubber marks on the pavement.

"If snot were brains, he couldn't blow his nose." I went back to the kitchen. "What kind of idiot is the manager of a big operation and he doesn't carry his cell phone?"

An idiot like Rob. I remembered Richard's offhand comment about Rob needing a helping hand. Whose story was true? Did Richard consider Rob a brother? Maybe Richard didn't feel he had *any* brothers. Given how he acted about PJ, it was probably true.

I tidied up my meal scraps and busied myself with kitten chores for the next hour, verifying they understood the litter box arrangements and food location and next introducing them to the basement. While they explored the various nooks and crannies of the main exercise area, I made sure the laundry room door was securely closed and the door to the unfinished storage area in the back of the basement. Satisfied they couldn't get into trouble, I went back upstairs and plunked on the couch with the bottle of wine.

My scrapbook sat on the coffee table where I left it that morning. I dragged it onto my lap and started flipping pages, sipping wine. Here was a picture of Will as a child, dressed up for Halloween in his Superman outfit. Here was a picture of my brother, holding Will on his shoulder. There was a picture of Maw-Maw, my father's mother, who ran a bait shop. I leafed through all the old photos and examined the other bits of memory tucked into the book, all the report cards, birthday cards, a dance program, a golf scorecard.

I dropped the scrapbook back on the table and leaned back, letting darkness settle around me. The kittens rejoined me, curling up on the couch while I stared through my front window, memories populating my living room.

No matter what Alan said, Will's death was a waste. He was a happy, committed, intense young man with an unwavering sense of right and wrong. Despite the cruelties he witnessed in the course of his work as an activist, he maintained a loving and kind nature. There was no reason on earth to end a life like his. There was no reason for him to die. And whoever killed him deserved whatever was dished at them.

I finished the bottle of wine and considered opening another, but I was too tired to get up and move. In the end, I curled up on the couch, two kittens tucked in beside me. Just when I was falling asleep, my landline phone rang.

I fumbled it off the end table and put the receiver to my ear. "It's your dime."

"I'm sorry Patrick's whore hurt you," a slurred voice said.

I propped myself up on an elbow. "Say what?"

"Sheriff Knott said you were hurt when that woman fainted. You should have let her hit the ground and take the fall. It's the least she deserves."

I screwed up my face, trying to remember where I heard this voice before. "Isabel?"

"I was married to him for twenty-five years. I was a child when I married him. I was only nineteen years old." A loud belch punctuated this pronouncement. "Pardon me. He knocked me up within weeks and I was chained to that son of a bitch ever since." Brief, loud, laughter made me pull the phone from my ear. "Son of a bitch. That is *so* apt. Have you ever met Eleanor? Oh, yes, he was a son of a bitch."

"Uh, Isabel, I'm not sure you want to be talking to me. You probably need to get some sleep." I managed to blink the exhaustion from my eyes to focus on the clock in the kitchen. "It's two in the morning. You've had a shock. You need sleep."

"The shock is he actually did it. I guess I should feel flattered, but let's face it, I didn't expect him to do it. The last time we slept together was years ago. I told him I wouldn't sleep with him while he whored around. I never thought he'd take me seriously and use a condom."

I shook my head, as much to shake sense into it as shake her words out. "I'm not sure I understand what you mean, Isabel. I think you need to get some sleep."

"Thank you for the advice, Miss Frye. I'll make sure Isabel takes it."

I dropped the phone at the sound of a snobby male voice. When I finally found the receiver again, wedged into the cushions of the couch, no one was on the line. I pressed the *off* button and replaced it in the charging base.

Richard Fitz was apparently keeping an eye on his sister-in-law. I only hoped it was what she wanted. I fell asleep, visions of a princess trapped in a tower dancing in my head.

Chapter 11

At some point during the night I meandered to the bedroom, peeled off my clothing, and dropped onto my bed. I was vaguely aware of two kittens leaping ahead of me to capture their spots before I got there, but luckily they moved before I flopped down.

I slept in the next day, not waking until almost seven in the morning, which was late for me. The sound of rain wakened me. I rolled out of bed and went to the living room, where I checked the indoor/outdoor thermometer. It was only sixty degrees outside. With a happy sigh I turned off the air conditioning and opened the window, letting in a summer perfume of wet grass, damp earth and freshness.

I made a pot of coffee and sat in the living room, working my way through the Sunday paper. The kittens romped with the discarded flyers on the floor, hiding underneath and pouncing on each other, racing away only to come back and pounce again. By the time I finished reading, most of the newspaper was scattered all over the house.

I cleaned up after the pounce-fest and headed for the bathroom. I paused on my way to the shower to examine myself in the full-length mirror. What I saw was disheartening, to say the least. A line of bruises covered most of my right hip and the side of my right leg. My right elbow was a livid yellow mixed with dark blue, scabbed over where I scraped it on the pavement. I winced when I tried to move it. I didn't notice the stiffness last night, but I definitely didn't have full range of motion. My right knee was puffy, and a hand-sized bruise was vivid on the outer side of it. I tried kneeling but gave up when pain zinged into my leg.

My face was the real shocker, though. My black eye was faded to a nauseous yellow and when I removed the bandage covering the sutures, I revealed the harsh red color, the small butterfly closures obviously keeping my cheek together.

"Not the sort of thing you want to see when you're sitting at a bar, having a nice, relaxing drink." I would need to keep the wound and the scrapes on the side of my forehead covered. They were definitely not appetizing.

I showered, grimacing when warm water touched my various boo-boos. It felt good, though, to wash yesterday's remnants of ugliness off me. A good shower can make any day feel like a fresh start, I decided, even one which started with bruises and scrapes. However, given the tender condition of my bruises, I decided on loose clothing for the day. So I tugged on a pair of old sweatpants and a large T-shirt which was washed so often it was shapeless.

I was on my second cup of coffee when Alan's gray Acura pulled into my driveway. Today he wore crisp denims and a pristine white shirt with rolled up sleeves, which contrasted with his tanned arms and face. He held a paper grocery sack in one hand which he kept under his umbrella while he hurried up the front walk.

1

"Leave the umbrella on the porch to drip," I said, pulling open the door.

He set it next to my lawn chair on the tiny porch. "How are you doing today?" He came in and handed me the grocery sack. "Your face looks like it hurts. Does it?"

I opened the bag. "What's this?"

"A get-well sack of feel-good food and fun. Poppy seed cake, a bit of crème fraîche, and a movie I watched I think you'll love. It's called *The Fall* and it's about a guy who takes a bad fall and what happens in the hospital."

I walked to the kitchen. "Thanks. I'm sure I'll empathize with the main character." I pulled out the paper plate and sniffed appreciatively at the spicy aroma. "I love your poppy seed cake."

"Guaranteed to cure whatever ails you." Alan turned cautiously. "Where are the little terrors?"

"The last I saw them, they were attacking the dust bunnies under my bed. Coffee?" I gestured to the pot on the counter.

"No, thanks. I drank my quota for today." He sat at the kitchen table while I got plates and cutlery. We each served ourselves a slice of cake and I added a healthy dollop of crème fraîche to mine. We ate in silence for a moment, savoring the marvelous flavors.

I sighed, breaking the spell. "There's something to be said for having a chef for a good friend."

Alan laughed. "I have to admit, it's rather nice having a bartender for a good friend, too. Are you doing okay, despite all your wounds?"

"You mean about Will?"

Alan nodded. "I talked with Owen. He said it was a positive identification."

I drew a fork-tined design in the leftover crumbs on my plate. "Am I okay? No, I'm not. I'm mad as hell somebody killed him. But I'm also worried. What if somebody comes after me?"

"Did you discuss it with Owen?"

"Not really. We were interrupted by Richard Fitz, who stopped by to inform Owen he expected the Sheriff's office to manage the investigation into PJ's death."

Alan blew out an exasperated, "Asshole. The Fitz family has had their way for more decades than I've been alive. I shouldn't be surprised Richard is still trying to run the show even though he hasn't lived here for years."

"He's running his sister-in-law, too." I explained about Isabel's phone call the night before. "Do you think I should call her and check up on her? You don't think Richard would be, well, holding her hostage or anything?"

"She has five children." Alan pointed out. "They can protect her."

"Yeah, but they're kids. Well, most of them are. Three is only, what, twenty-six or so? The others are college kids. They can't stand up to Richard."

Alan pointed his fork at me. "And there's no reason you should stand up to him, either. You don't owe Isabel Fitz anything."

"I suppose." I was still doubtful, though. True, I didn't owe her anything, but I remembered the wistful tone in her voice when we talked about careers. "Did you know she wants to be chef?"

"What?"

I nodded. "She trained as a chef. Maybe you should give her a job."

"I doubt if she'll be hard up for money."

"She will be if the Fitz company gets sued and they lose. Lee Knight told me a lawsuit was filed. The government has recalled millions of eggs. That can't be good for business."

"I'm sure Richard Fitz has it covered. Ah, there they are."

I peeked under the table to see Cayenne and Café sniffing at Alan's loafered feet. "They're getting quite a workout in the nose department," I commented. "Rob Huntington was here last night and Cayenne gave him a good sniff."

"Rob? What did he want?"

I pushed my plate to one side. "A shoulder to cry on. He and Marianne are getting divorced. Rob blames Guy for all his misfortunes, although to give him credit, he accepted a lot of the blame himself."

"Rob blames Guy for what misfortune? The problems at the factory?" Alan's lips twisted in disgust. "He can't blame Guy for it. It's his own damn fault."

"According to Rob, it's PJ's fault."

"What?" Alan shook his head. "Well, PJ is dead, so that's convenient. There's nobody to contradict him."

"Rob claims Guy gave him bad investing advice so he lost all his money. Oh, and Lee Knight told me Rob was selling the cabin. He sold it to Guy."

"What?" Alan's mouth sagged open in shock. "What the hell does Guy want with Rob's cabin?"

"He'll probably tear it down and build a McMansion. It's a nice location for it, up there on the bluff. Richard said he would have some kind of memorial talk for PJ at the town picnic. I told him not to bother." I hurried on when Alan started to grin. "Not everybody loved PJ. Why ruin a perfectly good town picnic with a talk about him? Is there any word on what killed him?"

"No." Alan sighed. "I contacted Marianne like you suggested and I gave her a statement. I'll be curious to see if it shows up in the paper."

"I'm sure it's not going to affect us much," I tried to reassure him.

"I hope not. So Owen didn't think you needed police protection?"

"We didn't discuss it."

"You should have. What if somebody finds you're related to Will? They might come after you."

"So what?" I'd mulled this over in the back of my brain all morning. "Just because I'm related to Will, it doesn't mean he would give me anything incriminating. And what kind of thing would be worth killing someone for? I mean, let's face it, that's a murder charge. What would warrant somebody taking a chance on a murder charge?"

"You're right. I never thought of it that way. What could he have possibly found which would cause someone to commit murder? Murder is *serious*."

"No shit." I ran my fork around the plate, dredging up the last lingering bits of cake and topping. "I've thought it over and I can't see any reason anybody would do it."

"I hope you're right." Alan stood and took his plate to the sink. "I want to get to the restaurant early today. I'm trying a new recipe with the radishes John Smalley brought me." He turned and smiled impishly at me. "I think John was disappointed when he came to the Parlor yesterday for brunch and you weren't there."

"Why would I be there?" I asked, flustered.

Alan shrugged. "I don't know. John came in and wondered when you'd be in to open the Pub. I think he wanted to talk to you about something."

"He never said anything to me about it." I tried to sound nonchalant but I was bubbling with curiosity on the inside. John Smalley? Wanting to talk to me? "Probably nothing special."

"You never know." Alan disentangled himself from small kitten paws attempting to play with the tassels on his shoes. "That might be quite a match-up. John's the biggest guy I know and you're the smallest woman I know."

I walked with him to the door. "Well, you know what they say. Everybody's the same height when they're horizontal."

He laughed. "I'll have to remember that when you and John embark on your love affair."

"Ain't gonna happen," I warned him.

"Right." He paused with his hand on the doorknob. "You know, if Isabel wants something to do, I could use another hand in the kitchen. I'd like time from cooking to work on the menu, try new recipes, and consider some redecorating."

"We redecorated in the Parlor five years ago!" I protested.

"Five years." Alan waved a hand. "So passé. I might give her a call after all the fuss dies down. With PJ gone, she may want something to occupy her time."

"With PJ gone, she may want to sit back and count her blessings."

"Cynic." Alan bent to air-kiss my cheek.

"Realist."

"Let me know if there's anything you need."

"I will." I watched him grab his umbrella and hurry to his car. Redecorating? We spent a bundle redoing the Parlor. I'd have to keep a rein on him if Isabel did come to work for us.

The thought occupied me for one more (tiny) slice of poppy seed cake. For some reason, I could easily imagine Isabel Fitz in a chef's coat, directing operations in Alan's kitchen. They would complement each other very well.

I went to the bedroom to gather my laundry. As if pulled from my thoughts, the phone rang. It was Richard Fitz.

"Isabel was not herself last night," he said after a curt, *hello*. "I hope you don't take anything she said seriously."

"I barely remember what she said." I was bent over the upended laundry basket, sorting clothes into Good Light, Bad Light, Good Dark, Bad Dark, my usual method of laundering. "I'm sure she's in shock. Is there anything I can do to help?"

"If there is, I'll be sure to tell you."

"If there is, I hope she'll tell me," I retorted. "When did God die and you get appointed in Her place?"

"Is that a joke?"

"No, it's a legitimate question." I straightened, holding my gold Acorn shirt which I wore the night Rob and Guy fought. It used to be a Good Light but now due to bloodstains it was a Bad Light, relegated to use on days when I was doing dirty work. "If Isabel wants me to help her, I hope she'll call me. She doesn't need you to run interference for her."

"Her husband was just killed." Richard's voice was sharp and admonishing, much like my old grammar school teacher who would remind me *young ladies don't talk that way, Tucker.* "She has a great deal on her mind."

"I understand that. Let her know if I can help, I'll be happy to." I hung up before he could so I could have the last word with that arrogant son of a bitch.

I dragged the dirty clothes in the laundry basket to the basement steps and opened the door. Two small furry bodies plummeted ahead of me, flinging themselves onto the steep steps without concern for life or limb, theirs or mine. I followed more sedately, laundry basket bumping behind me, and scooted into the laundry room, closing the door firmly. This room wasn't finished in any sense of the word. I had visions of tiny kittens worming their way into the wall studs only to end up trapped in the ceiling.

I got the Bad Darks started and came back into the exercise room. The kittens were tumbling around my treadmill. When I headed for the stairs the phone rang again. I didn't recognize the number on the display, but I figured, *hey, it's my day off. I have time.*

"Hello?"

"Tucker, this is John Smalley. I'm not bothering you, am I?"

For some stupid reason, I started to blush. "No, John. It's my day off. What's up?"

"I heard about someone being shot at the factory. I'm sorry to ask, but, was it your friend?"

His honest sympathy brought tears to my eyes. It also reminded me of his willingness to help in any way he could. "Yes, it was," I said with a mental prayer that I could trust him.

"I'm so sorry." There was a long pause. "I'm sure his death and PJ's death must have you shook up. PJ died at the pub, didn't he?"

"He died in the parking lot, but yes, it was pretty gruesome." I drew in a long breath. "I saw his body. I don't know if I'll ever forget it."

"Some things, well, they're hard to forget. I was in the Army when I was younger." Once again there a long pause. "I saw some combat time overseas. It can be, yeah, it can be gruesome."

This was a new side of John to me. "I didn't know that, John."

"I got out of high school and wasn't sure what to do with myself. So I figured I'd join the Army and see the world." He sighed a long, soulful breath. "Well, I saw the world and decided Barnsdale, Iowa, seemed awfully good in comparison."

"I can only imagine." Good heavens, think of it. Young John, sent overseas to fight. How did it shape his decision to become an organic farmer? How did it shape his decision to go for a degree in Philosophy? There were sides to John Smalley I never guessed.

"The reason I called is because I have an idea I wanted to talk over with you. I mentioned it to Rob and he suggested I call you since you have experience. Would you have some time this afternoon to come to the farm? There's something I want to show you that has to do with the idea." He sounded off-hand and diffident, like it really didn't matter if I showed up or not. Was it a ploy or did he really want to see me?

"Uh, maybe. What kind of idea?"

"Do you have a minute? I can give you the outline of the plan and you could think it over and we could talk about it. I guess you could call it a, um, a business opportunity."

This was intriguing. Somehow I never associated John Smalley—large, burly, slow-moving John Smalley—with a business opportunity. "Sure, I have time. Let me go upstairs, though, where it's comfortable."

I glanced over my shoulder. The kittens were sprawled on the treadmill, Cayenne on his back and Café ready to pounce. They would be fine. I went upstairs. "Go ahead, John. What's the idea?"

"I guess you could say you gave me the idea," he said while I settled myself on the couch and propped my legs up on the coffee table. "When you mentioned your friend at the Yoke and they were gathering evidence about—"

"I never said that," I interrupted. "I said I had a friend who was working there."

"I know, but I assumed . . . ."

"It's probably not, um, good to assume that."

A long pause. "Okay. Anyway, I have this idea. You and Alan did such a great job setting up the Acorn. I hoped you could give me advice. I want to do something similar."

"You want to open a bar?" I eyed my toes, wiggling on the coffee table. Maybe I should try some nail polish. As soon as I considered the idea, I dismissed it. I didn't have the time or the patience to fuss with polish.

"I want to open an organic destination."

"A what?"

"Here's the thing. Old Horace Pyle is retiring from farming and his farm is for sale. It's right next door to mine. Well, sort of next door. You know what I mean. It's near."

"Sure." I wasn't exactly sure what he meant, but some kind of assent seemed right.

"So I was going to buy it and turn it into a B&B. I could set it up as a destination vacation. City people could come here, stay on a farm, help run it. When it's harvest time, they could bring the produce to your restaurant and maybe Alan could show them how to cook it. It would be like a total organic experience for people. We'd have sheep and could do some shearing and maybe I could find someone to teach spinning or knitting."

"I can do it," I said, my brain processing through the points of his plan and seeing good and bad areas to address. "My grandma taught me when I was a girl."

"Wow. Yeah. That would be great. It could be like a working vacation for some people. Maybe we could do one of those community agriculture things, where people buy shares in the farm."

"You know, I read about B&B places in England where they do that. People pay to go stay at the farm during a certain time of the year like, you know, for planting or harvesting. And it helps pay for the farm."

"See, I knew you'd have some great ideas. Everybody thought you were crazy to open a pub in an old glove factory, but look at it. It's the best place in the entire county. Do you think—I mean, I was hoping maybe you and Alan and I could form some kind of business partnership and figure a way to get this idea off the ground."

I barely heard him. I was already envisioning an old-fashioned farmhouse with a big wraparound porch, painted white with blue shutters. Of course, Horace Pyle's house might not be anything like that, but it was a good image, regardless. A red barn would be nearby with sheep in a pen and cattle grazing on a hillside.

It would take renovation, of course, but I was accustomed to that. Heck, Alan and I turned a glove factory into a brewpub. We'd need additional plumbing for bedrooms, a big kitchen where Alan could prepare breakfast and . . . wait a minute. If Isabel Fitz was interested in working, maybe we could recruit her.

". . . expand my operation anyway, so this seemed like a natural for me."

"I'm sorry, John. I guess my imagination ran away with me. What did you say?"

"I said I wanted to expand my farming operation anyway, so when Horace told me he wanted to retire, it seemed like a sign that I should consider it. What do you think of the idea?"

"I think it has some real legs."

He laughed. "Does that mean it's doable?"

"It means we can at least stand it up and take a solid shot at it without the idea falling flat on its face." I laughed, too. "It has legs."

"Do you think you'd have time to come here sometime today? Horace is willing to let me come over to his farm. Maybe once we see it, we'd have a better idea if it has legs."

"Sure." I glanced at the clock in the kitchen. "Heck, I could come any time, I guess. What's best for you?"

"I have to go to Des Moines this afternoon, so the sooner, the better, I guess."

"Why don't I come now?" The laundry could wait. The things in there could sit until I got home. I would round up the kittens and go see him. That reminded me. "Hey, John. I inherited a couple of kittens. Do you need any barn cats?"

"Kittens? No, I like to get my barn cats as adults from the pound. I'm sure you can find a home for them, everybody wants kittens. Let me call Horace and see if we can go over there in the next hour or so. He mentioned he might go to town to visit his daughter, so I'll call right now and see if I can catch him."

"Okay, sounds like a plan. I'll see you soon."

I hung up the phone, buoyed by the idea of a new project. *Be cautious,* I reasoned while I changed clothes, trading sweatpants for jeans and my T-shirt for a loose summer blouse. *Don't get in over your head. Make sure to talk to Alan about it. Get his okay, too.*

Mental notes bounced through my brain while I shooed the cats from the basement, locking the door before heading for my car. As I drove north, my mind played with various B&B scenarios. I traveled in England twice and each time stayed in farmhouse B&Bs. If we could duplicate such a thing here, it might not be a huge attraction but I was sure it would pay for itself.

I turned right and headed east on County B, driving carefully on the rain-slicked paved road. John's farm was four miles outside of town, about two miles off the county blacktop. The ribbon of asphalt in front of me was dark gray, with deep ditches on either side which in turn led to farm fields and cattle pastures. I envisioned how a B&B operation might work, seeing in my mind's eye a house amidst the green fields with people sitting on a porch.

I can blame the accident on my preoccupation. I topped the hill and started to slow for the stop sign ahead. It was a four-way stop, with traffic coming from York ahead of me, from west of town on my left, from John's farm on my right, and me coming from the south. A long gray sedan sat on my left at the sign. The windows were dark so I couldn't see why the driver sat there, not moving. Since no other traffic was on the road, he was probably lost.

I stopped at my stop sign and flipped on my turn signal to make a right turn onto John's lane. As I did, the car on my left surged ahead. Two thoughts careened through my brain right before the impact: *That's Guy's gray car, isn't it?* And *Oh, shit. This is going to hurt.*

I was right on both counts.

Chapter 12

"How many fingers?" An insistent voice spoke from somewhere above me.

My head hurt. It hurt really bad. And my neck hurt. I was stiff, and bruised, and banged up. I was starting to recognize the feeling. Lord knows I should recognize it after the past week.

"How many fingers?"

I cracked one eye slightly open and closed it immediately when bright light zeroed in on my brain and exploded there.

"Miss Frye? I need you to open your eyes." That damn insistent voice spoke again.

I cautiously allowed my left eyelid to creep upward. Light swam into view then a dark silhouette replaced the light. "Huh?"

"Please open your eyes. Tell me how many fingers you see."

I eased open my other eyelid and squinted. "Three." I squinted some more. My vision cleared and I saw who it was. "You again?" I asked.

The emergency room doctor regarded me with somber dark eyes. "Yes, me again. Now close your eyes."

Asshole. First I open them then I close them. Make up your damn mind. "Huh?"

"What do you hear?"

Very, very soft. A chiming sound. "Bell?"

"Good. Now rest."

I can do that.

****

". . . mild concussion. Bruised ribs and two broken fingers, more bruising on her shoulders from the seat belt, a gash on her forehead. All in all, she's lucky." I didn't recognize the voice for sure, but I decided it might be Owen's.

"Lucky?"

Oh, I knew that voice. It was Alan, sounding as outraged as I've ever heard him. He was working up a full head of steam and getting ready to blow.

"Yes, lucky." Yep, that was Owen. Calm, quiet. "The ditch wasn't full of water. It's been so dry lately that when the car rolled, it didn't fill with water."

"Holy God," Alan said. "I never thought of that."

I peeked through my eyelashes, trying to analyze what I saw.

White walls.

Metal scaffolding around me with blinking lights and bottles and tubes.

Two men at the foot of my bed.

"Oh, shit," I whispered. "I'm in the hospital, aren't I?"

"Damn. We didn't mean to wake you." Alan leaned over me, his face lined with worry. "Sorry, Tucker. You should be resting."

"I think I already have." I smacked my lips, sensing that sweaters-on-the-teeth feeling. "Where am I? When is it?" I tried moving my head but it felt like I was wedged into place. "What's going on? Why can't I move?"

Alan's hand was warm on mine where it lay on the sheet. "They have pillows along your neck to keep you from moving. You have a concussion and they want you to lie still."

"Where am I?"

"Barnsdale Hospital," Owen said, coming into view. He moved behind Alan to regard me over Alan's shoulder. Now that I could focus, I could tell Alan sat in a chair on my left, next to the bed. "John Smalley found you in a ditch not far from his house."

"In a ditch?" I tried to sort through the conflicting images pounding through my brain, keeping time with the headache throbbing there. I was doing laundry. I got a phone call and I drove somewhere . . . I gave up trying to remember. "What happened?"

Alan squeezed my hand gently. "John said you and he talked this morning. You were going to drive to see him. When you didn't arrive, he got worried. So he drove to town and that's when he saw your car, in the ditch."

"Damn. What time is it?"

"Almost eight at night. You were knocked out."

I closed my eyes and tried to concentrate. "A car hit me, didn't it?" A sudden memory of a dark gray car closing in on my driver's door loomed in my brain.

"What car?" Owen asked.

"The one that probably left a big swatch of gray paint on my door." I closed my eyes again. "It shouldn't be too hard to find, Owen." I opened my eyes to see him smiling at me.

"Thanks for confirming it, Tucker."

"Was that a trick, Owen?" I whispered.

"A small one. Do you remember anything else?"

"It wasn't raining. I didn't have my wipers on. I was at John's corner and a car was sitting at the stop sign. When I went to turn, it hit me."

"Was there anything with you in the car?"

"Hmm?" I blinked groggily, struggling to make sense of what he said.

"Did you have a purse with you? A wallet? We didn't find any identification on you. The hospital found your insurance papers through their computer system."

"I had my purse with me. I always take it when I drive. Damn. Did somebody steal my purse? Why? I only carry one credit card and I don't carry much cash."

"Don't worry about it," Owen said soothingly. "You can contact the credit card company in the morning."

Alan's hand tightened on my hand again. "Why did you go to John's farm, Tuck?"

I struggled to remember. "It was something about a farm sale and property in England. I'm not sure," I said, my voice sounding weak even to me. "I think it was . . ."

****

The next time I opened my eyes, it was dark. I saw blinking lights near my bed and a night light over a sink. For an instant, I panicked. *Where was I? Who was I? Why was I here?*

Reason reasserted itself. I was in a hospital room. I wore a hospital gown, pale blue with white flowers. I was in a car accident. My car! How badly was it banged up? I needed to talk to my insurance agent and find a replacement car until it could be fixed.

These mundane worries helped my heart resume a normal rhythm. What time was it? I struggled to see the clock on the wall but the light was too dim. I wiggled my hands around on the bed, finally discovering a remote control device. I vaguely remembered somebody saying something about pressing a button if I needed anything.

Well, I needed a bathroom, for one thing, and answers for another. I squeezed the gadget in my hand and pressed buttons at random. I soon discovered some of them raised me, some turned on the TV, some adjusted the volume, and yes, one of them summoned a large female nurse, who appeared at my door with a startled expression on her face.

I explained my need for a bathroom and she explained the bedpan. I reiterated my need for the bathroom and she firmly suggested the bedpan. I tossed the remote control at her and started to climb out of the bed. She was about a foot taller than me and probably weighed close to two hundred pounds, but at that moment I was willing to take her on for the chance to get to a toilet.

"You shouldn't move yet." She hurried to my side. "Wait a minute. I need to get gloves."

"You're just touching me, you're not, you know, *touching* me," I said while I wavered by the side of the bed. I saw the bathroom, tantalizingly close, but I knew better than to make for the doorway on my own. I was wobbly and slightly woozy. With my luck, I'd do a header and land on the tiled floor and really mess up my face.

"Hospital policy. Wear gloves at all times. It's a lot easier now that we don't have to check on latex allergies because we have these non-allergenic gloves. There we are, hang on." She snapped a pair of gloves in place and came to my side, gripping my left elbow and helping me lurch for the potty.

"Are latex allergies common?" I asked, more to keep my mind off my churning stomach than from curiosity. *I will not puke. I will not puke,* I repeated like a mantra. *If I puke they'll keep me here forever. I will not puke.* It seemed to work. My guts began to settle and I focused on what the nurse said.

". . .than you think. Of course, I suppose it's like allergies to nuts. People are mildly allergic and they blow it out of proportion. They don't get a chance to be exposed to it so they can get over it. Nuts are in so many things nowadays. Of course, latex is, too, but not like it used to be. For some people the allergies are life threatening but for others it's a mild problem. Why yesterday they brought in a patient who . . ."

I tuned her out, focusing all my energy on getting to the stool and sitting. If that pot was another foot further, I would've collapsed. As it was, I was hard pressed to make a graceful landing. "I'm good," I said, leaning on the nearby sink. "You can go."

The nurse eyed me warily. "I'll be right here."

"And I'll be right here. Go. I need some privacy."

"There is no privacy in hospitals, don't you know that?" But she obligingly moved to the doorway and closed it part way.

Ten minutes later I was back in bed with the nurse tucking the covers around me. "I'll make sure to mention to the doctor in the morning you decided to take a walk," she said, disapproval evident in her voice.

"You do that. And tell him I want to go home."

"We'll see how you're doing in the morning."

"Yes, we will." I lay back and closed my eyes. I was asleep before she left the room.

By mid-morning the next day, I was ready to escape. I felt like crap, but I hated the hospital. There were too many sounds and smells going on around me. I wanted my own quiet little house with familiar sounds and smells.

I discovered that escape from a hospital could be accomplished in two ways: legally, by waiting for a doctor to appear and certify you to be fit to leave, or illegally, in which you get dressed and walk out. I was seriously considering the latter option when Isabel Fitz entered my room shortly before lunchtime.

She didn't seem like my idea of a grieving widow. In fact, she appeared pretty damn rested and relaxed. Her dark hair was pulled back into a bun, but it wasn't severe. It softened her features, with a few wisps free to dance around her cheeks. Her black slacks and black-and-white top probably fit the convention of widow's wear, but it was also perfect for lunch and a hand of bridge with the girls. All in all, widowhood was treating her just fine.

"I wanted to apologize for calling you the other night," she said, after a polite exchange of *I hope you're doing okay,* and *I'm fine, can't wait to go home.* "I drank a bit too much."

I waved it away. "Not a problem. It happens to all of us."

She smiled, her cheeks dimpling. I never noticed them before. Of course, I didn't spend much time with her and the last time I saw her, she was pissed off at her husband and not smiling. "It has happened very seldom to me. I wanted to thank you, too. Our conversation in your pub gave me, oh, I don't know, maybe a sense of hope?" She hesitated. "After we spoke I told PJ I wanted a divorce."

I gaped at her. I could barely remember our conversation in the bar. "Well, geez. That's a shocker."

She smoothed back her hair with her left hand, a hand now devoid of a diamond or wedding ring. "I realized the kids are grown and if I want to live my life, it's time I started doing it. So I told PJ I wanted a divorce. To my surprise, he broke down. He promised he'd be faithful to me from here on in." Isabel rolled her eyes. "I told him he was crazy. I was never sure if he used a condom. I told him that unless he used condoms, I'd never sleep again with him."

"Uh, makes sense to me," I said, mentally screaming *TMI, too much information, thanks for sharing, but I really don't need to know this.*

Isabel flicked a piece of lint off her slacks. "It would be poetic justice if sex killed him, wouldn't it?" She raised her head and I saw a hint of mischief? maliciousness? in her eyes before her expression smoothed and once again the proper society woman was in place. "But that's not why I came here. I was wondering if you know if Alan has any need for another chef."

I gaped at her again. "Say what?"

"Iowa is not a community property state. I can't expect a judge to side with me against the Fitz family. I may very well need to earn my living soon."

"I'm not sure. I mean, yes, I think he'd like help, but are you sure you want to plan that far ahead? After all, you're a widow. I mean, you'll inherit, won't you?"

Isabel's face stilled. "It all depends on PJ's will, doesn't it? And it depends on the executor of the will."

"But haven't you seen his will?" Surely she had, hadn't she? They were married, for cryin' out loud. Surely she knew what was in his will.

"It's irrelevant. Richard is the executor. I don't think I can expect any generosity from him." She didn't sound upset, but resigned to the fact.

"Lunchtime," a cheery voice said from the doorway. A different nurse than my bathroom partner swept into the room, tray in hand.

Isabel immediately got to her feet. "I wanted to thank you, Tucker, for giving me such encouragement. I'll give Alan a call in a week or two." She moved aside to give the nurse room to rearrange my meager furniture. "Thank you."

"Sure. Whatever." Then she was gone.

"Nice to have visitors," the nurse commented.

"Yeah," I said thoughtfully. *What the hell was that about?*

I mulled it over through lunch, which I barely noticed, probably a good thing because it was tasteless and unappetizing. If PJ wrote a will and excluded Isabel, she could contest it. But if she didn't have money of her own, how could she pay a lawyer? I guess a lawyer would take the case on contingency, but she made a good point. The Fitz family was a powerhouse not only in Barnsdale, but in the state. Would a lawyer want to butt heads with the Fitz family?

I tried to remember our conversation in the bar, but it had made little impression on me. Apparently it made a *big* impression on her, though. It took a lot of guts to ask PJ for a divorce. She had a good life, a cushy life, if she could ignore the son of a bitch and his philandering. I started to smile. Yes, it would be karma if sex killed PJ.

What killed him? I made a mental note to ask Alan the next time I saw him.

I napped for an hour or two before the doctor finally put in an appearance. "Yes, you can go home," he said in answer to my insistent question. "But I want to make sure someone is there with you."

This was a different doctor than my emergency room doctor. "I live alone," I explained. "There is no one to be there to take care of me."

"Can someone check in on you from time to time?" He regarded me with that patient, non-compromising stare all doctors are taught in med school.

"Can I go to work?" I asked. "If I can go to work, the whole town can see me."

He sighed patiently. "You have badly bruised ribs. Two fingers on your left hand are broken. You have a mild concussion. A cut on your forehead required stitches. Those are on top of the other injuries you've sustained in the last . . ." He examined the file on his lap, ". . . four days. I think you'd better take some time off."

"It's not hard work. I'm a bartender."

"Do you have to lift anything?"

I nodded.

"That's hard work."

"I'll get somebody else to do the lifting."

He sighed again. "Most people look forward to time off of work."

"Most people don't own the bar. I'll be careful. I won't work a full shift. I'll get somebody in to help." I glanced at the clock on the wall. "Heck, somebody already is covering my shift. I usually start work at two o'clock. It's almost four. So I won't go in today. That gives me a full night to rest up. Tomorrow is . . ." I hesitated, still not sure how much time I lost. "Tomorrow is Wednesday. I'll go in late, work a short shift. Thursday is my regular day off." I regarded him with a calm, *let's be reasonable about this* expression.

The doctor stood, leafing through the papers in his hand and signing them while he spoke. "I talked to Mr. Dale. He said he will either call you or stop by to see you regularly. If you experience any dizzy spells, nausea, or vomiting, call 911 immediately. No heavy lifting for a week. Try to keep your left hand immobile, at least for the first few days. I'll give you pain medicine to take with you and I can give you a prescription for more if you'd like."

I shook my head immediately. "I don't take pills."

"Your ribs and your hand will hurt once the injections we gave you wear off," he warned.

"I don't do pills." I didn't explain that my no-good brother was a drug addict and there was no way in hell I would set a toe on that path.

"I'll call in a prescription for you. You don't have to get it filled, but it will be there if you need it." He jotted another note on the file before closing it. "You had a bad accident. You need to take it easy for a few days."

Accident, my ass. "Will do," I lied.

I waited another two hours for all the paperwork to be processed. I sat there kicking my heels, clasping a plastic bag full of hospital junk—wash tub, toothbrush, tissues, and the like, which apparently were now mine by virtue of me touching them. I was dressed in the jeans and blouse I wore a day earlier, now wrinkled despite being neatly folded in the closet in my hospital room. Thank God they didn't cut the clothes off of me. Lord knows what I would have done if that happened.

When it came time to actually leave, I was surprised to find John Smalley waiting at the nurse's station. "What are you doing here?" I asked as the nurse piloted me in my wheelchair. We paused at the desk and the nurse in charge handed me an envelope.

"Here's your release papers and the pills the doctor wanted you to take," the nurse said. "And don't forget if you need to fill the prescription, the doctor called it in to the pharmacy."

"Great." I snatched the papers from her hand.

"I told Alan I'd make sure you got home okay. He's going to wrap up at the Parlor and come over as soon as he can." John took the bag of belongings I held on my lap and the envelope full of paperwork. "The doctor doesn't think you should be alone, at least at first."

"It's really not necessary," I protested while we rolled our way to the front door. "I'm probably going to go home and sleep."

"That's fine. I'll relax on the couch and watch TV while you nap."

"But you shouldn't have to."

"Relax, Tucker. Somebody has to drive you home and I volunteered. I'll go bring the car up to the door. Don't go anywhere." He hurried off, disappearing into the shadowy recesses of the parking garage.

"I could take a taxi," I commented.

"Lots of people volunteered to help," the young nurse said. "You must be popular."

"I own a bar. I have a lot of friends."

She giggled. "Lucky you. At least your friends aren't afraid of you. All of my friends are worried I'll practice giving shots on them." She wheeled me outside.

"I can see where it would put a damper on friendship. I'm surprised he let you borrow this," I said to John when he pulled up in Alan's sedan.

"I have a truck. I think you'd have trouble climbing in." John held the passenger door for me then tossed my plastic hospital bag and the envelope full of papers onto the back seat. He wedged himself into the driver's side, dwarfing the big sedan, which always seemed so roomy to me. Of course, when someone six-five and well over two-hundred pounds enters a car, there isn't a lot of room to spare.

"I'm sorry I caused so much trouble," John said while we drove through sun-dappled streets. "If you hadn't come to see me, this would never have happened."

I raised my face to the light shining into the car, reveling in it after a day in the artificial hospital world. "It wasn't your fault, John." I watched him from the corner of my eye. "It was Guy's car, wasn't it?"

The car swerved slightly when he gripped the wheel tighter. "No one is saying."

"It was a gray sedan. And you know, I think I recognize a Porsche when I see one. And there aren't a helluva lot of Porsches in the Barnsdale area."

He cleared his throat. "I heard the police were at Guy's house with a search warrant."

"I don't get it." I leaned back, once again allowing the flickering sunlight to initiate little movies in my brain. "Why would Guy want to force me off the road?"

"It was more than that," John said, his voice low and angry. "Someone tried to kill you."

Oh, Will. Did you know this would happen? My eyes got hot with unshed tears and I kept them closed. "There's no reason anyone would want to kill me," I whispered. "I don't know anything about anything."

"Somebody disagrees with you."

I let the sound of the engine lull me, willing reality to the background for another few minutes. John was right. It was a deliberate act of attempted murder. Owen would have to handle it. My brain felt so scrambled I couldn't think clearly.

"Did you leave your garage door open?" John asked a minute later.

"What?" I sat up straight in the seat while John pulled into my driveway. "Of course not. I always close it."

He stopped the car. "Let me go in and check. Do you have a key with you?"

I started to reach for my purse but I remembered. "My purse was stolen. I don't know about my car keys and key ring. Oh, damn. My garage door opener. I kept it clipped to my car visor."

"Wait here," John said, getting out.

I was so surprised I stayed pinned to my seat for a second then I hurriedly unfastened my seat belt and followed him into the garage. He turned when he reached for the door to the kitchen. "Do you normally keep this locked?"

I shook my head. "No. I know I should, but I've never gotten in the habit."

He opened the door and stepped inside. "Oh, God," he said in a strangled voice.

"What?" I pushed in behind him and stopped, aghast. My kitchen was a total trashed mess. The cupboards were all open, dishes were piled on the floor, canisters opened and the contents strewn about.

I edged past John, who was rooted to the spot. I turned to the right, to the living room, and stopped, appalled. The stench in the room was disgusting, a smell of rot and something I couldn't quite identify. The furnace was on full-blast, the heat so intense it felt like something was on fire.

I took a step forward and stopped. A pile of manure was stacked in the middle of the living room floor. I covered my nose and mouth with my left arm, choking. I reached for the thermostat and turned off the furnace.

"Dear God," John breathed.

I turned. He stood in the hallway, staring at the wall. I joined him. Red writing—bloody writing—stained the pale green walls.

You'll die too

Dried blood streaked from the letters, pooling on the floorboards. The smell of the blood and the other odor . . . what was it? "John, what—?" I turned to him, helpless with horror.

John was already moving, going back to the kitchen. He raced to the stove and slammed open the door. Smoke billowed out along with a gut-churning odor.

"Oh, God." He grabbed kitchen towels and pulled what looked like a burnt football from it, something compact and twisted.

It was an animal. I saw a small skull, legs, all burnt, all twisted.

"The kittens!" I whirled, peering into the living room. "Where are the kittens? Oh, God, it isn't—?" I stumbled, almost falling into him when he dropped the burnt remains on my kitchen table.

"It's a chicken," he said grimly. "I hope it was dead when it was put in there." He reached over and turned off the oven, waving at the smoke with big sweeps of his arms.

"What? A chicken? In the . . ." It was too much. My meager lunch wouldn't stay down. I raced for the door to the garage and pulled it open, stumbling to the lawn to vomit.

Chapter 13

I threw up everything in my stomach, leaning over with my hands on my knees to support me. It hurt so damn much because of my broken fingers and the bruises that I quit quickly, probably more from the pain than from the fact my stomach was empty. I drew in several long shuddering breaths before I could force myself to go back into the house.

I stopped in the entryway. John opened windows in the living room and he walked along the hall, stepping carefully over my strewn possessions. The burnt *thing* was gone and I saw the door to the back stoop open, letting air into the house.

"John?" I called.

He glanced back at me. His eyes were bleak and it seemed he alternated between wanting to weep and wanting to hit someone. "Stay there, Tucker. I want to make sure nobody else is here."

"The kittens," I said helplessly. "Where are they?"

"I'll find them. Go back outside. Don't come any further." He disappeared around a corner, into my bedroom.

I couldn't let him do it all for me. I forced myself, one step at a time, into the kitchen. I pulled open the door to the basement and turned on the light. The smell was there, too. Not the burnt smell but something else, something wet and bloody and horrible mixed with a smell of burnt feathers or hair. "John?" I called, my voice wavering. "Down here."

He emerged from the bedroom, ducked into the den then the guest room and came to me. "Go outside," he said, his voice grim. "You don't want to go in the bedroom."

"The kittens?" My stomach started to flip flop again.

"I haven't found them yet." He paused at the top of the basement steps and sniffed. His face paled. "Call the police. Wait for them outside."

"John, don't. You don't have to."

He gently pushed me toward the door. "Go outside. Wait there. Call the police." He descended the stairs slowly, warily.

Coward that I was, I obeyed. I grabbed my portable phone and went outside, dialing 911 with trembling hands. I managed a garbled plea for help then I pressed Alan's speed-dial number for his mobile phone.

I could barely hear him over the sounds in the kitchen at the Parlor. "Hey, Tuck. I'll be done here in an hour or so."

"Somebody broke in my house. It's awful. They killed—it's terrible. There's blood everywhere and it stinks and—" I started to cry, big gulping sobs. "I think they tortured the kittens. I can't find them. I can't go inside. John is in there and there are—"

"Oh, Christ," Alan breathed. "Tucker, I'm going to call Owen. I'll be there soon."

I checked the phone face and the time displayed there. It was six-fifteen, the height of dinner hour. "You can't come, you have to cook."

"Screw the restaurant, I'm on my way." He hung up before I could protest any more.

I sat on the damp grass in front of the house, careful to avoid the spot where I lost my lunch moments earlier. I hurt all over: stomach, hand, shoulder, face, my soul, my heart. Someone came into my house and tortured animals in there. They left shit and blood and entrails (yes, I recognized the mass of slimy pink and blood in the middle of the hall) everywhere, trying to poison my house, trying to poison me. They put something in my oven and maybe something in my washing machine or my dryer.

My stomach started to twist again. I got up and walked around on wobbly legs, pacing from Alan's car to the curb and back again. Who would do such a thing? Good God, if somebody wanted to get rid of me, shoot me or something! It wasn't like I was protected night and day. Anybody could take a gun and kill me.

As my thoughts slowed, so did my steps until I was standing in the middle of the street, staring blindly into space. What if John was right? What if someone tried to kill me in the car crash? I ran through it all, pacing it out. Someone—okay, let's say Guy, because it was his car—Guy hit me. His car was far bigger and heavier than mine. It pushed me into the ditch.

The drop into the ditch might have killed me. Those drop-offs were at least ten feet deep. Any car doing a nosedive into a ditch might easily result in death, especially if someone was stupid enough to not wear a seat belt.

It was a crazy way to kill somebody, though. How could he be sure it would work? People have car accidents all the time and don't die. If you want to kill somebody, wouldn't it be better to do something that was a sure bet? Did Guy have the guts to do that?

But why would Guy want to kill me? Why would he send me a threatening text message? I needed to show the text to Owen. I should have done it days earlier. Now I'd have to show him everything Will gave me.

I almost slapped myself on the head. I couldn't show him anything because my cell phone was in my purse and my purse was stolen. That explained how easily someone came in and did what they did. Forget the credit card and my identification. I could replace those. Holy crap, what else was in my missing purse?

Will's memory stick. My memory stick, with the copies on it. The knowledge settled over me like a pall. I actually shivered, standing there in the rays of the setting sun with the air hot all around me from the late June day. The information Will died for was gone.

I glanced back at the house then I resolutely marched inside. The light was still on in the basement and I heard noises from below, maybe John shifting something heavy. I tried not to think about what he would find. I made straight for the canisters, lying scattered on the kitchen counter. Flour clogged the sink, mixed with coffee and sugar.

I held my breath and sifted through it all, digging my hand into the canister and running my fingers through the mess in the sink. No memory stick and no list of files in a plastic bag. "Son of a bitch."

Sirens sounded in the distance. I drew in a deep breath, held it, and raced through the hall to my home office. My desk was a mess. Everything on it was scattered on the floor or in the chair. My monitor and the CPU tower were smashed. Broken plastic and shards of glass lay everywhere. Sitting right on top of the remains of the CPU was a big metal brick, ugly gray and heavy.

I kicked through the debris and went to the wicker basket, lying on its side in the corner. I upended it and cat toys rained out, bouncing and scattering. The red Angry Bird bounced, too, and I snatched it up, jamming it in my jeans pocket.

I next went into my bedroom, grimacing when I encountered another pile of manure, heaped on the middle of my bed. I delved into my dresser drawer, pawing aside my underwear, taking shallow breaths through my mouth. I found my cache of checks and the two credit cards I never carried but only used online. I jammed the credit cards into my back pocket and tore off one check to use for identification for my account. I stuffed the checks back into the drawer and left the room, gasping for air.

I emerged into the hallway and edged past the gory heap of stinking flesh outside my bedroom door. When I did, John came from the basement. He turned and I saw two kittens tucked into his enfolding arms, their front paws draped over his forearm. "They were hiding under the treadmill," he said when I hurried to him. "Scared shitless, I'll bet."

"Oh, John, thank you." I turned to view the wreck that was my home. "What will I do?"

He put his left arm around me, the kittens still nestled in the crook of his right arm. "We'll figure something out. First let me get these guys into their cage. We'll deal with it, don't worry." He went to the back stoop and gently pulled the kittens off his arm, setting them inside the cage there. "They'll be fine here for now."

"Are they okay?" I knelt to peer at the two faces, both staring at me in a faintly accusing manner. *Hey, lady. We come to live with you and look what happens!*

"They're fine. Your dryer, though . . ." John's mouth set in a thin, grim line, his beard twitching angrily. "They put a couple of chicks in there."

"Oh, God." I stepped onto the stoop, anxious for fresh air, anxious to get away from the torture house. My house.

Sirens blared and I jumped, almost knocking over the cat carrier. John put his arm around me again. It felt amazingly safe to have him there, holding on to me while I surveyed the carnage of my home. "We'll figure it out, Tuck. Don't worry."

I walked to the driveway to meet the squad car pulling up to the curb. Two officers emerged and I explained what we found. John went with them inside while I went to meet Alan, who pulled up at the curb behind the squad car in a large black pickup truck.

"Tuck, are you okay?" He sprang from the truck and raced to me.

I fell into his arms. He still wore his chef's uniform and I pressed against his chest, the welcome aroma of warm bread enfolding me. "I'm sorry, Alan. You should be at the restaurant, you shouldn't be here."

"Shh, shh," he whispered, hugging me gently. "What happened? Are you okay?"

As we walked to the house, I steered him around my barf pile but he noticed. "Were you sick? You know what the doctor said, if you're sick, it could be bad." He stopped pulling me to a halt with him.

"I'm fine. It's inside, it's what's inside. It made me sick."

One of the officers came outside and met me in the empty garage. He seemed so young, with his smooth-shaven, pink cheeks and baby blue eyes. Then I saw the gun belt with all the gadgets dangling from it and the steely gaze in those baby blues. "Ma'am, we need to get some information from you. Let's go over here and talk."

Alan looked uncertainly from me to the officer. "Can I go in? Can I help?"

The officer nodded. "Don't touch anything. We have to get fingerprints." He steered me to Alan's car. "You can sit in here, ma'am. You don't want to go back in there now."

I sniffled. "It's awful."

"Yes, ma'am. It is. We'll find who did it, don't you worry. There are bound to be fingerprints all over everything." He was so solemn and upset I wanted to hug him.

He opened the front passenger door for me and I sank down, my knees rubbery and weak. He started asking me a series of questions and I answered, my voice as weak as my knees. I was suddenly exhausted, overwhelmed by the sheer enormity of what was ahead of me. My house was a wreck. I had no car, no purse, no credit card. I still owed fifteen years of a thirty-year mortgage and I knew I couldn't ever live in that house again.

While I explained about my recent hospital visit and release, Owen pulled up in the same dark sedan he drove the other day. He got out and the officer excused himself, going to the curb to talk to Owen before Owen came to see me.

"This has been a rough few days, Tucker," he said, his voice gentle.

"I get the feeling it's going to be rough ahead, too." I ran a hand through my tangled hair. It came away with flour and sugar on it. I stared at it in horror. "They didn't just trash the house, Owen. They defiled it."

He nodded. "I heard. We'll find whoever did it and they'll pay."

I tried to laugh but it emerged like a strangled croak. "A fine and a slap on the wrist, I bet. While I'm left with—" I gestured to the house, the movement almost unseating me.

"You might be surprised. Sometimes the legal system is actually just. Stay here. I'm going inside." He turned to go to the house when Alan emerged, his normally tanned face pale.

"It's disgusting," he spat, coming to stand by the open passenger door. He leaned over it and regarded me. "You're not going back in there. I'll pack up your clothes and you're coming to my house to stay until we decide what to do."

I didn't even consider protesting. "Thanks, Alan. I don't think I can bear to go in there any time soon."

John came out, carrying the cat cage. The two kittens stared bug-eyed through the grate at the sight of the outside world. He set the cage at my feet and joined Owen and Alan, grouped around me in the car. "Why would someone do that to her house?" His gaze shifted from Owen to me. "It wasn't malicious. It was vicious."

"Whatever couldn't be ruined was defiled." Alan shook his head. "The oven. My God, what did they do? And the smell in the basement."

"They put a chicken in the oven and turned it on. Without plucking it or cleaning it," John said, his voice rough. "And I found the remains of some chicks in the dryer."

"Were they alive when they . . .?" I couldn't finish the question. I caught a glimpse of the anger in John's eyes and I had my answer. "What did they do to the computer?" I changed the subject so I didn't have to consider the death that happened inside. "They took a brick to it or something."

"It was a magnet. I've seen them in a factory where they need to separate metal from other material. A very powerful magnet. It probably wiped your hard drive."

"And with my purse gone, I have no backups. I used to keep backup memory sticks in my purse."

"Somebody has it in for you, that's for sure," John gently nudged the cat cage at my feet. "Thank heavens these guys hid. Who knows what might have happened."

I tried to pick up the cage, but my bruised ribs made such a movement impossible. I straightened, gasping with pain. Alan turned to Owen. "Is she needed here? Can I take her home? She just got out of the hospital. She needs rest." He turned to the house. "Not this."

"I'll check with the officers in charge," Owen said. "I think it would be okay, but Tucker will need to provide a sworn statement and she'll need to inventory the house to make a note of what was stolen."

I stared at him blankly. "Stolen? How would I know if something was taken? I won't know that unless I go in there." I swallowed, hard. "Owen, it's awful in there. I don't know if I can do it."

"We'll hire a clean-up crew," Alan said. "You won't have to do it. You come to my place and get some rest."

"But I can't stay with you," I protested. "What if I put you in danger?"

"I don't think it will be a problem, Tucker," Owen said before Alan could speak. "John was right. This was a vicious personal attack, designed to get you off balance. If someone really wanted to harm you, they'd have done it by now."

I nodded wearily. "Great minds think alike. If Guy wanted me dead, a car accident was a stupid way to do it."

For an instant, Owen froze, his face stiff. Then he relaxed. "There's nothing to prove Guy was the person driving the car."

I stared at him, amazed. "Who else would be driving it?"

Owen shook his head. "Don't make assumptions, that's all." He turned to Alan. "I'll check inside with the officers, but I think she can go with you. I'll have them come to your house when they're done here." He started for the house.

"I'll pack some clothes for you, Tuck." Alan followed him.

"Hold on a sec, Alan." John walked with Alan to the garage, talking earnestly. Alan nodded before going with Owen into the house while John rejoined me.

"John, I can't thank you enough." I reached again for the cage, but he beat me to it, lifting it easily and holding it so I could peer inside.

"I'm happy to help, Tuck. You let me know if you need anything else." He shook his head, his dark face somber. "That was nasty. Nobody deserves to have something like this happen to them, but especially you."

I craned my neck to regard him. "Why do you say that?"

"You love animals. Whoever did that" and he jerked his head to the house, disgust clear in his eyes, "they don't think of animals as anything but *things.*" He leaned slightly nearer me. "Did you lose any of the information you got from your friend?"

I struggled to remember what I told John about Will. It seemed like all previous conversations were shadowy memories, heard through a thick wad of cotton. My brain was fogged. "I don't know," I said, hoping it was non-committal enough.

He must have sensed my confusion. "I mean, you said your friend was at the factory and I assumed he or she would get information. You said you saw what they were doing."

"Not really," I hedged. I switched my attention to the cage, praying John would take the hint and drop the subject. "I'm amazed they survived. I was sure it was their blood on the wall in there. I was sure it was one of them in the oven. I couldn't have stood it. It's bad enough it was—" I couldn't continue. The day's accumulated stress combined to make my lip quiver while tears rolled down my face.

"Ah, I'm sorry, Tuck." John set the cage next to the door and knelt on one knee in front of me, taking my hands in his. "I shouldn't have talked about it. I'm sorry."

He was so worried I smiled. "I'm sorry, too, John. I remember you said you wanted to talk to me about something, but in all the excitement I forgot all about it. A B&B, wasn't it? We were going to go to a farm, right?"

"We can do it any time you feel better. You and Alan did such a great job with the Acorn. I can ask him about it sometime. You don't have to do it."

"I'll try to talk to him tonight about it." I shaded my eyes with one hand to stare at the house. "I don't know what I'm going to do, John."

"Try not to worry. I'm sure something will work out." He stood when Alan came from the house carrying two grocery bags. John went to meet him, taking the bags from Alan and stowing them in the back seat. Next John took the kitten cage and put it on the back seat then he and Alan exchanged car keys. "I'll talk to you later," John said, leaning in to talk to me.

"Thank you, John. For everything."

He clasped my hand. "Any time, Tuck." He straightened and walked to his truck while Alan slipped into the driver's seat.

"For a minute there it looked like he was proposing," Alan said in a teasing voice.

"Not hardly." I stared at the house in front of me. I knew I could never return. My life was irrevocably changed. I clenched my hand and grunted with pain when my two broken fingers protested.

"Let's go home, Tuck."

I wiped at my tears. "Yeah. Let's go." I turned to check the kittens on the back seat, but the pain in my ribs when I tried to turn made it impossible. I contented myself with angling the visor so I saw the cage in the mirror.

"They're fine," Alan said.

"Good God, after what they've been through, I'm surprised they let anybody touch them. I can't imagine it." I leaned my head against the car window. "It must have been done last night. So those poor kittens were in the house, smelling that awful smell all night and being scared and frightened." I shuddered again. "I should take them to a vet. I never thought about it because I figured I wouldn't keep them, but what if they were poisoned? I saw those innards." I shuddered again.

"They're wild animals, Tucker. They'll be fine."

"Maybe," I agreed doubtfully. "I guess my first priority is to figure where I'm going to live. I don't know if I could ever go back there, Alan. I know it's stupid but I would feel haunted or something."

"It's not stupid at all. I'd feel exactly the same way. And you don't have to worry about where to live. You'll stay with me until we figure it out."

"I have a mortgage," I said, thinking aloud. "I can't walk away from it. I'll have to remodel it and put it on the market. I'll have to get an apartment. Good Lord, I'll need to pay rent and mortgage." I started trying to do math in my head, but I didn't need to be precise to know it was going to be almost impossible. "Maybe if I clean out my savings account I can manage it."

Alan left Sherwood Acres and made a right then a left turn into his neighborhood, about a mile from mine. He owned a townhouse not far from the golf course. I knew he had ample space for me, but I was worried about the effects of two kittens on a house that was a designer's dream. "There's the third floor over the Acorn," he said. "You could move in there. The caretaker's apartment is still there."

For a minute I couldn't figure what he meant. "What?"

"Remember? The top floor has an apartment. We use it for storage now, but I'll bet if we fix it up, it would be perfect for you. There's a bathroom and a living room, a bedroom. There's even a tiny kitchen."

I visualized the space in my mind. When we bought the glove factory, the building had an apartment for an on-site manager, who presumably acted as a security guard when the factory wasn't in operation. The apartment was still relatively intact and closed off. We removed the floors on the west side of the building for pipes and equipment needed for the brewery.

"Do you think so? It's empty, but is it habitable?"

"I'm sure it is," Alan said confidently. "The health inspector goes through the building at least once a year, so we know it's passed inspection. I'm sure with a touch of paint and some cleaning, we could make it into a nice little home, at least until you know what you want to do."

The thought of painting, cleaning, and moving was so exhausting I just whispered, "Sounds good, Alan." I resolved to consider the idea tomorrow, when surely I'd have more energy to contemplate such a monumental task.

"Try not to worry about it, Tucker. Something can be worked out. Believe me."

"I hope so. My house is a crime scene and I'm not sure I can ever go back there."

"I know. But trust me. We'll figure something out."

I didn't answer. I didn't have that kind of hope left in me.

Chapter 14

When we got to his house, it took Alan a couple of trips to get me, the kittens, my hospital bags, hospital paperwork, and the grocery sacks with my belongings all moved to the lower level of his townhouse. I followed him down the stairs, relaxation increasing with each step. The dark brown carpet cushioned every move and a faint aroma of apples and cinnamon hung in the air, like a pie was pulled from the oven an hour or so earlier. It was such a startling contrast to the horror I just left.

"We'll put you in this bedroom and we can close the upstairs door so the kittens stay here." He put the two sacks on the immaculate bed in the tastefully decorated bedroom and set the cat carrier down. "They can run all they want around the TV room. I only use it to watch movies, anyway, so they'll have the room to themselves. I brought some of their food and toys and stuff here. They'll be fine." He opened the door to the attached bathroom, a room almost as big as my old bedroom. "I'll put the litter box in the corner over here."

"They might jump around or get into things," I cautioned when he opened the door on the carrier. For a minute nothing happened then Cayenne's orange paw cautiously inched out, testing the carpeted floor. He emerged from the cage, spied the bed, and made a beeline for it, pushing underneath. His sister hesitated in the door to the cage as though considering making a break for it, but in the end she followed his example.

"I'll be lucky if they ever quit hiding," I said glumly. "I can't imagine what it was like for them. Thank God my smoke alarms didn't go off, otherwise they'd be deaf."

"Yeah, the bastard who did that to your house must have figured the alarms would alert the neighbors. We found the batteries on the floor."

"Thank heavens for small favors," I whispered. "I feel sorry for them."

"They'll be fine. They can run and hide and do whatever it is kittens do. They'll forget all about it in a day or two. I hardly use this lower level anyway, so if something gets broken or messed up, it'll give me a good excuse to go and buy something new." While he talked, Alan pulled a couple of my blouses from the sack and hung them in the large closet near the bathroom. "I'll go back to your house tomorrow and get the rest of your clothes. You can use this space until we get the apartment whipped into shape."

I sat on the bed, my cracked ribs aching fiercely, keeping time with the headache that almost blinded me and the throbbing of my broken fingers. It was like I kept all pain at bay while I dealt with the house and once it was behind me, the accumulated aches suddenly landed on me in a heap. I longed to fall over and let the dark burgundy bedspread envelop me in warmth and softness.

Alan tucked a couple of T-shirts into a drawer and tumbled the rest of the sack into another drawer. *Oh, Lord. He was rooting around in my underwear drawer.*

I should have been mortified at the thought of him seeing my unders, but all I felt was exhaustion.

"There's a spare bathrobe here if you want to take a shower." He eyed me sympathetically. "Maybe you should wait until tomorrow. You might fall asleep standing up. Hold on." He left and soon returned, carrying the hospital sack and paperwork. "John said there are pills in here somewhere." He opened the sack and wrinkled his nose at what he saw. "Plastic ware. Oh well. At least you have a toothbrush." Alan put the hospital hairbrush, toothbrush, toothpaste, and tissues in the bathroom. "How about a nice glass of wine to wash down the pain pill?"

"That sounds perfect. Except I won't take a pill. I think a glass of wine will do the trick." I followed him into the next room, a big open area with two deep easy chairs and matching hassocks, a large flat screen TV and a coffee table. I eased myself onto one of the chairs and sank back with a sigh of contentment.

"You relax. I'll get us something to snack on." Alan went upstairs and I think I must have dozed off, because it seemed a while before he returned with an enormous tray, which he set on the coffee table.

"A feast." I eyed the wine bottle and two full glasses of white wine, the two bowls of chips and three bowls of dip, along with napkins and small plates.

He handed me a wine glass. "Here's to better times ahead." He raised his glass to mine. We clinked the rims, making them chime.

"I'll drink to that." I took a swallow, sighing when I felt taut muscles relax. The wine coated my tongue with a silky coolness which washed off the accumulated stress and fear of the day. "I'm so screwed up. What day is today?"

"Tuesday."

"I missed most of Monday, I guess."

"Being in the hospital will do that," Alan said.

"I missed work today. Who filled in for me?"

Alan waved that away. "Not to worry. Between Miller and the bar staff, we're managing. You sleep in for the next few days and heal."

"I'll be there tomorrow." I leaned forward and put a few chips and a healthy dollop of dip on a plate.

"You need to rest and recover. And we need to get you set up in a new place to live. The more I think about it, the more I think the apartment over the Acorn is just the thing."

"I don't know. Maybe a regular apartment would be better. I think I might feel safer if I have people around me." I dipped, nibbled, and dipped some more.

"There're people in either the Pub or the Parlor from about eight in the morning until two in the morning, sometimes earlier and sometimes later," he pointed out. "You may find yourself overrun with people."

"Well, yeah, I suppose." I sipped my wine. It was cold and crisp and faintly dry, a perfect complement to the chips and ranch dip. In fact, it was so good I took several sips.

"Besides, our building has security." Alan loaded up a corn chip with guacamole and sat back. "We have 24-7 security. All we have to do is call the service and they'll fix it so the third floor has its own system. Remember? They asked about it when we set up the service." He munched on the chip, dabbing his chin with a napkin.

"Yeah. I remember." I didn't remember, really, but I trusted Alan on things like that. I took another couple of sips of wine. "I am so beat." I yawned.

"You should be." He regarded me over the arm of his chair. "Did they get it?"

"Hmm?"

"Did you have something? Something they were after? Did they get it?"

A little voice in my head said, *Shut up. Don't talk about this. Nobody knew, right?* Another voice said, *Have another sip of wine and forget about worries for a while.*

"No, they didn't," I said, following the advice of the second little voice. I held up my glass. "Fill 'er up."

He obliged, tilting the bottle over my glass before taking my plate and loading it up with chips. "Is it worth all of this?"

I yawned again. "I don't know. But Will thought it was important, so by God, it's important to me. I won't let him die in vain, Alan."

He nodded. "I respect that."

We sat in silence for a few minutes. It felt so good to lounge there, sipping wine, staring at the darkened TV, and letting the quietness seep into my bones. "Alan?"

"Hmm?"

"Someone in town tried to kill me."

There was another long silence. "Yeah."

"It's hard to believe someone I've known for a long time might be capable of killing me."

Another silence. "Yeah."

"I shouldn't be surprised. I mean, people are probably capable of just about anything."

"Including good, Tucker," he said quietly.

Now it was my turn to be silent for a while. "Yeah." I drained the wine in my glass. "I think I'll lie down." I set the glass on the coffee table, noting it seemed quite distant.

Alan helped me to my feet and steered me to the bedroom. "I put a bottle of water here on the nightstand," he said from a far distance.

I realized I was lying in the bed, staring at the ceiling. "Don't turn out the light."

"I'll leave the lights on in the family room. Good night, Tucker."

I closed my eyes.

****

Once again when I awoke I wondered *who am I, where am I, why am I?* I lay in the unfamiliar bed, slowly peering around the unfamiliar room.

A small bundle pressed against my feet. I propped myself up on my elbows, which proved to be a big mistake because my right elbow was badly bruised and still sore. I managed to see along the length of the bed to the two kittens sleeping soundly against my legs.

I rolled over carefully and examined the rest of the room. I glimpsed a bathroom with a light on, a closet, a doorway. Suddenly I remembered. I was at Alan's house. I finally found the bedside clock and did a double-take. One? Was it one in the morning? Then I saw the small red dot next to "PM". One in the afternoon?

I never slept past six or seven in the morning. Good heavens. I inched away from the sleeping kittens and

213

sat up. I ached all over, from my head to my toes. I pushed aside the covers, surprised to see I was still in my clothes. I must have fallen asleep where I lay last night.

I got up, unsteady at first but gradually finding my balance by the time I reached the bathroom. A pristine white bathrobe hung on the door and I vaguely remembered Alan unpacking a few items of my clothing last night when we got to his house.

Yes, a shower. Please. I stripped off my clothes, which had been worn now for several days and left them in a heap on the floor. I peeled off the bandage over my elbow and examined the black-and-blue marks along my torso, showing where I slammed into something, probably the console in my car. A clear striping of bruising across my throat and over my chest showed where the seat belt dug in. And lastly there was a new bruise on my face, this one on my forehead above a nasty gash. "I'm the Bride of Frankenstein," I said as I peeled off bandages and discarded them.

I stepped into the corner shower, luxuriating in the expensive rainfall showerhead which gently pummeled my body. I simply stood there for several long minutes, delighting in the warmth and the soft massaging sensation. I carefully soaped and cleaned myself and my hair, washing off days of grime, fear, and hatefulness. When I emerged and wrapped myself in the fluffy white robe, I felt like a new woman.

I towel-dried my hair and patted it into a semblance of shape. That was all I really needed to do because its naturally curly nature meant it had a mind of its own anyway. I went to the closet and pulled it open, expecting to see a blouse or two.

Instead, half of my entire wardrobe hung there, a light scent of lavender wafting to me with the opened doors. A suitcase on the floor held underwear and shorts. It wasn't my suitcase. The last time I saw my suitcase, it was full of manure on the floor in my bedroom.

I turned to view the kittens, who still lounged on the bed. "Did you guys do this?"

"Hey, Sleeping Beauty!" Alan called from above.

I went into the family room. "I'm up and moving," I called back. "What elf brought my clothes here?"

"I figured you might like some selection. You were zonked, so I hung things up and left. Come upstairs and have lunch."

"Lunch? Why aren't you at the restaurant?"

"Get dressed and come on up. We have talking to do."

He sounded happy and excited, not glum. So maybe I wasn't up for another day of awful happenings. I hurriedly dressed, pulling on clean jeans and a button-on light cotton shirt, which was all I could manage given how dinged-up I was.

When I went into the family room, the kittens followed me, making a beeline for the food dishes now arranged near the patio door leading to the lawn outside. A new water bowl, kibble bowl, and two small heart-shaped dishes were arranged on a large rug which said *Spoiled Rotten Pets Live Here.* I examined one of the dishes and determined that yes, it was indeed porcelain. Trust Alan to use the fine china for the cats.

I climbed the stairs and opened the door leading to Alan's kitchen, closing it quickly behind me to prevent any kittens from escaping. They would take one look at

Alan's collection of angel figurines in his glass display case and havoc would ensue.

The roomy kitchen was empty but I saw Alan at his dining room table dressed in jeans and a pale blue shirt. "You seem better this morning," he said, getting up. "I have quiche in the oven, keeping warm. Have a seat and let me serve you."

"What are you doing here? Did you close the restaurant?" I filled a waiting ceramic mug with coffee while he went to the stove, opening it and releasing a mouth-watering aroma. I went to the dining room, a bright room with an expanse of windows with a view of the golf course in the distance.

"We did a buffet today." He put a plate in front of me with a large steaming slice of spinach-mushroom quiche. My stomach rumbled at the sight of its creamy texture. Alan's quiches were always moist and delicious and the crust was buttery and so flaky. The dish of fresh fruit next to it appeared almost as good. "I made up a bunch of quiches and the staff will pop them in the oven for reheating."

"You must have been up all night working." I speared a strawberry and bit into it, savoring its sweet juiciness.

"Oh, somewhat. It won't be the first time I was cracking eggs at dawn."

"Did you slip me a Mickey Finn last night? I was out like a light. I never sleep so good."

"I cannot tell a lie. I contacted your doctor and he said mixing one pain pill with a drink would not harm you. So yes, I slipped you a Mickey." Before I could express my reaction to this perfidy, he said, "I ran over to your house and got most of your clothes and a few other items. The police photographed everything so you'll know what I've taken. That way, when you do an inventory, you'll know what's really missing." He sat at the seat across from me and picked up his matching coffee mug. "Owen said they're done processing the scene so you'll be able to get a service in to do the cleaning sometime soon."

My first bite of quiche paused on the way to my mouth. "Who do I call? I've never even thought about it. Who can I get to clean up a mess like that?"

Alan pulled a memo pad from his shirt pocket. "I called around. There's a service in Des Moines which specializes in what they call disaster recovery. You know, floods, fires, and those kinds of things. They'll give you an estimate. And Owen said there are companies which specialize in cleaning up crime scenes." Alan grimaced. "You know, blood splatter and fingerprint dust and all that. So we can find someone. And I checked with your insurance company, and a large part of it will be covered."

"That's a start. I don't want to go in and inventory anything until it's at least somewhat cleaned."

"Absolutely," Alan said. "You don't have to worry about it. I have a team of volunteers standing by, ready to go in and get it cleaned enough so you can go through and check things."

"Seriously?" I said around a bite of delectable quiche. It really did melt on my tongue. Combined with the fruit and the coffee, it was ambrosia.

"Yep. When the police give us the word, they'll be in there handling things. After they're done, we'll call the real pros in and they'll get it all fixed up again."

"I'm going to have to sell it. I don't think I can live there." I swallowed hard, a memory of the horrid smell overriding the delicious scent of strawberries and coffee.

Alan nodded. "I don't blame you. I talked to Lee Knight. His brother, the realtor, said he'd list it for you at half his normal commission. I'm sure he can sell it, Tuck. Once the restoration people get in there and we buy new appliances, it'll be good as new."

"Okay. Maybe there is a light at the end of the tunnel." I sighed happily. "You are the best cook, Alan. Thanks for taking care of everything, not the least of which is my rumbling tummy. Did I tell you Isabel Fitz stopped to see me in the hospital? She wants to work for you. Oh, and I forgot to tell you about John's idea."

Alan held up his hand. "Hold that thought. Or those thoughts. First, tell me, what's your favorite color?"

I stared at him blankly. "Huh?"

"Favorite color. Come on, tell me."

"I like to wear gold but I like green around me. And yellow. Not bright but soft." I regarded my plate and the few crumb remaining. "Like your quiche."

Alan grinned. "Excellent. Hold on. I need to make a call." He dashed into the kitchen and I heard phone sounds, his voice so quiet I couldn't hear a word he said. He quickly returned. "Now tell me about Isabel and John."

"What are you up to?" I pushed aside my empty dishes. "Why do you care about my favorite colors?"

"Tell me about Isabel and John. Go on."

I told him about Isabel's visit to me at the hospital. "I couldn't make sense from what she said. I mean, she and I chatted but I don't think I said anything earth shattering."

Alan tilted his coffee mug, watching the swirls of cream. "I wonder about the allergy thing. I heard, and I won't say where I heard it, that PJ was allergic to latex."

"So?" I leaned back and burped softly, hands crossed my full tummy. I could get used to being treated like a princess. Fluffy white bathrobes, fresh clean sheets, food on demand. Yep, a girl could get used to this.

"PJ used a condom with his, um, girlfriend. A latex one. I *heard* she was surprised. He never used condoms before. He apparently wasn't worried about disease, only pregnancy, and she assured him she used the pill." Alan rolled his eyes. "Not that he should believe her."

"Why would PJ start using a condom now?" I stared at Alan, bewildered. "Wait a minute. Isabel said something about—"

Alan held up a hand. "You were under the influence of pain killers at the time. Who's to say what she said? I wonder who gave PJ the condom to use."

"But he must have known he was allergic," I protested.

"Maybe not. You know how he was about doctors," Alan said. "And everybody uses those non-latex gloves now, so even if he went to a doctor, he may not have known."

"True." PJ's aversion to all health professionals, medical and dental, was well known. He probably hadn't set foot in a doctor's office in a decade.

"Tell me about John and his idea. What's it about?" Alan asked.

I launched into a description of John's plan for an Organic Destination, complete with B&B, farm-to-restaurant connection, and lessons. Before I was halfway through describing it, Alan found a lined pad and was jotting notes.

"We could do cooking lessons, too," he said, writing furiously. "How to select and use produce when it's in season, how to use meat sparingly but to advantage. I'll bet we could partner with the culinary college in Des Moines and have students come and work here." His landline phone rang. "Hold on." He went into the kitchen and answered it, but soon came back to the door, phone held against his chest. "It's Owen. The police are done at your house. He's going to call in the troops for cleaning then he'll pick you up in two hours for the inventory. Sound okay?"

"Two hours? That won't be enough time for people to get it into shape."

Alan smiled smugly. "Trust me. We have enough people." He put the phone back to his ear. "That's fine, Owen. She'll be ready." He replaced the phone on its base. "Okay, what else do we need to do to get this idea off the ground?"

He and I spent the next hour going through John's idea, making notes, roughing estimates of costs, and scoping out a broad outline of a plan. After that I spent an hour on the phone with my bank, the insurance company, and the credit card company, trying to verify that my financial health was reasonably intact. To my surprise, there were no charges on the credit card and no withdrawals from my bank accounts.

My insurance agent evaluated my car (totaled) and my house (essentially totaled) and we discussed what I needed to do to get the claims processing underway. I was relieved to discover it wasn't as awful as I expected. I'd be out a bunch of money, but it wouldn't beggar me. It was a big load off my mind.

I took a few minutes on Alan's computer to email the files from the Angry Birds memory stick to my home email account. I didn't want to be responsible for whatever might be in those files, but I was damned if I'd hand it over without some kind of backup.

I returned to "my downstairs suite" and checked the kittens. They were curled up in the family room, faces pressed against the patio door to view the outside world. I scooped the litter, topped up the food dishes, and gave them a good petting before I left. As Alan predicted, they appeared to be none the worse for their traumatic experience. I made a mental note to have a vet check them at the earliest opportunity.

It was almost five in the afternoon when Owen's car pulled into Alan's drive. At my insistence, Alan went to the restaurant to work the evening shift. I promised to join him there after going through my house with Owen, an experience I dreaded but one I knew must be done. No one else could inventory it but me. I needed to suck it up and live with it.

"The police and my office are joining forces on your case and the shooting at the Yoke," Owen said while we drove to what I considered *the scene of the crime*, not *home*. "It isn't any secret that Federal agents are investigating what's happening at the factory because of the salmonella outbreak. If you're involved in that, it's important our department is involved, too."

"I was going to show you the message on my phone, but it's gone missing, along with my purse. I got a threatening text message."

He nodded like he expected that. "Is that why you wanted me to find the phone number?"

"Yeah." I dug into my jeans pocket and held up the Angry Birds memory stick. "My nephew Will gave this to me. I mean, he gave me these files. The original memory stick is in my purse, wherever it is. This is a copy."

Owen made no move to take the toy-gadget from me. "When we get to your house, there will be a detective from the DCI there. Give the memory stick to him for processing."

I lowered my hand, clutching the little rubber gadget hard in my palm. "Why not you?"

"I want to make sure there's a clear chain of custody for it. If you give it to me now, there's nothing to prove I didn't plant information. You'll hand it to an unbiased third-party and they'll take it from there." He glanced at me, his gray eyes intense. "I won't have it said that my relationship with Alan biased me in any way."

I nodded. "I'm sorry, Owen. I don't want to mess things up for you and him."

"You won't." He drove in silence for a few more minutes. "Did you go through what's on that stick? Do you know what's there?"

"Not in detail. Some of it was so nasty I couldn't." I stared glumly ahead. We pulled up to my house, where a squad car and a dark van sat at the curb. "Like my house."

"I'm sorry you have to go through this." Owen parked in the drive behind the dark van. "I meant to ask you, Tuck. Who knew you were on the road at the time of your accident?"

I shook my head. "Nobody. I told John I was coming out, but I didn't specify a time."

"Somebody knew you were going there."

"Only John."

Owen regarded me somberly. "You might want to be careful what you say to him."

I remembered John and the way he handled the kittens, making sure they were safe. I remembered the way he handled *me,* making sure I was taken care of. "You're wrong," I said confidently. "He would never do anything to hurt anyone."

"Don't be so sure about it. John has a lot to gain if the factory shuts down."

"Well, if he has a lot to gain, he'd be happy to have the contents of the memory stick made public. He wouldn't have any reason to run me off the road."

"That's if he's sure you have it and you'll make it public. If he could get his hands on it, he could see the information is released to the media."

I snorted. "Marianne? The media?"

"Or a newspaper in Des Moines, or any one of the national news outlets who are covering the salmonella outbreak."

"I haven't seen any breaking news, though."

"All I'm saying is you should be careful who you talk to. You can't be sure who your friends are in a case like this." Before I could frame a reply, Owen opened his door and came around to open my door for me. "We're going to walk through and see if anything obvious is missing. When you pack to move, either for the professional cleaners or to a new place, you'll have a chance to really evaluate what's here and what isn't. So this doesn't have to take long."

I followed him into the garage but stopped at the steps leading into the kitchen. Owen paused, too, and waited for me.

You can do this. Hold your breath, don't look closely, and you can do it.

I took a deep breath and followed him inside.

Chapter 15

Owen held the door for me and I walked through, steeling myself for the worst.

It was still a mess. Flour was everywhere, dark splotches were splattered here and there, and now a fine gray powder coated the fridge, the stove handle, the cabinets, the table and the chairs. Utensils were tossed around, food was strewn about, and the scrawled graffiti still splattered the wall, although it was hard to see because it was covered with a plastic sheet.

But the horrid, choking, nauseating smell was gone. The room was cool, not suffocating and hot. Now it seemed like an abandoned house, not a crack house or a torture chamber.

I turned to the chubby little man in jeans and a lab coat standing near the sink. "Detective Saxe," he said, nodding to me. His hands were full of brushes and tubes, various sized.

"Miss Frye has some evidence she'd like to have processed," Owen said, coming to stand beside me.

The detective set his tools into a big black case on the floor then he accepted the Angry Birds memory stick from me, putting it into a little clear baggie and labeling it. I filled in some information and signed a form, Owen signed a form, and the detective signed a form before the memory stick disappeared into the black case and he picked up his tools again.

"We're going to do a quick inventory," Owen said. "Then we'll leave it to you."

The man nodded. "Officer Norman is downstairs taking photographs. We're done up here. Terrible thing what happened, but don't worry, we found several fingerprints here. I'm sure we'll get the guy who did it."

"Thanks." I turned to the living room where a heaping pile of manure sat a day before. Now it was gone and the rug was covered with a sheet. My furniture was still ripped and torn, but it didn't bother me for some reason. Today it was just a mess. It wasn't a personal insult. I don't know why it changed in a day, but for some reason, it did.

I walked along the hall. The spot where the guts had sat was gone, cut from the carpet runner to expose bare floor. In my bedroom, my bedding was gone and the bed remained, stripped and naked in the middle of the room. The dresser drawers hung out, damaged beyond repair, the flimsy wood showing where someone kicked through the base of each drawer.

"Whoever did this was pissed off. I didn't notice that yesterday. I was so surprised, I guess."

"Yeah," Owen said. "This was personal."

"Thanks for confirming that." I walked slowly through the other rooms, noting what was changed, what was rearranged. When we got done, I told Owen, "The only thing obviously missing is the scrapbooks."

"Scrapbooks?" He pulled out a notepad and so did the detective.

"Photo albums and scrapbooks on the coffee table. I skimmed through them the other night. They're gone."

Owen and the detective exchanged a look. "We didn't find anything like that around."

226

"Anything else, Tucker?" Owen asked.

"I don't think so."

"Okay, good. We need to get your fingerprints so we can eliminate them." Owen led me back to the kitchen where the black case now sat on the table. He left to make a phone call and talk to the officer on duty while the detective briskly arrayed various pads and papers on the table. Before I knew it, I was fingerprinted and cleaning my hands with the little handy-wipe towelette he handed me.

"Thank you," I said, wiping off my hands. "I hope we find who did this."

"Oh, we will," he said cheerfully. "Criminals really aren't smart. We usually get them in the end. You don't worry about that."

"Of course, even if you catch whoever did it, it still means my life is totally screwed up," I commented when Owen and I drove through downtown to the Acorn.

"True. But maybe it'll make you feel better if you see the guy who did suffer a bit." Owen flashed me a quick grin. "I know it always makes me feel better when I see that."

"I'll keep it in mind. We've got a good crowd tonight," I said when we pulled into the parking lot, which was almost full.

"Alan said you should meet him in the restaurant. I called him while you were being fingerprinted."

"It's six o'clock," I protested. "It's the middle of dinner hour."

"He insisted. And you know how he gets if he doesn't get his way."

"Okay, okay. Thanks, Owen, for helping me through all this. I appreciate it."

"It's what I get paid for, Tuck. Sometimes it's worth it, like now." He waved good-bye and drove off while I entered into the back door of the Parlor. I darted into the kitchen, glancing into the dining room as I went. It was a full house tonight, and Alan certainly didn't need to take time to bother with me. I'd grab a quick bite to eat then go.

He spied me when I entered. "Finally! Are you all done at the house?" He hurried over to me, wiping his hands on his immaculate white apron.

"Yep. Now I can have the insurance people go in, take their pictures, and figure what the next step is. I can't stay in your basement forever."

"Lower level, please. Basement sounds so middle class. Speaking of which, come with me. I decided to take a swipe at the apartment upstairs. Come see what you think."

"But you're busy," I protested. "It's dinner hour."

He untied his apron and hung it on a hook near the door. "A few minutes won't hurt. Come along, come on." He took my arm and almost dragged me to the far corner of the kitchen and the tiny freight elevator located on the exterior east wall. "I checked with our insurance agent, and he assured me the policy can be expanded to include residential as well as commercial property." He nudged me into the elevator, a five-by-five metal space with padding on the walls.

Alan touched the "3" button and the cage lurched upward, groaning slightly. "We need to oil this because you'll be using it."

"I can take the stairs," I said half-heartedly. The stairs were steep, narrow and the worn wood of the risers made them treacherous.

"Nonsense. We have an elevator. You'll use it. Now I did some tidying up, as you shall see. And there were volunteers."

"Like the ones at the house? Whoever did it, they worked a miracle. It didn't stink at all and I could barely tell anything even happened."

"I put out a call for volunteers, and I have to tell you, it was gratifying." He seemed very satisfied with himself. "Very gratifying."

"Really?" We chugged upward, past the second floor. "You'll have to tell me who it was so I can thank them."

"Too many to name," he said with an airy wave of his hand. "Now we did what we could in the time we had, so don't expect too much," he warned when the car rumbled to a stop.

"I don't expect anything." *Dust, disuse, closed up smell, airless and ugly, ancient wallpaper, dirty shower.* Those were my memories of the last time I was in the third floor apartment. I had retreated hastily when the aroma of stale cigarettes, old spaghetti, and disuse filled my head.

"Voila. Your new abode." Alan flung open the elevator door and I stepped . . .

. . . into a dream world.

I walked through a small entry foyer wallpapered in a cheery yellow stripe. It was large enough to hold a table, an umbrella stand, and a coat rack on which hung two of my summer jackets. I peeked through the doorway and goggled at what I saw.

The room in front of me was once shades of brown: brown carpet, dirty beige walls, faded brown-and-white wallpaper, dusty faded white woodwork. I walked into a bright, shining, clean room.

"What the hell?" The last time I saw this space it was bare, dusty, and it reeked of *old*: old wallpaper, old floors, old woodwork, old dusty windows, years of disuse which settled into its cracks and seams.

Now it sparkled. A fresh coat of creamy yellow paint made the walls glow. A cheerful flowered border paper hugged the gleaming white crown molding near the ceiling. The wood floors were burnished a deep cherry color and area rugs in shades of pale green and dark burgundy contrasted beautifully with the shining wood. The woodwork was polished and appeared positively warm to the touch. The windows were so clear I blinked twice to make sure they were actually closed.

"What happened?" I walked forward into the living room. I turned, marveling at the overstuffed chintz sofa, the matching hassock, the two armchairs with high backs, the television mounted on the brick wall between two tall windows.

On the far side of the space was a little dining area where a white table and four mismatched white chairs sat, each with a different happily patterned cushion in yellows and greens. Next to it and through a doorway was a tiny galley kitchen, which shared a wall with the Pub's third-floor storage. I could hear the hum of the machines on the other side of the wall, and there was a faint aroma of hops.

The last time I saw the kitchen it screamed *old*, with grimy brown cupboards and a chipped countertop.

Now the cupboards were all whitewashed and the counter, a dark rose color, shone with a soft glow from the lights under the cabinets. The petite fridge and stove were older models but gleaming white and so clean. At the far end of the room sat a large water dish and two kitty bowls.

"Everybody pitched in," Alan said, laughter in his voice. "All the bars in town stocked your glassware. Isabel Fitz donated the dishes. The Dog and Pony restaurant donated the silverware. Marianne Archer gave you the desk. The ladies' golf league bought the couch and the chairs." He kept talking, walking around the apartment, touching furniture, paintings, an afghan, all donated by someone I knew.

"John and I chipped in on a new computer," he said, going to the desk positioned against the wall near the elevator. He opened the lid on a bright red laptop. "If you want a monitor, we can get one and hook it up so you can have a desktop system again."

"No, I'd love to have a laptop. I always wanted one but never thought I could afford one. But I don't understand—when did you—how did you—why—"

"Come on, I'll show you the bedroom." Alan led the way through a doorway opposite the kitchen. A tiny hall led to a bedroom on the left and a bathroom on the right. The bedroom was small, barely containing a double bed, a large dresser, and a standing mirror and an armoire. "All the furniture came from the Forest and Glen antique store. It was a steal. The baseball team bought it and set it up."

I turned slowly, taking it all in. The four-poster bed was angled in the corner, sitting on a pale green braided rug. To the right and to the left of the bed was a window through which streamed late afternoon sunlight. "I don't believe this. It's like night and day."

Alan went back into the tiny hall and opened the door to the bathroom, a long, narrow rectangular space. A claw-foot tub with shower arm above, a toilet, a tiny sink were all immaculately white and shining in a room with pale green walls.

"There's even a closet here." He opened what appeared to be a wall to reveal a ten-foot length of closet space in which my clothes were neatly aligned, shoes underneath and my two spare purses hanging on a hook. "It's not convenient in the bedroom, so that's why we got the wardrobe. And see." He pulled aside a four-foot tall screen at the far end of the space to reveal a covered litter box. "Kitty place."

I gaped at it, and at him. "But when did this all get done? The last time I saw this place it was a mess." I turned around the tiny but *glowing* bathroom, light streaming in from the tall windows over the bathtub.

"All night. We got started on it before you fell asleep." He touched the tub and rubbed his fingers. "We finished about an hour ago. The two drugstores in town donated the shower curtain and all the other stuff." He pulled open the old-fashioned medicine chest to show me the bottles of aspirin, boxes of bandages, tweezers, nail files, and other assorted bathroom miscellany.

"But—but—"

"Come here, let me show you this, it's really cool." He led me back to the bedroom and picked up a remote control from the low bedside table. "See, it controls your heating and air conditioning. It's one of those special self-contained units. I figured the temperature up here might be iffy because there's only radiator heat and you know we keep it cool downstairs. And in the summer it's liable to be warm because of all the windows."

"It feels comfortable now. And it's so full of light. How?"

He clicked a few buttons and I noticed a large white box set high on the wall began to hum. Cool air drifted to us. "See. It's called a ductless air system. You can heat or cool each room individually." He pointed to a booklet on the side table. "Read all about it. Come on. Let me show you how the TV works."

I followed him into the living room and sank onto the sofa, onto *my* sofa, twisting on the seat to examine the space. "Oh, who did that?" I pointed to the two kitty condos, one positioned at each window above the street below.

"John did. He said you needed matching cat furniture."

I sat back. "But why? Why would all these people help me?" I turned to Alan.

"At one time or another, you've helped almost everybody in town."

"Oh, no." I leaned forward to examine the wooden steamer trunk which served as a coffee table. "I haven't done anything."

"Sure you have. You've listened to the woes of the world while bartending." He stood near a window, smiling at me. "I think you need to eat your words."

"What?"

"Remember when I said people can surprise us by the good in them, too? You didn't believe me, did you?"

I shook my head, unable to speak.

"Guess we proved you wrong."

I stared around the room, awestruck. "You sure did. I don't know what to say."

He sat down and put an arm around my shoulders. "You deserve it, Tuck. You've never asked anybody for any help. This time we decided to help you whether you want it or not."

I leaned my head on his shoulder. "Thanks, Alan."

The loud clanking of the elevator broke our tender moment. I twisted around at the sound but grimaced when I found I couldn't twist because of bruising. "Damn, I can't wait to feel better," I griped while I stood.

"We'll have to get a key for the elevator," Alan said. "You need privacy up here and security." He walked to the small foyer and I followed.

We waited as the elevator made its laborious descent then reversed itself to rise up. When the door finally opened, the packed space emptied of people, laughing. "Send it back for more," Lee Knight said as he left. "We've got a crowd waiting downstairs."

"I'll take it down and get back to work." Alan kissed me on the cheek. "Enjoy your new digs, Tuck."

I was swept into the living room on the tide of people who all told me how they conspired to get the apartment ready for me in record time. I discovered that my liquor cabinet, an old refinished icebox near the kitchen, was fully stocked and soon the elevator disgorged another group and a party was in full swing, complete with cake, snacks, and music provided by a new portable MP3 player stuck into portable speakers.

"I can't believe you guys did all this," I said for the hundredth time to another townsperson who gleefully showed me yet another feature of my new apartment. "I'm overwhelmed."

"We were happy to help. Heck, everybody has something they can donate, even if it's only their time. I'm so glad you like the color. John Smalley thought you'd like green."

"Where is John?" I looked around the crowded room.

"Oh, he'll be by later, I'm sure. He was here all night, painting and cleaning and directing traffic. Between him and Alan, we knew this place would be finished in time."

I drifted to the kitchen and leaned against the counter, still marveling that all of this was *mine*. I now had a place to live. I didn't have to worry about going back and trying to forget all that happened in my house. I could stay here, get the house ready to sell, and not have to worry about a mortgage payment once I sold the house.

Well, of course, I did have a mortgage payment. We had the loan on the building, but it was the Acorn's mortgage, not mine. I made a mental note to talk to Alan and Miller about that and see if I couldn't chip in more, since now I owned a residential interest in the place.

Rob Huntington poked his head around the corner. "There she is, the woman of the hour." He came into the room, a drink in hand. "How are you feeling? I heard you were in a car accident and in the hospital. What the heck happened?"

"Car accident, home invasion. You name it, I've had it." I raised my hands to take in the immaculate little kitchen. "And now here I am. How are you doing?" He seemed exhausted, but at least it appeared he'd shaved and showered at some point, because he no longer was wrinkled and tired.

He shrugged. "I'm hanging in there. Waiting for the axe to fall, I guess."

My good cheer began to evaporate. "You mean at the factory?"

He nodded and took a sip of the amber-colored liquid in his glass. "You've got a lot of great friends. People donated almost everything. What wasn't donated, Alan or John bought." He examined the small stove, a miniature apartment-sized model in sparkling white. "A tragedy like what happened to you really shows you who your friends are."

"I was totally shocked by what happened to me at my house but I think I'm even more shocked by how generous people have been. I had no idea people would help me like this."

Rob frowned, eyeing the dishes stacked on the counter. "Who gave you these?"

"Isabel Fitz. She said she didn't use them anymore. Aren't they pretty?" I didn't tell him what was in the note Isabel tucked in one of the elegant coffee cups. *I hope you enjoy using this china, Tuck. PJ bought it for me a long time ago and I never got around to using it.* I suspected more of a story than her simple explanation, but I wasn't going to pry unless Isabel offered more information. I planned to enjoy the pretty floral pattern on the Noritake dishes, a big step up from the department store ceramic dishes I used to have for daily use.

"I wonder what people would do if it was me in trouble," Rob said, taking a swallow from the glass in his hand.

"What?" I dragged my attention from the china and back to Rob.

"You see how people came out of the woodwork to help you. I wonder if the same thing would happen if it was me."

I stared at him, confused. "I'm sure they would, Rob."

"Would they?"

He seemed profoundly depressed by the idea. "Pray you never need to find out," I said. "Believe me, you don't want to have your house trashed in order to find how people feel."

He took another swallow of liquor. "Why was it done, do you know?"

"I have no idea. I think it has the police stumped, too."

"The police?"

"Yes, the police. They were over there, taking fingerprints and pictures and God knows what. I know I saw some footprints in the flour tossed all over the place, and the print was a much bigger size than mine." I held up my foot, wiggling it so he could see my size five sneaker. "Given all the forensic gadgets they've got, I'm pretty sure they'll track down the person who did it. Heck, I'll bet they can tell what cow the shit came from. At least, that's the way it seems like on TV when they do their forensic stuff."

"Cow?"

I wrinkled my nose. "You don't want to know."

"I never thought of that. I mean, I never figured the police would investigate."

"Holy crap, of course they would. What did you think I'd do, pack up and run away?" He must be *really* drunk if that's what he thought. "John said it wasn't only a malicious prank, and I agree. It was personal and it was targeted at me. Of course I called the police."

"John? John Smalley? He saw it?" Rob took another swallow, dribbling some onto his chin. He wiped the dampness with the sleeve of his pale yellow shirt.

"Yes, he drove me home from the hospital."

"Hospital?"

"Car accident, remember?" How many drinks did he have? I'd need a lock for the liquor cabinet if I wasn't careful.

"Oh, yeah. That's right." He seemed to perk up, nodding vigorously. "I heard Guy hit you yesterday morning. Have the police arrested him?"

I frowned. "I don't know. So much has happened between now and then, I sort of lost track." I made a mental note to ask Alan or Owen about it. "The last I heard, somebody mentioned the police had a search warrant and they were at his house."

"Why would he want to hurt you?" Rob asked.

"I have no idea. I also have no idea why he'd want to steal my purse." I shook my head, exasperated anew at all I lost when someone took my purse. "I spent an hour today trying to get replacement identification and credit cards. Tomorrow I'll tackle the cell phone. There's no way I can go back and get my backups, though." As soon as I said it, I wanted to take the words back. *Well, why does it matter who I tell? I turned in the files, so I'm off the hook.*

"Really? You carry backups in your purse?" Rob's voice was faintly mocking.

"Yep. Lucky for me, it wasn't the only copy of some really important files."

He took another swallow of his drink. "Yeah, lucky you. How bad was it at your house? What about your home computer? Maybe you can get your backups there."

"No, the computer was trashed. But the backup I stored in the house is fine. Now the police have it, so I don't have to worry anymore." I started to move past him to rejoin the party. Rob stood in my way, though, filling the small kitchen with his inert body.

He seemed to shake himself from his trance. "You made backups of your backups?" He tilted his head and frowned, obviously confused.

"Yeah. Silly, but I'm glad I did it. What's the word about PJ's death? Have you heard anything else? Did you talk to Richard Fitz? How's it going at the factory?"

"We talked by phone," Rob said. "I haven't seen him, yet. I'm sure if I could talk to him in person, if I tell him what PJ did, maybe Richard and I can figure a way to handle it."

"Don't you think the best way to handle it would be by telling the truth for a change?" Marianne asked from the doorway.

Awkward. Feuding husband and wife at the same party. Oops. I attempted to alleviate the tension. "Marianne, thank you so much for the desk." I moved to her side, hoping she'd go with me, back into the living room, away from her drunken husband. "I'm sure I'll get so much use from it."

"You're welcome, Tuck," she said perfunctorily. "Well, Rob?" Marianne seemed to float when she moved, the effect of her gossamer skirt composed of many layers of lightweight, sheer pink-flowered cloth. "Why don't you tell the truth for once?"

"You're a fine one to talk about truth, Marianne," Rob said in a controlled, low voice. "You've lied to yourself and to me all your life." His eyes went to her hand and the ruby ring. "You lied about that. Guy gave it to you, didn't he? Why did you lie about that?"

Oh, boy. We're hitting too close to the bone here. Time to break this up. "This isn't really the time or the place to discuss this." I held up my uninjured hand. "I'm sure you both have a grief or two you'd like to air, but don't you think you should save it for a marriage counselor?"

"Counseling?" Marianne's voice dripped with disdain. "Why would I bother? Rob has lied to me since the day we got married. Why would I believe anything he said in a counseling session? You told me we were broke, Rob. Why did you lie about that?"

"What?" I turned from her to Rob. "You said you were broke."

"We aren't," Marianne snapped. "He wanted me to think it."

"You don't know how bad it is," Rob said. "Guy told me to invest—"

"Guy did nothing of the kind. He told me all about it." Marianne seemed afire with indignation. "Right before he left town, he told me how you lied."

"What do you mean?" Rob asked, eyes narrowed and his shoulders taut. All trace of drunkenness was gone. He seemed as predatory as Marianne was angry.

"He told me about the bank account you set up. You saved all the money you got from the sale of the hardware store. There were no debts to clear up. You lied to me."

This is getting bad. "I think you need to take this somewhere else."

"Why do you believe Guy but not me?" Rob demanded. He advanced on Marianne, his fists clenched.

"Wait a minute, wait a minute." I stepped between the two of them. "Marianne, you go to the living room right now. Rob, back off."

Rob tried to grab Marianne's arm. I pushed at him and banged my broken fingers against his shoulder, almost fainting from pain. "Damn it, Rob, get back," I wheezed.

Marianne was suddenly jerked to one side and John Smalley filled the doorway, his white shirt strained across his chest, emphasizing his heavy forearms. "Go sit down, Marianne," he rumbled. He turned to me. "Need some help, Tuck?"

I nodded gratefully. "Keep Rob in here while I get rid of Marianne."

"No problem." John crossed his arms, fixing Rob with a steady gaze. "Relax."

I went to the living room in time to see Marianne disappearing into the foyer, joining some other guests getting in to the elevator. I returned to the kitchen. "She's gone." I stared at Rob, who glared at John.

"What did she mean about the money, Rob? You told me you were broke."

"It's none of your damn business," he snarled, brushing past me and almost knocking me over when he bolted from the room.

"It makes no sense. Marianne is talking about secret bank accounts. What the hell is going on?"

"I have no idea, Tuck." John regarded me shyly. "Do you like your new place?"

"John, I love it." I impulsively reached over and tried to hug him. Of course, there was so much of him it was hard to do.

He returned the hug, not squeezing much, which was good because I was bruised just about everywhere he might squeeze. "Good." He stared down at me and I looked up at him.

I almost got up on my tiptoes to kiss him. I saw his hesitation then his head began to bend to meet me. But someone called my name so I left, glancing back at him. He winked at me.

Hmm. My future might be getting interesting.

Chapter 16

I spent what remained of Wednesday evening settling into my new apartment. The guests were gone by nine o'clock when Alan brought the kittens and my few belongings from his house. He lingered for a while, helping me clean up from my Welcome party.

While we washed dishes, I told him about Rob and Marianne's argument. "Rob gave me this big sob story about how broke he was and now Marianne is saying he's got money salted away. What's that all about?"

"How would Marianne know?" Alan asked. "Unless Rob chose to share information with her, the only way she'd find out is if he died and she inherited, right?"

I considered it. "True. If he opened accounts in his own name, she might not ever know. Wouldn't it be awful, to be married to someone and then discover he's living a double life?"

"And especially for Marianne." Alan folded his dishtowel and hung it on the stove handle. "Don't forget, she waited years to marry Rob because he said he didn't have enough money. I think she finally gave him an ultimatum and it's what pushed him into marriage. I'm sure she's regretted it all these years because if she played her cards right, she could have married Guy and lived in the lap of luxury."

"Poor Rob. And poor Marianne." I took my wine glass and went into my living room. *My* living room. "Have a seat," I said, gesturing to *my* new armchairs.

"Nope. You're tired and so am I." Alan yawned. "I was up most of the night decorating. You know, John did a lot of the work himself. I think he has his eye on you."

I shook my head. "Don't play matchmaker, Alan."

"Oh, I don't think that's needed. I think John will take care of it all by himself."

I smiled while I walked with him to the elevator. This place already felt like home, with magazines from my house on the coffee table and a kitten curled up on each condo, a small heap of fur silhouetted against the window. "Thank you so much for doing this, Alan. It means a lot to me."

"I was glad to do it, Tuck. Now don't forget. Miller will set the security alarm when he closes the Pub tonight. I'm usually the first one here in the morning so I'll deactivate it. If you need to go out in between those times, punch in the security code in the restaurant and leave."

I nodded. Alan already drilled me in security procedures twice. "I'm going to take a pill and go to sleep," I promised.

"We'll get someone to examine the elevator and get a key system set up. I don't want anyone having access to your apartment unless you give them the okay."

"Good idea." I wasn't really worried since the only people who might possibly come upstairs were restaurant employees, but he was probably right. "I'm surprised how quiet it is. I was worried I might hear the

Parlor or the Pub. Or smell the food, which, delectable though it might be, I don't want to smell all the time."

"They made these old buildings to last." He stepped into the elevator cage. "Solid and impenetrable. Good night, Tuck."

"Thanks again, Alan." I leaned in and kissed him then the door closed and I was alone.

I went back to the living room and curled up on the sofa, relishing the quiet, the cleanliness, and the cozy little space. It was probably half the size of my house, but it was adequate. Hell, it was more than adequate, it was charming. My house was a mish-mash of furniture and styles, but this apartment had Alan's touch, which somehow managed to coordinate the odd assortment of furniture and furnishings into one cohesive, relaxing whole.

I sipped a glass of wine, content to simply watch the windows darken while the sun slowly set. The last few days were filled with a jumble of emotion: grief, fear, anger, anxiety, and confusion were the ones that sprang immediately to mind. It seemed like everyone in this drama was hurt in some way.

Poor Will, killed in a farm field.

Rob Huntington, who now faced censure or jail time.

Marianne Archer, who apparently was betrayed by the man she married.

PJ Fitz, who died in the back of an SUV.

Isabel Fitz, who now faced a life totally different than the one she knew.

The only one who wasn't hurt was Richard Fitz, who appeared to be managing all the bumps with amazing calmness and aplomb. If things continued like they were going, he'd get off scot free, his factory would probably be exonerated of all charges, and the Fitz conglomerate would continue making money hand over fist.

I glared at my dark TV screen, angry at fate.

Then I remembered the moment with John Smalley in the kitchen. I think it embarrassed both of us a bit, but it also intrigued me for sure, and I think it intrigued John, too. I got ready for bed in my new bedroom, wondering what it would be like to have a man in my life again after so many years without. I decided it might be interesting as long as he wasn't there full-time. I wasn't cut out for a full-time relationship anymore.

"May not be an issue," I said to the kittens, who made themselves at home at the foot of the bed. "Let's cross that bridge if we get to it."

With that comforting thought I swallowed the last of my wine and went blissfully to sleep.

****

Thursday morning dawned clear and bright with a crisp coolness in the air, unusual for Iowa in June. I opened all the windows in the apartment, something that worried me at first lest small kittens push against a screen and tumble out. But I checked all of the windows and the screens appeared to be super strong and held quite firmly. So I decided to hope for the best and I opened up the apartment to allow the cool morning breezes inside.

I didn't have my exercise room anymore, so I'd need to find a substitute until I could figure what to do. I dressed in shorts and a blouse then went to the Parlor's kitchen at nine o'clock. I found Alan already sitting at the center island, sipping a cup of coffee while he considered today's menu.

"We can move your exercise gear to the second floor," he said when I mentioned my concern. "There's room underneath your apartment for it. We'll have to rearrange some of the things we have in storage there. In fact, it might be good to let the cats prowl around there, too. We've been lucky so far with controlling mice, but having two hunters patrol the space would be useful."

"Isn't it against city code or something?"

"Nope. They can't be in the food and drink part of the building on the first floor or the equipment for the brewpub on the second floor. We can easily block off a section and let the cats into the exercise area."

"You think of everything." I filled a cup of coffee before pulling up a stool and sitting.

"I've worried about the second floor storage for a while," he admitted. "We only go up there once a year or so to get holiday decorations. It would be a perfect place for mice to nest. Having two cats checking it on a regular basis should handle any problem."

I sipped my coffee and marveled at how Alan's mind worked. I tended to focus on day-to-day things like stocking the bar or handling customers. Alan always thought a month or two ahead, anticipating problems before they arose. I told him as such.

"That's why we're successful," he said. "You notice the here and now. I think about the there and then. I contacted the football coach at the high school. He said some of the boys like to earn extra money doing moving. So I asked them to handle the exercise stuff. I hope that's okay. I figured the treadmill and your elliptical machine might have to be disassembled and maybe jocks could figure it out." He grinned at me.

"I would never have thought of it," I admitted.

"Actually, Owen suggested it. I implemented it. So what are you going to do today?"

"Work."

"Oh, no. You need to rest. Besides, today is Thursday. It's your day off."

"I've had a lot of days off lately. I'll just drop in and see how things are going."

"Well, as long as that's all you do. I think Miller planned to come in and open. I know he has someone lined up to take over later on. Maybe you can drop in before tonight's party."

"What party?"

"Did you forget? It's the kickoff for the town's Dodransbicentennial celebration. We're closing the Parlor early so the staff can go."

"I can't believe you can pronounce that. I didn't even know there was a word for a 175th anniversary."

"I practiced it. There's a party in the park tonight to kick things off. It starts at five or so. From what I've read in the paper, Richard Fitz is slated to speak after they get the celebration rolling. First they're going to present the Golden Arrow award."

"Who's getting it this year?" I asked. The Golden Arrow was voted on by the city council and was presented to a business person who helped Barnsdale's economy in the previous year. It was like a Businessman of the Year award, but with our own local Robin Hood touch. I secretly wanted the award, but so far we never got it. That golden arrow would be a nice addition, hanging over the cash register in the Pub.

"I *heard*," and here Alan winked at me, "it might be John Smalley's turn."

Any envy I felt about the recipient vanished. "Oh, that would be nice. He's worked hard to get his organic business running smoothly. It does a lot to have a business like his offset the reputation of the Yoke."

"No kidding. We could use some good publicity."

I sipped my coffee. "I might call John and see if we can go to the farm he's thinking about buying, to get an idea of how much renovation it needs. If we want to really consider his plan, we'll need to start thinking about a budget."

"Good thought," Alan said with an impish grin.

"What?" I demanded.

"Nothing, nothing. Make sure you don't overdo it today, doing whatever it is you're going to be doing." He dodged my playful slap. "Seriously, take care of yourself. You're still pretty banged up from the car accident. Speaking of which, when do you get wheels?"

"Today, I hope. I need to go upstairs and make some calls." I glanced around the pristine kitchen. "I'll try to stay out of your way with my comings and goings."

"I've been thinking about it." Alan pulled over a notepad on which was a rough diagram, drawn in pencil. "We could put in an outside entrance for you. That way you won't have to go through the kitchen to get to the freight elevator. See, if we get rid of the window here and move the sink, we can put a doorway in. You'll be able to come and go without having to be in the middle of traffic, so to speak."

"That's perfect," I said. "And I'll pay for it."

"No, we'll pay for it."

"I'll pay for it," I insisted. "And I'll pay rent."

We quibbled amiably for a few minutes, then it was finally decided I'd pay for the construction and would contribute four hundred dollars a month into a special savings account which we could use for redecorating or remodeling. "There's no need to pay on the building mortgage," Alan said. "We already have it covered through the business account, so why muddy the waters?"

"You're right. This way we can build up a little fund for repairs and redecorating."

"I know you won't let me touch the Pub, but I have ideas for the Parlor." He grinned when I groaned. "It won't be anything huge, just a tweak here and there. But it's for later. Now you'd better shoo, I need to get going for the day."

I went back up to my apartment and called my insurance agent, who assured me a loaner car was ready for me whenever I wanted to pick it up. A check would come to me for a replacement car and a separate check coming for the damage to my house. The second check would be relatively small because there was no structural problem, only a psychological one. I decided to use the money for redecorating and getting the house ready for sale.

I marveled again at how much like home this apartment felt. Although it was only half the width of the building, it felt light and airy. Tall windows on the north, east, and south meant the space was almost always bathed in brightness. I heard and felt the vibration of the machines on the first floor while our beer was brewed, but it wasn't intrusive. The faint aroma of hops, mash, and barley mixed with the grass and flower smells from the outside world.

"I'm home," I said to Cayenne, who was stretched full-length in the front window, staring down at the street. He yawned in agreement and settled in for a nap.

I took a few minutes to make a shopping list then I grabbed one of my old purses from the closet. Armed with my remaining credit cards and my shopping list, I headed out.

I walked first to Staibler's car dealership, not far from the pub, where my loaner car awaited me. "I'm glad to see you up and around," Harry 'Horse' Staibler said. "It sounded like a bad accident."

Sounded like meant the news of my car accident and house trashing was probably all over town. *Gotta love the Small Town Telegraph.* "I'm walking and I'm happy," I said, holding up my bandaged hand. "A couple of broken fingers is a small price to pay."

"The insurance folks said to get you something like what you used to drive and I figured this was close." He winked elaborately at me.

I regarded the sleek new sporty Malibu. The only thing it had in common with my old Malibu was the fact they were both red. This newer, updated version was more like a Mustang than a Mom-Mobile. "Thanks, Horse."

He gave me a few lessons on where the bells and whistles were, including the keyless ignition which I immediately loved. I signed a bunch of papers and an hour later I was driving again. I headed for town and my bank. It would be only a short walk from the bank to the clothing stores, where hopefully I could score the items I needed to replace from my old purse. I could tackle the cell phone problem by going to the mall on the outskirts of town. With luck, I'd be done in an hour.

That was optimistic. I didn't anticipate the amount of paperwork involved when one loses one's identification. I needed to open new accounts at the bank, transfer things, get a new driver's license at the courthouse, put a hold on this, and put alerts on that. And there was the whole problem of my mobile phone, which I had to prove was lost by producing the police report.

By early afternoon I replaced almost everything except for my peace of mind. I returned to the Acorn and made my way through the kitchen, which was starting to slow after the lunch rush. I resolved to make sure the construction work was done quickly on an exterior entrance. I went upstairs, showed the kitties my purchases (they were not impressed) and settled in for a quick nap.

Two hours later, I woke up, groggy and grumpy from oversleeping. But the rest did me a world of good. My ribs still hurt, but they didn't remind me with every breath. My broken fingers hurt, but now they only throbbed. And my scraped elbows and face now tingled slightly instead of burning with every movement.

I was on the mend. I decided to celebrate by going to work. I dressed in sneakers, capris and a gold Acorn shirt and went downstairs. It was almost empty, which confused me at first until I remembered the party and the Parlor closing early.

Alan was in the dining room, turning the *Open* sign to *Closed.* "I called a guy to come and give me an estimate on the doorway. And I talked to the elevator company, which, surprise, is still in business. They can re-key it on Monday."

"I should have done it. I'm the one who's loafing around. You're busy."

"You know what they say. Give the busiest person the most work. They'll get it done fast." He grinned when he said it so I knew there were no hard feelings. "Where are you off to?"

"I'm going to check in at the Pub before going over to the park."

"I think I'll join you. That sounds like a good plan." He waved me ahead of him and we passed through the Parlor door and entered the Pub.

I was only gone a few days, but it felt like years. I swept my gaze around the room, expecting to see changes. But it all was the same, from the burnished wood to the mirrors behind the liquor walls in between windows by the brewery.

Miller was behind the bar and he waved when we came in. "How are you doing?"

Alan and I took seats at the far end of the bar. "I'm doing okay." I held up my taped fingers. "I can't get into a fight for a while, but other than that, I'm mobile."

Miller filled two glasses with wine and set them in front of us. "On the house," he said with a grin. "It's good to see you, Tuck. We were worried about you for a while."

"It's good to be here, Miller. Thanks for filling in for me. I'll come back on duty tomorrow."

"No worries. We'll set a schedule. You can't do full time for a while, but we'll figure something." He meandered off to fill a barmaid's order.

I took a sip of wine, savoring the feeling of home, once again. I spent most of my waking hours in this pub and I enjoyed it. I didn't consider this work. This was Home with a capital H. Now I didn't have to separate Home from home. I had it all. Life. Is. Good.

"Here comes trouble," Alan said softly a few minutes later.

I followed his gaze and saw Richard Fitz enter the pub, an older woman with him and behind them, Isabel Fitz and Rob Huntington. They were all dressed in what I thought of as "the sporting set" clothing. Pressed dark pants for the men, tailored summer skirts for the women, and crisp shirts and blouses. I was surprised to see Rob in anything other than jeans and a summer shirt. He seemed out of place, like the Professor next to Thurston Howell the Third.

They took a table in a quiet corner, and placed orders with the barmaid. I watched Miller fill the order. One white wine, one Deacon's Downfall, a gin and tonic, and bourbon straight with water on the side. The gin was Old Raj, our best stock, and the bourbon was Maker's Mark. I shook my head when the bar maid set the bourbon in front of Rob.

"That's a mistake," I said.

Alan peered over his shoulder. "I haven't seen her in years."

"Who?"

"Eleanor Fitz. She's Richard's mother. And Isabel's mother-in-law."

I eyed the quartet in the corner. "Gin and tonic."

"And I'll bet she asked for the best in the house. That's Eleanor. Only the best for her and her children. I think the only reason she didn't send the kids to private school was old Henry, her husband, insisted they be raised here among the people they would later enslave."

I raised an eyebrow. "That's a bit harsh."

"So is she."

"I'm going to thank Isabel for the china," I said, slipping off my bar seat.

"I'm not sure that's such a good idea," Alan cautioned. "She may not have told Richard or Eleanor she donated it or to who."

I hesitated. Isabel saw me and waved me over to them. "Well, here goes."

"Don't say I didn't warn you." Alan turned, smiling at Isabel and nodding at Richard and Eleanor. The old woman gave a frosty nod in return.

I made my way through the crowded pub, greeting people while I went. The old woman watched my progress with thinly disguised disapproval. She reminded me of Maggie Smith, who played one of the professors in the Harry Potter movies—tall, thin, white-haired, sour-faced, and oozing with good breeding. Like my momma would say, she was so stuck up she could drown in a rainstorm.

"Isabel, thank you for helping me get back on my feet again," I said when I reached the table. "I appreciate it so much." *There. I was tactful. No mention of fancy china.*

"I was happy to do it." Isabel smiled warmly at me. Her dark hair was once again pulled back into a chignon and she wore dangling gold earrings which sparkled when she turned her head. It made her seem youthful and energetic despite the dark pants and staid blouse she wore. "I don't know if you've ever met my mother-in-law. Eleanor, this is Tucker Frye, the proprietress of the Acorn."

The old woman nodded regally to me. "Miss Frye. I heard you've had a series of unfortunate accidents. How terrible for you."

"Not really accidents. Oh, Guy hit me by accident, and a woman fell on me by accident, but the car crash was deliberate."

"Guy Gibson?" The old woman shifted her attention to Richard. "Guy?"

Rob cleared his throat. "Guy and I were having a disagreement and Tucker unfortunately got in the middle."

"They were fighting," I clarified. "And I stepped in. Guy hit me." I shifted a bit, wincing when my bruised ribs made themselves felt. "And he kicked me. I think he kicked me on purpose. My momma always said that I draw trouble to me like a magnet draws iron. I guess my talent hasn't faded with time." I smiled at Richard, who frowned at my ill manners.

"It's hard to believe," Eleanor said. "Guy was such a nice boy."

I almost laughed. I'm sure she remembered Guy differently than a lot of his contemporaries did. "My condolences on the loss of your son. I'm sure his death was a shock."

She drew herself up, the very picture of an aristocratic woman bearing up under severe distress. "Thank you. Yes, Patrick's death was unfortunate."

Yeah, dying in the back of an SUV with his pants around his ankles. That's unfortunate, alright. I caught Isabel's eye and choked back my laughter at the suppressed humor I saw there. I turned to Richard.

"You said something about a memorial? I want to attend if I can."

A shocked stillness settled over the table. Richard regarded his beer glass. "I planned to speak tonight but I was told it might not be appropriate. So we will have a private service tomorrow before the burial."

"Oh." I wasn't sure what else to say.

Rob had his own ideas, though. "Yeah, apparently the city council didn't think it would be good to let Richard talk about PJ—Patrick—at the party. I don't know why. PJ was a leading citizen in town. It only makes sense Richard should be allowed to talk about his brother." He sipped his bourbon, his expression a mix of defiance and complicity.

Richard raised his eyes. "It's irrelevant what the city council thinks."

Okay, Rob. Leave it, I silently pleaded.

But no. Rob needed to put his whole foot in it. "I still say despite everything that's happened, it's only fair you be allowed to talk about Patrick."

"After what, exactly?" Richard's icy tone would have frozen me in my tracks, but Rob was either too drunk or too anxious to score points to notice.

"Well, the issues that came to light at the factory in York. I overheard the discussions between you and the Federal investigators." Rob turned a pitying look in Eleanor's direction, like he commiserated with the old harridan. "I was manager at the plant but I only did what PJ said to do. I'm sure once the investigations conclude, they'll show—"

"They won't be able to show anything, will they?" Richard said coolly. "Patrick is dead so he can't defend himself. It will be your word against a dead man's.

How will we know what is real and what isn't? How will we know who told you to do what?" His steely gaze held Rob's.

My stomach lurched. So that's how it would play out. Rob would be tossed to the dogs and the Fitz family would be exonerated of any wrongdoing. Poor Rob. So much for Richard treating him like a brother. It was like watching a puppy being thrown to the wolves.

Rob sat in frozen shock, disbelief evident in his slack face, his wide-eyed stare. "What?" he whispered. "What do you mean?"

"You heard me." Richard glanced at his mother, who gave a slight tilt of her head. "You were given the job and given authority to run the factory. Now there's a lawsuit pending against the company because of gross incompetence and dangerous business practices. Our accountants have discovered some unusual entries during the latest audit. And my brother, a man who was in a position to reveal the true facts about the workings of the factory, is now dead. His death is quite a convenience, isn't it?"

Rob lurched to his feet, almost falling over when the chair fell behind him. "What are you saying, Richard? I did what PJ asked me to do. What are you saying?"

"Rob—" I put a hand on his arm but he shook me off.

"I suggest you hire a lawyer, Rob." Richard said it softly. "The Fitz Corporation cannot be responsible for your legal fees. It wouldn't be right for our lawyers to represent you while they also represent the interests of the company."

Rob stared down at Richard. Isabel paled so much two bright spots of pink showed on her cheeks where her blush was applied. "Richard, that's wrong," she whispered. "Rob had nothing to do with PJ's death. You know it."

"Be quiet, Isabel," Eleanor said. "Let Richard handle this."

Rob took a staggering step backwards. "I won't let you do this to me. I won't." He turned, pushed me aside, and raced for the door.

I started after him but stopped and turned to face Richard. "What are you doing to him?"

Richard raised his beer glass. "Me? Nothing. Rob has done it all to himself."

I looked from him to the old woman, who merely stared back at me like I was some form of insect.

I picked up Rob's glass of bourbon and tossed it in Richard's face. "You're the sort of man who would steal straw from his mother's kennel. Get out of my bar."

Chapter 17

"Apologize to my mother," Richard said, his voice deadly quiet. His face was so red I thought it might explode. His hands, clenched on the table, told me what would happen if he got those hands on me.

"Like hell I will," I spat.

Richard stood, glaring at me over the table. "How dare you insult her or my family." He moved behind his mother, heading for me.

"Are you threatening me?" I drew myself up to my full height, facing up to him when he towered over me. "Go ahead. I'm not afraid of you."

"You'll hear from our lawyer. You can't act like this." The old lady stared up at me, her chin quivering. On any other old woman's face, I'd say she was hurt. But on this woman's face all I saw was anger. Her son stood behind her, one hand protectively on her shoulder.

"I did act like this," I corrected. "Isabel can stay but I want you and your son to leave."

Richard leaned over and put a hand under the old woman's arm. "Mother, let's go." He straightened, helping his mother to her feet. His eyes met mine and I saw pure, unadorned hatred there. "You haven't heard the end of this."

"Bring it on. It's my bar. I can serve who I want."

"No, it's our bar."

I turned and saw Alan and Miller behind me. Alan met Richard's stare with one equally as cold. "Get out, Richard. Now. You aren't wanted here."

"Here?" Richard peered around the bar, his disdain saying volumes about what he thought of our establishment.

"Yes, here," Alan said. "I'm sure this will come as a surprise, but the Fitz family isn't exactly loved in this town."

Eleanor grabbed her purse from the table. "Isabel, we're going."

Isabel remained seated. "I think I'll stay. I see no reason to leave."

"We were insulted," the old woman said.

"Isabel wasn't insulted," I said. "I've got nothing against her."

"Fine." Richard gently tugged his mother toward the door, pausing to regard his sister-in-law. "Isabel, we'll talk to you later. I hope you know what this means."

"Oh, I think I do, Richard." Isabel swirled the wine in her glass. Her hand was trembling but she managed to place the glass on the table without spilling any. "Good night."

Richard paused to fix me with an angry glare then he and Eleanor left, the door slamming shut after them. "Well, that was a bit of Victorian drama, wasn't it?" I said loudly, my gaze intercepting several curious glances from the other patrons. "Sorry about the fuss, folks."

The silent bar around me suddenly broke into a buzz of conversation. Isabel laughed shakily. "You're in trouble now, Tucker."

"I meant what I said. Bring it on. I can't believe that son of a bitch is trying to blame all of his problems on Rob. It isn't fair."

"Shit, life isn't fair, Tucker." Alan held up a hand when I rounded on him. "I'll tell you what. I'll call our lawyer to give her a heads-up in case Richard decides to make good on his threat." He walked away, pulling his cell phone from his pants pocket while he went.

"That asshole." I sank into Rob's chair, trembling. "I guess I shouldn't have thrown the bourbon at him. That might have been over the top."

"Nah. I think it was perfect. He wouldn't have taken you seriously otherwise." Miller gave me a little tap on the shoulder before going back to tend to the bar.

"You don't want to have Richard as an enemy," Isabel said.

"Look who's talking. You're related to him."

"That doesn't matter. He and his mother will get rid of me as soon as they can." When she saw my alarmed expression, she laughed. "No, not that way. They've made me an offer I can't refuse. Richard is the executor of John's will and he's free to interpret it however he likes. He made it clear they'd like distance between me and the Fitz family. I'm getting a big chunk of money to get out of their lives. They'll pay for college for the kids, and Henry Three will get a good job with the company. But I think Richard and Eleanor would like for me to just vanish." Isabel raised her wine glass. "I think I'll take them up on their offer."

I sat back in the chair and sighed. "Probably best for you, for sure. I talked to Alan about the chef idea. He might be interested."

Her eyes lit up. "Do you think so?"

I nodded. "Yeah, we discussed it a bit." The door opened and John Smalley walked in. He seemed different and it took a second for me to notice he'd trimmed his beard closely. It was no longer bushy but instead was more of an outline for his chin, revealing a strong jawline. It made him less outdoorsy and more stylish, especially with the sporty dark brown shirt and the lighter colored khaki pants. *He cleans up good. Real good.*

He carried a large framed certificate and a long narrow case, like one used by florists. I waved him over to join Isabel and me. "Why don't you talk to Alan about it yourself?" I said to Isabel when John paused by our table. "He won't bite. I'm sure he'd be happy to discuss it."

"Did you insult Richard Fitz?" John looked from Isabel to me.

"She did it," Isabel nodded toward me. "And I watched."

"He's madder than hell. He and his mother are ranting about it to Lee Knight. Richard is talking about suing you." John's dark brows drew together into one line when he frowned. "I wouldn't be surprised if he called the cops."

"What? That stupid idiot." I got to my feet. "I'm not going to let him slander me." I glanced at the bar. I saw Alan in the back hallway, near the staff room. "I'm going to the park, Miller," I called out. "Tell Alan, okay?"

He nodded. I turned to John. "Where was Richard? I don't want him yammering all over town without me there to tell my side of the story." I headed for the front door.

"Tucker." I stopped when Isabel put a hand on my arm. "Tucker, be careful. When Richard gets angry, he can be dangerous."

"I'm not worried about him. What's the worst he can do to me?"

"He can make it hard for people who want to do business with you." Isabel nodded when I turned to her in disbelief. "Seriously."

"He doesn't even live here. What does he care?"

"He believes in carrying grudges. Be careful."

"I'll go with you," John volunteered. "Richard has no beef with me. I'll talk to him."

"You don't need to fight my fights for me. I can do it."

John put a hand on the back of my neck and squeezed gently. It was a surprisingly calming gesture and my indignation died. "I'm not fighting any fights," he said. "I'm just helping. You're not weaker because somebody helps you." He moved his hand to my back, and gently urged me to the door. "Let's go deal with him."

Isabel's lips twitched in a faint smile. "Good. Take care of her, John."

"I can handle this." I pushed open the door. Then I remembered my manners, drummed into me so many years ago by my grandma and mama. "But thanks, John, for being my backup." I glimpsed his pleased smile and sent a thankful prayer to my female ancestors for their guidance.

"I saw Richard's mother and Lee leaving the park. Richard and Rob were heading for the other side of the park. I think they were going to the Priory," John said when we emerged from the bar to the street. People were walking in the direction of the park on our right and the band shell in the middle where speeches would be made.

"The Priory?" That was a tiny, ten-foot square building which used to be a coffee shop on the far side of the park. It was deserted now and rundown, mainly housing garden tools and used as a Fright House at Halloween. "Why are they going there? For that matter, why are Richard and Rob even talking to each other? The last time I saw them, Rob was so pissed off he was either going to split a gut or split Richard's face."

"I don't know. Did you know about this?" John showed me the framed certificate.

I took it from him, reading while I walked. "The Golden Arrow award. That's great, John. I wish I was there to see it."

"Totally surprised me." John took the certificate back from me and tucked it under his arm. "I didn't expect it at all."

"Where's the arrow?" I asked, careful to keep an eye on the crowd. The last thing I needed was another fall. With my luck, I'd break something else and there wasn't much on me that was unbruised or unbroken. I needed to preserve what working parts I had.

"Here." He handed me the long green box. I stopped under a tree to open it and peek inside. A long metal arrow, painted gold, lay nestled in white satin lining. Several people walking by stopped to congratulate John while I examined his prize.

"Wow. It's like a real arrow." I hoped my envy didn't show. Damn, that arrow would sure be nice over the bar.

"Except there isn't any fletching." He took the box back from me, wedging it under his arm with the certificate.

"Fletching?" I tried to see through the crowd but couldn't glimpse either Richard or Rob. Most people were heading to our left, where the band shell sat. All of the picnic tables, about a dozen, were full and in the distance I saw people at the softball diamond, the bleachers starting to fill up. It was a perfect night for a picnic and a game, with a gentle breeze, low humidity, and only a few wispy clouds in the pristine blue sky. "What's a fletch?"

"It's the feather part of the arrow at one end, near where you nock the arrow to shoot." John turned aside to talk to a couple who stopped to congratulate him.

I shifted impatiently from one foot to the other, waiting for him. When he finally resumed walking, I said, "I didn't know you knew anything about archery. Where are they?" I tried to peer through the clump of people in front of us but saw nothing but more people.

"I studied archery in college."

"Really? I'm surprised you didn't get recruited for the football team." I dodged a group of teenage girls, all giggles and cell phones.

"The coach tried to recruit me. I didn't enjoy getting tackled. There they are." John pointed ahead but once again he had to stop to accept congratulations. It was several minutes before we shook free from well-wishers and resumed walking.

"Where are they? I can't see anything."

John peered over the heads of the people around us. "I saw Marianne following them. The last I saw they were going to the far side of the park."

"Maybe we should call Owen or somebody. Rob was really pissed off. He might take a swing at Richard." I grinned. "On second thought, let's not call Owen and let Rob take a swing at Richard."

"What happened between them? Rob always idolized Richard. It must be something awful to make him so mad." John moved slightly ahead of me and I followed, letting him cut a path for me through the crowds.

I couldn't think of a quick way to summarize it so I settled for, "Rob thinks Richard is setting him up to take the blame for what happened at the factory."

"Why am I not surprised? Richard always did manage to avoid trouble without getting shit on himself. I think he's led a charmed life."

"Well, if Rob has his way, the charm is ending. He was really mad." There were fewer people on this side of the park, which was on a bluff over the river. A couple of picnic tables in the distance were occupied with wisps of smoke rising from nearby grills, but otherwise all the action was behind us. Most of the townspeople were now grouped around the band shell where the high school band lurched into a rendition of the school's fight song.

I turned slowly, trying to find Rob, Marianne, or Richard. I couldn't see them amongst the different groups. John and I stopped outside the Priory. It was a small building that was rickety and appeared ready to collapse if someone sneezed. There were two windows on each side of the tiny structure, but the broken-out ones nearest us were covered with cardboard and tarp. "Where do you think they are?"

John held up a hand. "Shh." He leaned toward the Priory. "In there," he whispered.

"Should we go in?" I whispered in return, reaching for the faded green door.

"I think you'd better," John said. "Otherwise Richard will make your life miserable."

"True." I opened the door as Rob said,

". . . to happen this way."

"What did you do?" Marianne said in a sobbing voice. "Rob, what did you do?"

"Is Richard here?" I glimpsed Marianne, standing on the far side of the empty ten-by-ten room, near one of the remaining intact dirty windows. Two saggy wooden chairs were against the wall on my left and a line of garden tools leaned against one window near her, but otherwise the place was dusty, musty, and empty.

Rob faced her, something long and wooden in his hands. "Where's Richard Fitz?" I moved inside. "I need to talk to him."

My words faded when I saw Richard in front of me, lying on the scarred wooden floor.

He lay in a pool of blood.

I tried to back up but John pressed against me from behind. "Rob, what happened? Is Richard . . .?" John's voice faded when he saw what I saw.

Is he dead? Oh, yeah, I think he is. I tore my eyes from the sight of Richard Fitz, his neck mostly missing and blood flowing from what used to be his Adam's apple. Rob stood a foot or so from Richard's body. I couldn't tell what he held. It was like a long pole, red at the end. My shocked eyes focused and I saw it was a hefty wooden rod with what appeared to be the remnants of a hoe at the end. It wasn't one of those flat-bladed ones, but the triangular kind for really digging into the dirt.

Or digging into a man's throat. I put a hand to my own throat and gulped.

Marianne's normally pale face was even paler than usual. Bright splotches of blood dampened her pale pink skirt and her hem where the fabric was torn.

"What did you do, Rob?" I croaked.

Marianne turned slightly. "What are you doing here?"

"I needed to talk to Richard." I glanced down then up, swallowing at the sight of Richard, his eyes open and staring, his throat missing.

"It wasn't supposed to happen like this." Sweat poured along Rob's face and his shirt was wet with it, dark rings around the neck and arms. His desperate eyes met mine through the dust motes glittering in the filtered light in the gloomy room. "I didn't mean to kill him."

"What?" I made the mistake of glancing down at Richard, my gaze darting from the awful sight. "What do you mean? He wasn't armed. Did you attack him? It wasn't self-defense, was it?"

"Not him. Guy."

I gaped at him. Behind me John made an odd, strangled noise. I pressed back against him, suddenly anxious for his solid bulk.

"You killed Guy?" Marianne whispered. Her face paled even more and I was sure she might faint. "When? How? Oh, Rob. What did you do?"

Her mournful words made me shiver, not because of the sadness but because of the wealth of knowledge I heard in her voice. *Marianne guessed. She knew something was wrong.*

Rob stepped forward, brandishing the hoe. I retreated again from the pool of blood. For one crazy second I was worried if I stepped in it, I'd be contaminated, like when we were kids and we played lava-on-the-floor. Sanity reasserted itself. "We should call an ambulance. Maybe Richard is alive."

"That night." Rob stared at Marianne, his eyes haunted. "I didn't mean to. Guy came to the cabin. He told me he knew about the embezzlement. He was going to tell Richard. I hit him and he fell. I wasn't sure what to do."

I remembered his frantic phone call. "You panicked and wanted my help but then you changed your mind. That's why you called me the second time. You decided not to admit to it."

"It was an accident," he insisted. "I just didn't tell anybody."

John shifted behind me, moving quietly. I couldn't tell exactly what he was doing, but I prayed he was either dialing a cell phone or getting ready to back up and get help.

"What have you done, Rob?" Marianne asked, horrified. "Aren't you taking your medicine? You promised me you'd take your medicine."

Oh, shit. Marianne told me he was taking medication. For what? "Are you okay, Rob?" I struggled to keep my voice from cracking.

"I'm fine." Rob breathed heavily, almost gasping, like a man who'd run a brisk mile and was recovering from the effort. "I didn't need the pills so I stopped taking them."

Oh, shit. John must have thought the same thing I did because I heard his sharply indrawn breath. "Was it an accident, Rob?" he asked in a soothing, calming voice while he eased forward one tiny inch at a time.

"Yes and no," Rob said. "It was an accident Guy came to my house. And I guess it was an accident he died. But I'm not sorry I threw his body in the river. It was all so convenient. I saw his note to Marianne. I knew he was going away, so nobody would miss him. It was like fate." He nodded thoughtfully. "Yeah. Like it had to be."

"But why?" Marianne took a step closer to Rob, her hands outstretched. "Was it because of me? Rob, you know our marriage was over. It didn't matter about Guy. Even if he wasn't here, I wouldn't be happy." She appeared oblivious to the man who was either dying or dead, lying at her feet. Marianne appeared oblivious to anything but Rob, who stared at her, the hoe still upraised. "Why?"

"Of course you wouldn't be happy. Nothing I did ever made you happy. You were always the princess, waiting for her Prince Charming."

"Marianne," I said softly. "We should leave. Rob needs help. We should go."

John started to move, bending over. When Rob swung to face him, John said, "I'm just setting down my things, Rob. There's nothing to worry about." He set the framed certificate on the floor but kept the box holding the arrow. "See what I got. It's nice, isn't it?"

I don't think Marianne even heard John speak. Her mind was too preoccupied with her own worries. "I filed for divorce but I'll have to testify against him at a trial, won't I? I don't know if I can do it." Tears dampened her cheeks. It made her seem helpless, vulnerable, and weak.

How much of this is real and how much staged? I chastised myself for such uncharitable thinking. Good Lord, her husband was a murderer and her lover was dead. If anybody had a right to cry, Marianne did.

I tried to move back but my bandaged hand came in contact with the doorframe, sending a bolt of agony through my arm. That painful reminder fueled my anger. "You son of a bitch. You hit me with Guy's car, didn't you? Did you trash my house?" I started forward but John's hand on my arm held me back. "We were friends, Rob. How could you?"

His attention fixated on me. It felt like I was being skewered. "When John told me you were on your way to his house, it was too good a chance to pass up."

John tensed next to me then he shifted. I realized he was inching his way to the right, edging around Richard in the middle of the room. The green box holding his arrow was clutched in John's left hand, almost crushed by his grip. "I trusted you, Rob. We all did."

"You all thought I was a fuck-up. Poor Rob." His voice was sarcastic and bitter.

I winced. How many times did I think that?

"What do you think you're doing, Rob?" John asked softly. "You can't get away."

"I can if I kill you."

I stiffened but John only shook his head, like a ponderous bear worrying over annoying bugs buzzing around his face. "You know I won't let you do it. I won't let you hurt Tuck." He looked down at me, his face calm. Only his eyes betrayed his worry, his fear. "Get out of here, Tuck."

"If you do, I'll kill her." Rob raised the hoe, twisting toward Marianne.

Marianne gasped. "Rob, you wouldn't. You love me."

Rob took a step forward. "You betrayed me just like Richard did. I only did what PJ told me to do. He knew the factory was contaminated. He told me to cover it up. I knew someone would start digging in and looking more closely at the factory. My money would be discovered."

"Your money?" Marianne could barely voice the words around her sobs. "You don't have any money, Rob. You told me we were broke."

"What happened, Rob? I don't understand." John edged slightly to the right. *Be careful,* I wanted to say. *Don't get hurt.*

"Guy knew I was cooking the books at the factory. I was investing with a company in New York and Guy knew them. A friend of his mentioned that somebody from Guy's hometown was getting rich in the market. I didn't plan to kill Guy, but then he showed up. It made sense." Rob's gaze shifted to me. "That brought you into play."

"Me? I don't know anything about investing," I protested.

"But you did know the guy who snooped around the office, copying files. I saw him in there and I pulled his file. PJ told us to watch out for undercover activists, so I called the private detective we have on staff and he told me the kid grew up in Louisiana. You confirmed it for me the other night when you told me where you used to live. Those scrapbooks of yours were proof." He said it like I was the guilty one, not him.

Oh, shit. That's the only thing I could think of. *Poor Will.*

"I called the kid using Guy's phone and promised him some information. He met me at the factory and I knocked him out. I called the Sheriff's office because I needed to make sure somebody competent would show up."

I'll have to remember to pass on that compliment to Owen. If I get the chance.

"I turned the guy loose in the field. I fired a shot, then Owen fired a shot and well, you know what happened next."

I nodded weakly. Rob shot Will and Owen fired his gun, too. But it was Rob's gun that killed Will.

"I didn't mean for it to happen," Rob said softly. "Things started to fall apart. I needed Guy to take the blame for my finances. I needed PJ to take the blame for what happened at the factory. I didn't think Richard would turn on me. I thought he'd support me. He knew PJ was incompetent. I don't understand it." Rob sounded like a hurt, bewildered child.

"But PJ died and an accountant came in and it all started to come apart. I needed a little more time. I was going to leave town, let Guy have Marianne. I wanted to start a new life. I was even selling the cabin to Guy. But that's null and void now because Guy can't sign anything." Rob suddenly smiled. "That's right. I can keep the cabin." His shoulders relaxed and he sighed but then he tensed, his frantic eyes peering around the crowded room. "No, I can't. I have to leave. That's right. That's why I sold it."

"Rob, how could you?" Marianne's anguished words were almost incomprehensible through the sobs that made her gasp. I wasn't sure if she was crying for Guy, or Rob's betrayal, or Richard's death. *Shit. Who cares why she's crying? God knows she's got reason enough.*

Rob's head moved slowly to face her. Any indecision or weakness suddenly vanished and a steely resolve replaced it, changing him to some kind of avenging angel. "I decided to finally live my life." Rob straightened and the hoe in his hands came crashing down, slashing across the empty space over Richard's body.

Marianne reeled back and I caught a glimpse of her startled face, the blood spurting from her neck when she slammed against the window on the side of the building. Glass exploded around her, and she slumped on the frame for an instant then sank, blood flowing on her chest to stain her pink blouse.

"Holy crap, Rob!" I shouted. Rob turned to me, the hoe upraised. "This isn't right. Don't do this. What are you doing?" I was babbling but I couldn't stop myself. Marianne was only slightly closer to him than me and she—

Oh, God. She was gurgling or her blood was gurgling while it spurted from her neck.

"You stupid bitch. If only you'd left it alone." Rob raised the hoe.

"Rob, this is insane." I turned to Marianne, who struggled to talk, her hands making little grasping gestures on the rough wood floor. Blood dribbled off the side of her neck near a gaping hole.

John lunged forward, the golden arrow in his hand. Rob swiveled to meet him, but the hoe was too awkward to use in close quarters. He shifted his grip and met John's assault, using the hoe to block John's downward thrust with the arrow. I tried to move around them to get to Marianne, but between Rob and John fighting and Richard on the floor, there wasn't much space to maneuver.

I jumped over Richard's body but Rob and John turned, Rob slamming into my right shoulder. It must have caught him off-balance, because he dropped the hoe. John made a lunge for him, but Rob ducked, glancing around for the hoe. I dove for it, grabbing it before he could. I dragged it out of his reach, sliding it behind me so I got my hands free to help Marianne.

I knelt over her. She was so terribly pale except for where the bright red blood flowed from her throat. I grabbed a handful of her skirt and tore, wadding up the soft fabric to put against the wound. Her eyes were focused on me and all I saw in their pale blue depths was surprise, like she couldn't understand why she was dying here on a dirty floor with her loving husband fighting for his life.

"It's okay, Marianne. I'll get a doctor. It's okay." I turned, my knees scraping on the splintery wood floor. I gasped in pain but kept moving, keeping low and aiming for the doorway.

Rob suddenly tore the arrow from John's hands. They were fighting above me. John's legs were right in front of me, inches from my face. I grabbed him around the knees and pushed with all my might. He went down like a falling tree, dropping to one side, when Rob stabbed forward with the arrow.

I flailed around behind me and found the hoe. When Robin leaned over John, preparing to stab him, I circled the hoe over my head and brought it crashing against the side of Rob's face. He spun backward, the arrow flying from his grip. Dust rose up in thick clouds when he slammed into the wall before he spun again, hitting the remaining intact window and sending fragments showering over us. Rob dropped face forward, his legs buckling and his body landing heavily on Richard's.

I sprang to my feet and leaned over John. "Are you okay?"

He nodded, blood running from a cut on his swollen lip. "Fine. Get help."

I headed for the door.

****

A week later, I broke my rule and opened the Pub at noon. It was the least I could do. Our loss was so staggering I felt it deserved at least one private drink for us to encompass it all.

I set the portraits at the end of the bar, each in front of an empty barstool. First the dead: Will. Rob. Marianne. PJ. Richard. Guy. Although PJ was not directly part of Rob's craziness, it wasn't for lack of trying on Rob's part. I hoped the last two would rot in hell, but I included them for closure as much as anything. They died in the melee that was Rob Huntington's schizophrenic life and I guess they deserved to be acknowledged.

I straightened Rob's picture. He smiled into the camera, his hair mussed, and his eyes guileless. Who knew this man led a double life? We all trusted him, we all felt sorry for him. We had no idea he salted away two million dollars in a secret bank account. We didn't know he forged and stole from PJ for years. No one guessed what he was capable of, from murder to home invasion to murder again. Rob seemed like a hapless fool, but we were the fools, not him. There was a monster near us, a monster that lurked, the monster held in check by medication.

Rob walked a fine line all his life and no one knew how close he was to falling off without medication to keep him balanced. Now he was in a high security mental hospital awaiting evaluation. He'd probably stay there or in a similar institution for the rest of his life.

I raised my glass of Friar's Folly, Rob's favorite beer. Alan, Miller, Lee, Isabel, John, and the others who gathered all did the same.

"To lives snuffed out before their time," I said.

"Hear, hear." Alan sipped then set his glass on the counter.

Guy's picture fell over. "Karma?" I asked..

"We can hope." Alan regarded Isabel, who was talking with Miller. "I'm surprised Eleanor didn't kick up more of a fuss when Isabel told her she was going to apprentice as a chef with me."

"I think the old woman is in shock," Lee said. "With both Richard and PJ dead, there's no one left to run the company. I expect PJ's son will learn some harsh lessons very quickly."

"Let's hope Three doesn't turn out like PJ," I said fervently.

"He might surprise Eleanor. Shutting down the factory and giving the employees a good severance package went a long way to settling the bad feelings in town." Alan looked past me to John, who stood behind me. "I still can't believe you guys were almost killed by him. We're lucky to have you still with us."

John smiled at me. "You saved my life. You're no bigger than a gnat. How'd you do that? How'd you knock me over?"

"A gnat can drive a bull to distraction. It just has to know where to push."

John's eyes met mine and I swear I saw an invitation there. "I'm willing to be distracted."

I smiled in return and raised my glass. "I'll drink to that."

A word about the author…

J L Wilson is a Midwestern author who writers "mystery with a touch of romance, romance with a touch of gray."

She can found out and about the Interwebs at her web site (www.jayellwilson.com) or Facebook page (https://www.facebook.com/jayeAtPlay).

Check her character list to see who's who in this book (and other Remembered Classics): http://bit.ly/character_lists.

Other Remembered Classics from The Wild Rose Press are Dogged, Flyer, and Laked.

She has several other books with the Wild Rose Press

www.ingramcontent.com/pod-product-compliance
Lightning Source LLC
Chambersburg PA
CBHW060522260626
47161CB00003B/726